Family
OF THE
Heart

K.L. WATKINS

NEWMAN SPRINGS PUBLISHING
320 Broad Street
Red Bank, NJ 07701

First originally published by Newman Springs Publishing 2021

ISBN 978-1-63692-378-9 (Paperback)
ISBN 978-1-63692-379-6 (Digital)

Printed in the United States of America

To my children: Ryan and Zanna

CHAPTER 1

$\mathcal{T}$he summer I moved to Sarasota, Florida, 1971, I was reborn. I was twenty, pale, overweight, insecure. I had never had a relationship with a boy as a boyfriend or friend, nor had I made good choices in girlfriends. That summer, I made a friend. Zan: strange name for a most exotic, beautiful woman; she a woman, I still a girl. I had two years before completing college; she had just graduated. Both new to Florida, she chose me as her friend, giving wings to thoughts I'd never had—maybe I wasn't an ugly duckling after all. The first morning at my job at a bank, a woman swirled into the room, wearing a long skirt, a scarf that came to her knees, and so many colors I felt I had fallen into a rainbow. How she kept from getting entangled with the scarf was beyond me. With all the colors, she contrasted with my beige slacks and buttoned-down blouse.

"My name is Zan," she sang, and as I stuck out my hand, she reached beyond it, gripping me in a tight hug. "Zan Dora!"

I stuttered, in awe of this thrilling being, "I'm Katrina Wheeler. Do you work here?"

Zan threw back her head and laughed, a melodic chortling as she trilled, "Yes!"

Next, the boss, Mr. Krighten, introduced himself while Zan gave me a curtsy, her scarf entwining around her knees, her skirt kicked up in a bloom of color, saying, "We process files. Now that you're here, things are looking up!"

After I had been there for a few weeks, she was the first to ask, "How come you are tanning when you never tanned before?"

"My doctor prescribed suntan pills so I wouldn't burn. Being tan changes the way I think about myself—I don't have to hide my bread legs."

We were sitting at our worktable, sifting through files, just the two of us, when Zan screamed, "Bread legs? What are you talking about?"

"Pasty white, fat, no shape—my college roommate calls me Bread Legs, says her legs are beautiful while I'm stuck with these!" I brought my legs out from under the table and straightened them, embarrassed to point them out, making sure she saw the offending body parts.

"They look curvaceous to me! Sounds like all you need is a new roommate!" We had our own apartments, both of us living independently. Zan lived in a little cottage I thought looked like the home of Snow White's seven dwarves. The house, unlike most Florida homes, had gingerbread cutouts along the roofline, similar to what I had seen in Candler and Inman Park, Atlanta. The house was painted a peach color and the cutouts an emerald green. It was fanciful!

"I can't believe you found this place! It must cost a mint. How can you afford it?"

"It's my mom's college roommate's. I clean her house so I don't pay rent."

I lived on the beach by the bay: three small cinder-block rooms, none of the charm of Zan's cottage—if I wasn't used to dorm living, I would have been claustrophobic. Zan exclaimed, "You think mine's great? You live right on the water!" She talked me into sneaking onto the pier of the condominiums next door. "If anyone stops us, pretend we live here. With two gorgeous women, who'll doubt us?" I was thrilled to be included in her "gorgeous women." We snuck over so frequently people thought we lived there.

We worked together at the bank, earning our own money. The bank had no idea how much fun we'd have after they hired us and shut us in a large room with no windows to straighten out neglected mortgage files. We were so focused on our own conversations we made bad files worse. Mutt and Jeff, Straight and Narrow, Sugar and Spice, Coffee and Cream. Despite our short history, we left our mark. In the end, it was I who left, compelled to go back to college even though I loved the beach, the taste of freedom, my independence. Things happened that summer that were irrevocable, sealing me away from Sarasota for twenty-five years. Alas, I'm getting ahead of my story. That was later. It's hard to believe that that summer was only eight weeks long. I could hardly believe only eight weeks changed my whole life. I need a break, or my emotions will overcome me. I promise—if you are still reading—to continue. If you are not interested, I will write anyway, and you can put my book aside, but stop now or read to the end. That's all I ask.

*****

That summer was about friendships: deep, complete connections. The bank vice president introduced number four to our work environment a few days later, a large gentle bear of a man, who lit up when he saw us.

"Mr. Goodard, this is your workroom. You will be working with these two ladies: Katrina Wheeler"—I nodded—"and Zan Dora." Zan ran and circled Wally in a hug just as she had me.

"Thank God you've come!" she cried dramatically. "We need you!" Wally flushed red.

"This is your boss, Mr. Krighten." Mr. Krighten was a boy genius—eighteen years old, leaving for Yale in the fall. Steeped in intellectual knowledge, he had the personality of sawdust.

"I'm new to Sarasota," Zan started talking as soon as the door closed behind the executive. "So is Katrina. What's your story?"

Like Zan, Wally had finished college and needed a summer job. His mother, Vanessa, owned an art gallery across the bay on Anna Maria Island. She had contacts at the bank that landed him his job. Wally had an easy grin, an infectious giggle, and exuded goodwill. He completed our group at the bank:

> The boss: Mr. Krighten—dubbed by the bank as the smartest, most efficient. We never moved past calling him Mr. Krighten—I don't remember his first name because of his stern stature, his constant frown, his total disdain for us;
>
> Zan Dora: gypsy, salt of the earth, bound by nature to bring out the best in all of us. She was the freest spirit I'd ever met. When she walked into a room, the lights seemed to brighten, and she drew attention to herself without knowing it. How? She was enchanting—in her dress, in her smile, in the glow that shone around her (she would call it her aura);
>
> Wally Goodard: a native to the area, funny, self-deprecating, intelli-

gent beyond measure. He was more left-brained than me or Zan, having an engineering degree, but he thrived on our impishness. His biggest asset was his infectious giggle, his love for us despite his rational mind;

Finally, me: Katrina Wheeler— coming of age with this group who by adoring me made me love myself. That was a major lesson I learned that summer, though future challenges made self-love an ideal that was hard to hold on to, a concept I never stopped striving for.

"Welcome to the club! We should give ourselves a name!" Zan exclaimed.

"Like what?" I asked. "Newcomer's Club?"

"Dull, dull, dull. Sounds like the Welcome Wagon. Something clever. Sea Oats?"

"What about Bank Notes?" Wally's suggestion was applauded; we cheered. By giving us our name, Wally sealed himself in our inner circle: Bank Notes, forever, that's how we referred to one another.

I had a defensive wall around me as large as the seawall at the end of my street, my wall so secure no one penetrated it. Why the wall? I ran with beautiful people but was not one of them. I had bread legs and ran with French baguettes. Wally and Zan descended the wall without compromising me—I hardly noticed their dance of friendship because they stole in, leaving no room for me to push them out. They climbed over, swam under, poked holes but never charged, never forced me to do anything I was unwilling to do. Wally and Zan, though beautiful, were different enough from what society accepted, that they embraced me, never saw my insecurities—or never allowed me to express them. In their blind acceptance, they refused to enrich themselves at my expense.

I asked the group to come over to my apartment that night, the first day Wally came to work. Although I liked living by myself, the nights were long and boring.

"Sure," Zan and Wally answered together, and Zan made arrangements to ride with Wally. Zan, though free-spirited and zany, surprisingly relished a life of security. Her summer cottage was a friend of her mother's; she preferred parties at my house even though her cottage was bigger and she didn't often drive. She rode with Wally, which rapidly became two even three times a week. Wally loved it—he had just bought a Porsche and, thrilled with its power, was proud to chauffeur around a woman as stunning as Zan.

That night Mr. Krighten did not stay long. Zan and Wally arrived with a bottle of Boone's Farm, cheap but tasty wine. That's when Mr. Krighten left, muttering about drinking with coworkers—conscious he was underage. We waited for him to leave before bringing out marijuana and, after we smoked, fell into giggles and unfinished stories.

"I want a hit," I said as Zan leaned over me to hand me the joint. She let out a piercing scream right in my ear. "What the hell!" she yelled, pointing at a flying roach.

"Florida's specialty," Wally said. "Palmetto bugs, fancy name for flying roaches."

"Christ, I could navigate that one. Find a seat and pull on my seat belt!" Zan's eyes were huge. I grabbed a can of bug spray. "We have damn big roaches in Alabama, but I've never seen one fly." Zan was screeching as I waltzed after the roach. Zan and Wally collapsed into laughter.

"What's so funny?" I joined in the laughter, hitting the bug as he dipped and dived.

"Who else would go into battle with a roach for me?" Zan giggled. We looked like hell the next morning at work, and no one spoke except Mr. Krighten. Now that he had a captive audience, he never shut up. He talked about the debate club, going on and on about his different topics— both sides for and against the Vietnam War, legalizing abortion; he didn't stop for three hours. We could hardly keep our heads up so didn't listen.

*****

I knew from the beginning Wally loved me. He was deep, warm, trusting. I bloomed under his smile. He called me Kat; no one had ever given me affectionate nicknames before. He loved me, even more than he loved Zan. Wally and Zan gave me self-confidence I'd never had. Even though I knew he cared deeply, I did not want his attention in a romantic way. I had never experienced recognition from the opposite sex so found myself wanting his friendship first. My own father is a self-centered man; my mother's life built around him; therefore, I had never had attention from either parent. An only child, my parents lived their lives without including me. That summer, I needed Wally as a friend; I found lustful attention in other places.

The next Saturday, I met a man on the beach who had large eyes, curly hair; Adonis came to mind until he opened his mouth.

"Hey, you!"

"Who, me?" I stuttered, losing my finesse immediately. Zan had disappeared to find a restroom. I looked behind me to see if that gorgeous man was talking to someone else. He wasn't.

"See anyone else around here?" He winked. I wanted to kill Zan for leaving me alone.

"Your name?" He struck a pose straight from a muscleman magazine, showing off.

"Katrina. Yours?"

"James. People call me Dog. You here alone?"

"Ur, no—there's my friend."

"Who's this?" Zan asked as she walked up.

"This is Johnny."

"Excuse me, dimwit, the name's James, but call me Dog." He turned to the side and flexed his muscles so we could see his definition. Zan shot me a look I chose to ignore.

Zan sneered. "You're like a character in that Edward Albee play, *The Sandbox.*" She meant the character who was a muscleman standing on the beach, flexing his muscles, grunting.

"You free tonight?" James—er, I mean Dog, asked me.

"Sure." My heart nearly leapt out of my chest—it beat faster, straining my rib cage with an ache. "Where to?" I ignored the fact that he called me dimwit, thrilled just to have a date.

"There's a new club at Lido Beach. Temperance. You want me to pick you up?"

"Sure." I wrote down my address. I had no phone.

He was half an hour late, so I paced, sure he would not come. I nearly smoked a whole pack of Marlboros and was rolling a joint when he knocked. I hid it, not sure of his persuasion—friend or foe regarding weed.

"Got any pot?" he asked. He stood so close I backed further into my apartment. He leaned over staring at my face, and I was immediately uncomfortable. To avoid further intimacy, I uncovered the joint and lit up.

"Ummm," he scooted closer, blowing smoke into my mouth. "Forget Temperance," he groaned, squashing me, pressing his body tight against mine.

"Uh," I verbally stumbled, aware for the first time that we were alone in my apartment—not in a dorm with the protective regulations of the early '70s. I realized I had made a mistake, but that didn't stop Beach Boy; he grabbed me, forcing me down on the bed, tore off my clothes, and thrust himself inside. No preamble, no foreplay—just a quick, dry fuck. "Shit fire, man," he yelled, "are you a virgin? God, this is great!" he crowed. I scrambled off the bed, tears streaming down my face. I shoved him outside when he finished and told him I did not want him to come back. Ever. Who but me would lose their virginity to a man whose nickname was Dog?

*****

The next man, I met at Temperance. My French baguette friend was visiting, and I wanted to impress her. We were drunk by the time two men joined us. "Who are you?" they slurred.

"Frances and Katrina," French baguette trilled at the cute one. "And you?"

"He's Bobby, and I'm Ben," the cute one said, ignoring Frances and leaning towards me.

"Sounds like a cartoon." Frances smiled directly at Ben then pointedly swung her French baguette legs from under the table to make sure he saw them and her very short skirt.

"What the hell are you talking about?" Ben instantly disliked Frances. This was a first. I always got stuck with the leftovers any time I went out with Frances.

As the waitress came up to our table, I ordered Chardonnay. The waitress brought my fourth glass; Frances's third as I leered at Ben.

"Wanna dance?" he asked me, and I stood up. Sat right down too, regrouping, finding my balance then stumbling to the dance floor. It was a slow dance, and his hand cuddled my rear. I was almost too drunk to notice. Almost. We sat down at the table alone as Frances and Bobby danced a fast one. Frances looked like a New York City Rockette.

"Your friend got a mouth on her, know that? What'd she mean by cartoons?"

"She's nuts about Saturday morning cartoons—she was flirting with you." I reached over to pick up my wineglass, knocking it into his lap. Horrified, I grabbed a napkin and began wiping him off, noticing his penis was ramrod straight, hard as granite. I shivered, he groaned, but he couldn't take me home; Frances was spending the weekend. Frances was furious the cute one chose me, so she was ready to go.

"Let's go, Joe." She grabbed my keys, leaving me just enough time to write down my address.

"That bitch go home tomorrow?" Ben asked. I could tell by the knob in his pants his penis was still hard. He leered at me and tried to stop me from leaving.

"Monday," I said as I untwisted my arm from his grip. There was something unnerving about how intensely he clutched me; my arm was bruised when he let go. I knew then I shouldn't have given him my address.

"I'll come by Monday," he said. "You didn't give me your phone number."

"No phone." Frances grabbed my arm right where he had, corralling me to the car.

"What a waste," Frances insisted on driving us home, furious Ben had chosen me.

I didn't say a word. I was afraid I'd given a sexual invitation to Ben. I invited Zan and Wally over Monday to stop Ben from thinking he was going to score. He showed up right on cue, banging on my door. I ran to answer it, but when he saw Zan and Wally, he turned mean. "I thought we were going to fuck," he hissed then turned away, slamming my door.

At eleven, he returned. "Finally," he said as I answered. "Who the hell were those goons?" he roared as he shoved his way in. As he came inside, he stripped off his clothes then tore mine off and fucked me on the floor. What was with me? Two men in a row so similar it was like I had a needle stuck in a record, spinning around and around in the same groove. "Tight little bitch, ain't you?" he said. I pushed him out, telling him I had an early morning job.

In my vast experience of two, I was tired of mindless fucks, deciding it was time to ditch him. Ben had other ideas: Tuesday, Wednesday, Thursday—he banged on my door. "Hey, cunt, open up." He circled the apartment, screaming. I hid in the bathroom on the floor.

By Friday, Wally decided to get involved. "I'm spending the night so when that bastard knocks, he'll think we're fucking our brains out." Wally, my best, my only male friend, giggled in anticipation. Ten, eleven, midnight—it was four in the morning before Ben began his knocking. Wally woke up, quickly slipped out of his jeans, tousled his hair as he ran to the door.

"What the fuck do you want?" I could hear as I ran to my bathroom hideout. "She's my woman. That's what I get for going out of town. You can't let a babe like her out of sight." Wally loaded it on.

"She's your girl?" Ben was so stoned he leaned on the side of my apartment to keep from falling over. I peeked out of the bathroom, but he saw me and glared. "Fucking two-timing cow," he slurred, "this guy says you're his."

"A detail I forgot to mention." I cringed.

"Fuck you." He stumbled to his car, the tires pushing violently on the gravel in his retreat.

"I don't think he'll be back, but you've got to be more careful."

"You're right about that." I decided then and there no more Temperance.

******

Zan and Wally talked to me about my indiscretions the next time Mr. Krighten left for an early lunch. "You can't pick up just anyone," Zan said.

"It's unsafe, Kat." Wally looked at me, concern filling his eyes. "I'll introduce you to someone." So the next two men I dated were friends of Wally's. I should have fallen for Wally; he was ready, but a male friendship was so enlightening, I was unwilling to let it go.

That summer was spent in discovery of the wonder of the turquoise ocean, white-sanded beaches, and other things Zan and I had never experienced. We visited all the beaches in the Sarasota area, having a tough time deciding on our favorite. Wally preferred Anna Maria Island, so though it was a drive, we often went there for sunsets and long, quiet walks. We quickly agreed with Wally, and it became our favorite too.

One evening, Wally invited us to a bonfire at his mom's place. "Most public beaches don't allow bonfires, but we get around it because it's Mom's private beach," Wally told us. Wally's mom, Vanessa, owned a large stretch of land right on the ocean. Wally grew up there so took it for granted. Not

Zan and me. Zan and Vanessa had a spark the minute we met her; I took longer to discover her friendship, but it was powerful and meaningful to me throughout the rest of my life. Even later when I found it difficult to return to Sarasota, Anna Maria Island and Vanessa called to me: her friendship, the turquoise ocean, the salty smell, sand like sugar, her private beach with its quiet peacefulness.

Midsummer, Zan was summoned home for her sister's engagement party. "You have to go with me," she begged. The first sign something was up was when we stopped at a rest area near Parrish, Alabama, where Zan changed clothes into a pencil skirt, ruffled blouse, black tights, Mary Janes. If I hadn't been riding with her, I would not have recognized my friend.

"What's with the change?" I asked.

"My parents are Bible-thumping Christians. Call me Suzanne, not Zan Dora."

"Do I need to change?"

"No. You're more conservative than I am. You're so clean-cut, they'll love you."

I was overwhelmed by the small-town Alabama engagement party. First clue again were the clothes: lots of lace, lots of expensive jewelry, six-inch heels. I faded into the background with my beige skirt, peach blouse, and flats. Second was the prayers over everything: the food, the presents, the marriage, future offspring. How had Zan come from here?

When we finally got back to her room, Zan read my tarot cards. I knew she wanted to tap into her Sarasota personae, not lose herself in the Alabama air.

"Your first card is death, but that's not as it seems. It means extreme change, not actual physical death. You have two men in your future: one's extremely dark—dark hair, dark eyes, dark personality. There's some dilemma between you that stretches…" Zan's door flew open, and her mom entered, talking nonstop about the gifts until she stopped dead in her tracks.

Have you ever heard of knocking on someone's door? I wanted to ask.

"What in the blazes are you doing?" her mother asked Zan.

Zan scooped up the cards as fast as she could as her mom moved towards them—I'm sure to destroy them. Her mother knelt by the bed in prayer, lifting her arms in supplication. "Get thee behind me, Satan," she intoned then lunged again for the cards.

"These are mine, Mom," Zan told her as she hid them behind her back.

"Either you give me those Chronicles of Satan or you leave right now."

"I'll move them to my car and never bring them to your house again," Zan promised.

"All right, but only because I approve of your friend. Get them out of here—now!" I never did get my reading finished, never heard about the men who were to be my future.

We left Sunday after a Southern lunch, left without another reference to the cards. Zan said we skipped church because Parrish was so small the preacher came once every two weeks. "It's a service you'd never forget. Folks prostrating themselves, talking in tongues, embracing the Holy Spirit." I was almost sorry I missed it.

It was great to get home to Sarasota. Zan and I both breathed a sigh of relief leaving Alabama, embracing the smell of the salty air as we drew closer, ready to go to Anna Maria and sit on the beach we'd come to love.

CHAPTER 2

$\mathcal{N}$ext, Wally introduced me to Joe, a disc jockey at a Sarasota radio station. He had coke-bottle-thick glasses but a voice that gave teenage girls wet dreams as he purred across the airwaves. He was a complicated soul who always drank. He didn't care that I wanted to take it slow sexually, but I didn't realize that it was because when he drank, he couldn't seal the deal.

After two weeks of nothing but kissing, I planned my seduction carefully—dropping by the radio station where he worked, decked out in my shortest shorts and my most revealing halter top. His mouth dropped as I flounced into the soundproof studio. He turned on a record and asked, "What are you doing?" as he kissed me and his hand wandered inside my top.

"I thought I'd catch you in action." I giggled. He returned to the airwaves, his voice husky.

"I put three records on in a row." His mouth encircled my nipple as it hardened beneath his touch. He slipped his hand easily inside my shorts.

"I've never done this at work," he said, quickly running his tongue down my belly, unzipping my shorts, and rolling me down on the couch. His tongue lit a fire as I writhed beneath him. The third record ended; he went back to the airwaves and answered a few calls from hot teens responding to the yearning they heard in his voice. He put on more records and returned. We fucked with abandon; I barely stopped from screaming.

He hardly noticed Janis Joplin had stopped her wailing, so he had to quickly rejoin the listening audience, cracking jokes that implied there was more to life than the blues.

"What the hell is going on?" an outraged man burst through the soundproof door and gaped at my red mound pumping furiously, Joe's butt airborne. "You're fired. You are desirable to the ladies, but this"—he pointed at me, barely stopping from ramming his finger into my face—"is ridiculous." The radio manager picked up right on cue, but calls began to pour in for Joe.

"Mo' Jo"—Joe's radio handle—"had an accident on the set," the man said.

Joe dragged me out the door. "I lost my job, and it's your damn fault," he said as he advanced threateningly. "You lousy cunt!" I was afraid of him, so I ran to my car and locked the door behind me. Never heard from him again. Months later, the calls in Sarasota still came in. "Where's Mo' Jo? He always sounded like he was screwing his brains—" The radio quickly shut off the commentary.

Wally kissed my cheek, squeezed my hand. "Joe wasn't worth a damn. He's a drunk."

*****

Wally introduced me to another man two weeks later, Jonathan, so good-looking I couldn't talk when I met him. He had long, silky black hair, intense black eyes, and a deep tan. He was a foot taller than me, six foot two. When we met, he leaned down to peer in my eyes. I immediately thought of the interrupted tarot reading Zan had started. "You must be Irish! You're so pale and such a redhead!"

"I'm tan for the first time in my life," I protested.

Zan snickered, hardly able to contain herself at my nervousness.

"Tan?" Jonathan laughed and stood up. In my mad race around the apartment, I backed into him, stepping on his foot. He grabbed me as I fell into his arms. "I think you're perfect, little one!" he said, and I blushed wildly, unable to prevent my face from turning scarlet.

"I'm Seminole," he continued, talking intimately as if I was the only one in the apartment, "the only true Floridian. That's why I'm so dark. Only dated a few pale faces." He sighed deeply. I figured he was the kind of man who created a stir just by entering a room. He knew it too, conscious of his own sensuality, sure of himself. He had my nerves zinging, blood coursing through my veins. I thought, *What's so sensual about him touching me?* It was as if he had thrown my head back, kissed me wildly, stripped me naked, yet he had only caught me when I tripped. I knew instinctively that Jonathan wanted to set me on fire, knew he could!

The next day, Zan said, "I have something for you," as she handed me a sack. "It's a love potion for you and Jonathan." I opened the sack and was hit with a pleasant odor.

"What is it?"

"A secret potion I've been working on. If I tell you, I'll have to kill you." I recognized clover and sunflower seeds but nothing else.

"By the way," Zan asked, "with all the sex you're having, do you use birth control?"

"I've never needed to. Guess I'll get on the pill when I get back to Atlanta."

Once I got to my apartment, I brewed a stiff pot of tea just as Zan instructed.

"What's this?" Jonathan noticed the tea as soon as he walked in.

"A tea Zan brewed for us. Would you like some?"

"Love a cup. I was raised on herbal teas but never knew white women brewed them."

"Zan's not like other women."

"She's bright and sensitive, isn't she?" He snuggled me under his arm and whispered, "Bright and sensitive like you, eh?" Next, he asked, "Ever tried magic mushrooms?"

"No, but I'll give it a try," I answered, not wanting to sound naïve. The mushrooms were tough. My hand shook as I popped the first one in my mouth. "They don't taste so hot, do they?" I tried gallantly to swallow.

"Chew it up while I make another pot of tea. That'll help it go down." He went into the kitchen and mixed more of Zan's brew. I stayed on the couch, drifting into the cushions.

"Here's your tea. You okay?" Jonathan peered into my eyes. I could not stay focused, my eyes darting around the room. Once Jonathan handed me the tea, I took a gulp. Jonathan began to slurp my neck as I nuzzled him, pulling up his shirt, circling his nipple with my tongue.

"Can I do that?"

"Suck your own nipple? I don't think you can reach it." We laughed, loud, pealing ripples, which I saw heaving through my body in bright purples, greens, and yellows.

Jonathan pulled off my T-shirt, his mouth beginning a search for the center of my nipple. His tongue landed on its target, and he began to banter and nip until my nipple stood up. He sucked noisily while I tried to untie the string on his drawstring pants. The tie began oozing colors—purples, blues, reds, so I gnawed at the tie with my teeth, finally untying it, stopping when his pants fell to the floor. His erect penis was orange with yellow lightening.

"Are you always like this?" I asked in wonder, my eyes wide.

"Just when I do 'shrooms. You're not so bad yourself, little one." He pulled me to him gently and peeled my clothes off, following their descent with his tongue as he tugged off my shorts. I followed him lethargically with my eyes, colors popping everywhere.

Jonathan was very deliberate, his tongue darting in and out every crevice of my body, teasing me until my sexual center ached with longing. I raised my pelvis as he drew his tongue closer, finally, tauntingly, landing on my wet, pink mound, finding me open and ready. "You're an eager little thing, aren't you?" he whispered as he drew closer and entered me with his tongue, in and out in an offbeat rhythm.

"Come on!" I screamed, pulling him down, eager to take him in. He teased and withdrew, making me beg, finally thrusting inside me just as I thought I would burst into flames. I screamed, clawing his back, watching my fingers trail colors up and down his powerful shoulders, pulling him closer. We rocked back and forth, glistening in each other's energy, yelps and cries savagely escaping from deep within. As soon as we finished, we began again. After another escapade, we fell, exhausted, wrapped tightly in one another's arms.

Jonathan and I stayed in bed all the next day, exploring parts of our bodies I'd only dreamed of examining with the opposite sex. He knew a different dance every time we made love, thrusting, pulling, pushing, teasing me to a crashing cymbal before finding his own music.

"I forgot Irish girls carry on so." He gave me one final kiss on a private part of my body and got dressed. "Gotta go to work," he whispered in my ear after the day turned into evening. "See you soon." He left, and I fell asleep, exhausted, energy spent.

"Go with me to Oklahoma," Jonathan urged at the beginning of August. We'd been together a few times, and it was always amazing—unlike anything I'd ever experienced.

"What for? I have to go back to college."

"When do you go back?"

"September 20."

"Worrywart! It's only August first. Come with me!" he begged.

"Why Oklahoma?"

"Indian dances, celebrations. I'll pay half of your ticket back to—where do you go to school?"

"West Georgia. How are we getting there?"

"I'm driving my Mustang."

"Think it'll make it to Oklahoma? How far is that anyway?"

"Just over one thousand miles. It'll be a holiday—we'll camp under the stars, make love. What'd you say?"

The stars and the lovemaking sounded wonderful, so I agreed. Zan let me leave my little VW bug, Queenie, at her house. She and Wally would bring it to me once I got back to school.

Jonathan and I left Saturday, early. Wally, Zan, and I vowed to stay in touch, forever.

The trip was slow. Every hundred miles or so, we ran into car trouble. The first was a flat, and we walked ten miles before finding a filling station willing to help. Jonathan did not have a spare. The next was the water pump and so on. We were hot and tired but included the car as part of our adventure. We finally arrived in Miami, Oklahoma; it was midnight, yet the dances were just beginning, and at least a dozen dark-haired women surrounded us, recognizing the car, looking for Jonathan. He was hugged and kissed by all of them.

Jonathan changed the minute we stepped foot on Oklahoma soil, strutting, dancing, moving to a rhythm I'd seen when we made love, something I thought reserved for me. Whenever he left our tent, ten women circled him; two in the front beside him: one who was tall; the other, plump with dimples and hair so dark it was almost blue. I followed because I didn't know what else to do. I finally asked, "When did you make reservations for me to go home?"

"Wednesday night. You'll have to take a bus to Oklahoma City." I hadn't realized I needed a bus, and I was ready to leave. We didn't even sleep at the same time, so forget any lovemaking. Jonathan danced all night, so I'd return to the tent early, sometimes before the dances even began. He wandered in by nine the next morning, falling across the covers, sleeping all day. On Tuesday, he said, "We'll have a special farewell tonight." He smiled, tweaking my nipple through my shirt playfully. I turned away, and he was angry at my rejection. He began to search under my blouse for my breasts, but I left the tent. I lit a cigarette as he stomped out.

"The hell we'll have a special farewell," I grumbled, knowing that if he came back, I'd go with him even though I felt like murder—his—was what I really wanted. Needless to say, this trip had not turned out the way I'd hoped.

I didn't see much of Jonathan the rest of the day; when I did, he was with the tall, dark beauty or the short plump one. "The tall one's Miss Miami this year," an older Native woman told me, "she'll probably win Miss Oklahoma." I remained silent as I watched the dances, the games, the children playing. I got my things together and caught a ride with her to check out the bus schedule to Oklahoma City. I wasn't going to ask Jonathan for a ride.

"Bus leaves every hour beginning at 8:00 a.m. You want a ticket?" the man behind the counter asked, and I bought one for the next morning at eight, the earliest I could escape.

"I'll be coming to town tomorrow morning if you want a ride," the old woman said. "Don't get your hopes smashed on Jonathan. He's been 'the one' ever since he could walk. Only one other competes with him." The woman's face took on a distant look, and she seemed to stop herself from saying more. "He's never brought a white girl home, and I guess he couldn't take the pressure. The Native girls expect him to be there for them."

Jonathan came in early that night, but the minute he did, something felt off. I couldn't figure it out, but the magic wasn't there. My skin crawled when he kissed me. He stroked me tenderly and hummed in my ear, but I felt uncomfortable, wanting to peel off his touch. The heat he usually generated was gone. I stood up in the tent and walked out.

"What's going on, little one?" He came up behind me and nuzzled my neck. "I'm sorry I've been such a jerk."

"That's part of it," I said, "but something just isn't right."

"Come with me," he whispered and took me to the top of a hill overlooking the dancers where he rolled a joint, offering me a hit. I drew in deeply, and some of my edginess disappeared.

"Follow me," he coaxed. We walked in silence for a long time until we came to a field; Jonathan laid down a blanket and pulled me down beside him.

"Where are we?" I whispered.

Jonathan laughed. "Why are you whispering? We're not far from the dances but far enough that no one will hear us." He pulled me close, and I began to respond, quickly taking off my clothes. Soon all I noticed was his enormous penis, erect, ready. It was as if I was surrounded by him as the moonlight danced on his smooth chest. As I kissed him there, I tried not to think of how many times he'd been with other women the past few days. I surrounded him with my tongue. He groaned, almost sobbing. Fortunately, I didn't smell sex, other women.

"You are lovely, little one," he whispered as he circled my ear with his tongue, softly sliding in and out. "Are you ready?" I nodded, and he climbed on, entering me deeply, riding me slow. Just as he came, his huge rod thrusting deep inside, spewing his magic, I looked over his shoulder and saw a deep scar on his back. I touched it with my fingers, ran my fingers over the pulpy, tight skin. I had never been aware of it before, and I thought I'd explored every inch of him.

As we finished and rolled back on the blanket, I asked him, "What's that?" reaching under him to touch the scar. He smirked, his smile having a nasty edge.

"Pretty astute, aren't you?"

"What do you mean?"

"Jonathan doesn't have a scar."

"What the hell are you saying?" I stood up to gain a better advantage and began to notice other differences between this man and Jonathan. His hair was curlier, longer, darker— if that could be possible. "Who the hell are you?"

"Jonathan's older brother, Brett. We're just eleven months apart. What is it you call us? Irish twins?" He offered his hand for me to help him up, but instead I drew my hand back and slapped his face as hard as I could.

"Nice little trade between you and Jonathan, wasn't it?" I snarled.

"Feisty little bitch," he said as he rubbed his cheek where the mark of my hand remained. "You're every bit as good as he said you'd be, maybe better." He was so smug I tried to slap him again, but this time he grabbed my arm tightly and held me back. "It was as good a goodbye as you were going to get. He wasn't going to tell you goodbye, and I'd have hated for that to happen." I threw on my clothes and stumbled back through the fields, following the noise of the dancers to find my way. Even so, I heard his last words: "We always make a trade, every summer…but never one as good as you." I tripped over branches, almost fell on the sloping terrain, but was so intent on reaching the tent, I finally made it. I noticed someone sitting in the tent as I drew closer.

It was the old lady who'd taken me to town. "What are you doing here?" I asked rudely.

"That's what I was trying to tell you yesterday." She pointed outside as if she knew Brett was there. "It would not have been right for me to warn you about his brother. You must live your own experiences." Here, I had no idea how uncanny and ironic her words were to turn out. "Try to sleep tonight. We'll get up with the sun, and I'll take you to the bus. I've grown fond of you. There's something mystical about you." Her voice was soothing and calm, and I leaned against her knees, nodding off as she stroked my hair. I don't know when she left, but felt her presence again when she came back to wake me. She arrived just as the sun rose. When she dropped me off at the bus station, she looked painfully in my eyes. "Sometimes I'm not proud of Brett or Jonathan, but I am their grandmother." I choked back tears, not knowing why she made me feel so sad.

CHAPTER 3

*W*hen I got home, I had two weeks before school started, so I slept late, went to bed early. I avoided calling Wally or Zan, too sad to connect. I was moody, but my parents didn't notice. They were going to Scotland for a year, my dad studying Scottish literature. They left me to close up the house and settle affairs. Since my parents were gone for a year, I could use their car until Zan and Wally brought me Queenie. When I got back to school, I realized my period was late—real late. I called Zan. "Where the hell have you been?" she demanded.

"Zan, it's been so awful, I couldn't talk to anyone. Now, it's worse."

"Shit! It can't be so bad you can't talk to me. What happened?"

"The whole time I was in Oklahoma was nasty. Jonathan ignored me, hooked up with Native women immediately. Then, he came back to fuck me goodbye, and it wasn't Jonathan."

"What do you mean it wasn't Jonathan?" she snarled, disbelieving.

"He has a brother, Brett. They're only one year apart and look alike. I caught on when I saw a scar on Brett's back, but not until after—"

"God, I hope you're over Jonathan now, aren't you?"

"I'm pregnant with Brett's baby. Not Jonathan's—Brett's. I can't go to the infirmary. If they find out, they'll kick me out of school. Abortion's illegal."

"Oh Christ!" Zan sounded like she was crying, so I started too. "Don't freak out," she reassured me. "We'll get out of this. You're my best friend. Let me think. God, just let me think."

"One good thing is my parents are out of the country for the whole year. They expect me in Scotland at Christmas, but I can beg off. They can't afford my ticket anyway, so that'll be okay. What the hell am I going to do?"

I cried louder, and someone knocked on the phone room door. "Quiet hours." I shut up; I didn't want anyone in the dorm asking me what was wrong.

"I can send you some herbs. Nothing poisonous or anything but some that might help you miscarry."

"You sure?"

"I'll try to find a recipe. I've only used herbs as birth control, to stop the problem before it happens. I should have shared those with you long before now."

"God, how stupid can I be? Why did this time end in pregnancy and none of the others? If my calculations are right, I'm eight weeks pregnant—I was in Oklahoma August 5, and it's October 5. I know I can't have a baby and keep it. I thought I could finish winter quarter then come to Sarasota, take spring quarter off and have the baby there. The baby would be due in April. I'll put the baby up for adoption then finish the school year during summer quarter. Tell my parents I need to go to summer school."

"You want to live with me? You can, you know."

"I'm still thinking about it, but right now, that's the only thing I can come up with. God, I wish abortions were legal. Would you mind if I move in? I know your place is small."

"Not too small for you and me, lovie. Abortions will be legal soon. I know they will."

"I'm not sure an abortion would be the right answer for me even if they were legal. You know what I mean?"

"Yes, and without them being legal," Zan said, "the alternatives are horrible."

"What?" I asked.

"I've heard there are underground doctors who perform abortions illegally, but we'd have to find such a doctor. Vanessa might know of one."

"That makes it even more complicated. I'd have to come down there soon, might have to drop out of school. And, what if something went wrong? Is there any way to get help after an illegal abortion?"

"It's one hell of a dilemma. Do you think adoption's what you want?"

"It's what I think is best, and I don't think I'll change my mind."

"You need me to fly up there?"

"No, I'm okay. I'm okay," I said as I hung up, softly crying myself to sleep, knowing okay was far from how I felt.

I finally decided not to take the herbs Zan sent me—no abortion for me, with herbs or an illegal doctor. Even though I had decided to give the baby up for adoption, I was already attached and couldn't bear the thought of ending its life. I stayed by myself most of fall quarter, barely speaking to anyone, shutting out my old friends. They finally quit asking me to go out. I got a single room to make it easier to hide my pregnancy, but Frances dropped by, asking questions and pushing me to go out with her. "What's up, girl? It's not like you to be a hermit. I usually have to hold you back!"

"I need to bring up my grades. I don't feel well either."

"I've noticed you're putting on weight. Don't get any fatter." I became aware that when Frances visited, she spent all her time preening in front of my mirror.

I stopped smoking pot and cigarettes because they made me nauseated. I almost quit eating since I didn't want anyone to know I was pregnant. As an art major, I finally took a pottery class and soon discovered it was my passion. I spent all my free time in the studio, signing up for as many clay classes as my schedule permitted. It was during this sad time that I discovered I had talent with clay.

Katrina, Zan wrote,

> *Come to Sarasota for Christmas! It'll be fun and I want to see you—need to see you terribly! Wally's spending Christmas with me—and his mother and my parents. It'll be like old home week and once the folks go, we can talk and carry on! What ya say? I can drive up in your car and we can drive back together. We can do that over a weekend!*
>
> *Write soon!*
>
> *Love—your big sis, your forever family, you are my heart!*
>
> *Zan!*

Zan met me in Atlanta, and we left my parents' car at their house then drove down on Sunday in Queenie. I told my parents I was behind in my studies and couldn't fly to Scotland. They only asked once.

Wally was at Zan's when I arrived, decorating a miniature tree with ornaments. He hugged me tight.

"Zan told me you're pregnant, but I never would have guessed. You don't show."

"I haven't put on much weight. They'd kick me out of school if they found out."

"Is it okay that I know?"

"Sure, I told Zan she could tell you. I just couldn't write it in a letter. It's too emotional to put in words. Only thing that's keeping me sane is pottery."

"Did you bring any of your work to show us?"

"Just wait. It's Christmas, remember?"

"Whose baby is it? Jonathan's?"

"No, fortunately for me, it's not. It's his brother's—Brett. Seems he likes to fuck Jonathan's women, and I won the swap meet. Do you know Brett?"

"He was raised in Oklahoma—not here with Jonathan. I knew Jonathan had a brother who's almost identical, but I never met him. What do you mean by swap meet?"

"They are identical except for a scar on Brett's back. He said I'm the first woman who noticed the scar and picked up he wasn't Jonathan. Seems they trade women every summer."

"Why do you say it's fortunate it's not Jonathan's baby?"

"I'll answer the swap question first. Seems Brett targets Jonathan's women every year to see if the women realize he's not Jonathan. Brett loves to take advantage of their resemblance. I think Jonathan swaps with him too. I'm the first one that caught on it was Brett. I'm glad it's not Jonathan's as I would be too attached. I think if this was his baby, I'd want to keep it, couldn't give it up. It's better this way—it'll be easier."

"I have another idea for the baby, Katrina."

"What?" I did not smile. I had spent many hours thinking through my options and wasn't sure Wally could offer anything I hadn't considered.

"I could marry you. Father the baby. Give the baby a name. I've always loved you. I'd love a baby, and I'd love to take care of both of you."

"God, Wally, oh God!" I sat down and cried. Finally, I squeaked out, "I'm so touched! I cannot believe you. I don't know what to say."

"Say yes, goofball. I'd love to marry you!"

Wally was one of the very best friends I'd ever had—my first and only male friend. Though I seriously considered his offer, I was leery, worried that our marriage would be the demise of a beautiful friendship—a friendship I could not live without.

I squeezed him but did not answer, deciding to tell him no when I was headed back to Georgia.

We had a great Christmas with Wally's mother, Vanessa, and Zan's parents, who arrived from Alabama. When Zan's parents arrived, she transformed again. She put on a straight skirt, a lacy blouse, black pantyhose. I wondered if this was her costume for them. She hid her gypsy clothes in the back of her closet. "I have to do this for my mom. She'd freak out if she knew what I'm really like. Fortunately, her college roommate has sworn to keep my secret."

"My parents are like that too. They have no idea I'm a hippie, and they'd have a fit if they knew I was pregnant. They don't think I've ever kissed a guy. Thank God they are out of the country for a year."

"Thank God for small favors," Zan echoed.

I gave everyone pottery for Christmas. "I can't believe this is the first time you've taken a class!" Vanessa said. "This is as good as anything I carry in my gallery. Have you thought of selling it?"

"Not really. I just started."

"Well, send me some, and I'll sell it for you. Get some money in your pocket." The way Vanessa smiled at me I knew she knew I was pregnant. Zan shot me a silent look; I guess she was trying to tell me Vanessa was cool. She was. I also took that look to mean that Zan's parents certainly didn't know, didn't suspect. Thank God I didn't show yet.

"I'll do that! I'll send some pots, but you price them. I'm not used to the business side. I wouldn't know what price to ask."

"You'd better get used to it—learn the business. I think you've got real talent."

"Thanks."

"I think so too," Zan cooed. "You really ought to do something with this. The pieces are exquisite."

"It's hard work, but it calms me, gives me something to think about other than myself. I'm taking another class next quarter."

"Any way you can major in it?" Zan asked.

"I think so. I'm in my junior year and have already declared art as my major, so I can graduate with a major in art, emphasis in pottery."

"I'm glad you found something you are passionate about," Zan said.

"I think if I keep making pots, I might be okay."

"Then promise you'll make time for that," Zan said. "Promise?"

"Yeah, I promise. I know it's important for my sanity."

When I was ready to go back to Georgia, I asked Wally to walk me out to the car. Zan discreetly disappeared.

"I can't marry you, Wally. I'd love to—it'd be the easiest solution. But, I can't—I'm too young. I don't want to tie up your life with a friend, not a lover. You deserve someone who loves you from the bottom of her heart. I love you from the top of mine." I tried to laugh, to ease the seriousness that had come over him. "You deserve better. I'm only twenty. I'm not ready for a baby and the responsibilities that go with it. Thanks for loving me so much!" Wally tried to convince me, to bring me around to his solution. Although I wouldn't agree, I saw his pain and anguish in the way his shoulders drooped, the grimace on his face, and in the deep wrinkle between his eyebrows. It would be so easy to say yes—it would solve almost all of my problems, but I knew marriage between us wouldn't work, mainly for him. I hated leaving him in such despair but knew in my heart my decision was best. Our friendship had become one of the most important things in my life; I did not want to jeopardize it in any way, least of all solving my problems selfishly.

Driving back was hard. The few friends I had at university left me alone because I didn't party anymore. I was isolated, and my two best friends were more than five hundred miles away. They were also the only two who knew my secret, and I had rejected one of them. It took me all day to drive back to school, and it was one of the saddest days of my life. I stopped for gas and crackers, singing Janis Joplin and other blues songs all the way, talking to the baby, reluctantly, unwilling to get attached but unable to avoid it.

When grades arrived, I was shocked! I made all As for the first time in my life. It would be hard to convince my parents I needed summer school, so I just told them I was taking spring quarter off. I wasn't asking them, and they were so far away, they couldn't interfere.

Winter quarter was as dismal as fall, but I dreaded spring quarter more; I had no idea what childbirth would be like, and if I was honest, I knew it would be hard to give the baby up. If anyone noticed I was pregnant, no one said a word. I was sure I looked it, but this was a time when such things were ignored, never mentioned; no questions asked. It was not that problems were overlooked or unobserved; they were closeted, avoided. Even my teachers never made comment. In the early '70s, we did not use the word *dysfunctional*; we would not have known what someone was talking about if the word came up. However, ironically, we were a culture of dysfunction, a passive-aggressive generation who did not yet have the tools of self-discovery that would later be available. We accepted our lives without knowing we had the ability to change them. We were a generation of victims where later our own children would rise against such labels and take charge of their circumstances, fighting their demons and coming out victorious.

I arrived in Sarasota on April 1—appropriate, I thought, since I felt like a fool! Zan had outdone herself—she built herself a loft so I could have her bedroom to myself. Everything was clean and beautiful, herbs hanging from the ceiling, fresh flowers in every room, spilling out of vases in every color.

"I couldn't wait for you to get here!" Zan practically crowed, and my spirits lifted in response to her enthusiasm. "I do have to work at the bank, but we'll go to the beach at night and talk, just like old times! I've learned all kinds of new teas for the last month of pregnancy. I'm so glad you're here!" Zan bustled around, giving me clean sheets and towels, fixing a fruit salad for supper, and talking nonstop. I didn't want to talk but didn't need to as Zan didn't give me a chance.

"How's the bank?" I finally asked.

"It's the same place, but Mr. Krighten went to Yale, so I've got a new boss. I don't know where they found her— not from the same hole where they discovered Mr. Krighten, thank God. She's just like you—funny, silly. We have a great time—it's just the two of us, working on those files. Remember Ronnie Jones and Mrs. Treat? Well, it turns out..." Zan went through all the bank gossip, mimicking the people as she talked about them, making me laugh as I remembered each of them and their various quirks. "You ought to be in theater, Zan! Your imitations are spot-on!"

On April 22, Zan looked at me and said, "Today's the day! That baby's coming today! I'm staying home from work. I feel it in my bones."

"What the hell do you know? Today's no different from any other day." A few hours later as I left for a walk, my water broke all over the kitchen floor.

"Damn good thing you stayed home from work. It's all your fault. Shit! I'm not ready."

"Lordy, Lordy, what'd I tell you? If you ain't ready now, you never will be. That baby's happening."

Zan took me to the hospital, and I was surrounded by medical personnel in lab coats, nurse's uniforms, hospital whites, masks. I felt alienated. It was 1972—a few years before women took arms against the medical establishment and forced them to humanize the birthing process. No one was allowed to stay with me; I was given a shot in my cervix so I couldn't feel anything. I wasn't asked about any of the medical procedures that day.

Zan wanted to help with breathing exercises, but the doctor laughed at her. "Breathing? What are you talking about? She won't even know she's having a baby. She won't be thinking about breathing, I promise you! Now, don't worry your little head," the doctor said as he shoved Zan out of my room and began to roll me down the hall to the delivery room. I was a mere instrument in a cold, sterile event.

As the baby arrived, I looked up just as the doctor cut her umbilical cord. I thought I was screaming in agony, but none of the doctors or nurses responded, so it must have been an internal cry. The baby was dark-skinned, a beautiful little girl with a head full of dark, black hair. As they cleaned her and withdrew her from my room, I felt a grief so severe my stomach cramped and roiled; I pitched forward and threw up all over myself. For the first time since the baby's birth, the nurses turned to me, hurrying to clean me up, washing my face with a cold rag. I felt as though my eyes had blasted from their sockets; the tears steamed behind my eyes, but none fell. I could not weep.

It wasn't until I was wheeled back into my room that Zan was allowed to join me. That's also when we met Ilana, the social worker on the maternity ward. She was so different from Zan and me that we teased each other that she was from another planet. She whirled into my room, applying her lipstick as she entered, wearing four-inch heels and a low-cut silk blouse under a classy suit. "It's obvious she doesn't live on a social worker's salary," Zan whispered to me eyeing her. "I saw her drive in this morning in a brand-new Mercedes. Rich husband or a promising sideline," Zan snarled. We laughed together, imagining various scenarios.

Ilana never once talked to me about my emotional state; she ignored my questions about the adoption process and the adoption family. She spread the paperwork over the hospital bedside table and nonchalantly asked Zan to sign as my witness.

"Hell no, I'm not signing! Katrina's giving her baby up for adoption over my protest! She has to sign, but you have to get someone else to sign the witness line. Not me! I object."

I began crying, and Ilana said, "Dear, we go through this every day. Pull yourself together. It'll be over soon, and you'll forget it. Sign right here, and I'll find a witness since your friend here"—she glared at Zan—"is uncooperative."

"Get the fuck out of here," Zan advanced on Ilana like she was going to hit her, and Ilana moved faster on four-inch heels than anyone I'd ever seen. She waited over an hour to return, hoping Zan had left.

"Now, are we ready, dear?" Ilana's condescending tone crawled through my skin, sending shivers of anxiety up my spine. I hated to think my little baby girl would be in her arms for even a moment.

This time, following close behind Ilana was an older woman. "What am I signing?" the woman asked and looked from Ilana to me. "Are you sure you want me to sign this?" She waved at the paper and my tearstained face.

"I don't have a choice. It's okay." The woman would not sign until I reassured her that it was what I had to do, the first person in the hospital to give me even a moment's notice.

"Now, Ilana," Zan again advanced towards the social worker as the witness exited; Ilana began to follow her, but Zan stepped in her way. "You do know what Katrina wants for this baby, right? Nice stable home, lots of love—"

Ilana interrupted, "It's been taken care of. A nice family wants the baby; the arrangements are final. There is no changing your mind now." She pointed her finger at me, then at the document in her hands, just to solidify the finality of my decision. "I believe they are leaving with the baby as soon as I finish the paperwork," she haltingly spit the words at me. I could not respond because my spirit was shattered. I signed the papers after taking time to read everything, even the fine print. I refused to let Ilana shake me up, but when I could find no more delays, I signed. I did not cry while Ilana was in the room because I refused to give her the satisfaction.

After four days in the hospital, I felt ready to go back to Zan's cottage. During my time in the hospital, Zan tried to stay with me, but every night at midnight, the nurses ran her off. Finally, after a week, they released me. Zan drove her car around to pick me up at the departure door. I craned my neck to see if I saw a family with a brand-new baby, especially one with a head full of black hair. I had no idea then that I would crane my neck looking for a dark-haired girl for the rest of my life. My dark-haired baby girl, my firstborn.

Zan took me home and made a hot herbal tea as I sat with my feet up. "It's the toughest thing you'll ever do, Katrina. I know that. Are you sure you're okay? Want to talk about it?"

"I can't. I'd fall apart. Just thanks for being here, thanks for going through it with me."

I did not see Wally the rest of the trip, but I didn't stay in Sarasota long once I left the hospital. I couldn't. I was going crazy, thinking at every turn I'd see her, see the baby, thinking every young family with a dark-haired baby girl had my baby. Zan decided to drive me back to Atlanta then fly home to Sarasota; she did not want me to drive home alone. While she drove, I slept. I moved in with an old high school friend during the month of May and returned to West Georgia in June. My parents extended their stay in Scotland through September, so they were glad I went to summer school, none the wiser of anything going on in my life.

Frances came down to my dorm room as soon as I moved back in. "Hey, Bread Legs, where've you been? Boy, have you lost weight! You were getting hefty there for a while, thunder thighs. Want to smoke some pot?"

I wanted to scream, pull her hair out. Instead I gritted my teeth, calming down, reminding myself she did not know what I'd just been through. I politely refused the pot, the partying. After three invitations, she finally quit asking.

Zan, I wrote,

> *It is tough being here without you,*
> *without the baby. You are the best friend a*

41

woman could ever ask for, you know that,
don't you? Most difficult, of course, is being
here without the baby, I still think of her as
mine—my baby. Going nine months carry-
ing a tiny human being inside me, getting
so attached, talking to it when I had no one
else to talk to (which was most of the time
until I moved in with you)—it's so damn
hard, I still cry all the time.

God, what a living hell! How can I
ever date again? Marry? Shit no! Not on my
horizon!

Love,
Katrina

Although my brain knew I had made the right decision giving up the baby, my heart did not agree with this decision, making me continue to struggle; although my decision—my brain's decision—was final, the battle in my heart was ongoing, one I might never relinquish.

Katrina,
None of my friends—truly, not one of
my friends—has ever gone off the deep end,
so neither can you! You cannot be the first
friend to land in the looney bin, got that?
I know your strength—God! I lived with
it—watched you make the hardest decision
I've ever witnessed. And, you did it, girl.
Best decision—not for you, but for the baby.

*Know I love you and always will. You
are PIONEER WOMAN, Queen of the Pack!*
Love,
Zan

After giving birth to the baby, once again I turned to pottery for release. My pots changed noticeably in design, the artwork taking on a distinct maternal feeling. The baby's influence was evident, at least to me. I wrapped outer bowls around inner bowls, outer cups around inner ones, as if my pieces longed for an embrace. I made vessels, artwork that appealed to women, not men. And that's who I sold to—women were my main source of revenue. Vanessa sold a lot in her shop and found several galleries willing to carry my work on consignment so much of my income came from South Florida.

I made lots of abstract art as well, sculptured pieces of mothers reaching for their children or mothers longing for children who were not there. I know it's hard to express how you could tell what the mothers were longing for since the children weren't there, but it was easy to see. I can't explain it. "Empty Arms" was a frequent title, and such pieces became one of my trademarks.

The next year, my senior year in college, was tough. Not only did I shy away from friends, I wrestled with a deep self-loathing.

Dear Zan, I wrote,

> *It is hard not to hate myself—a con-
> stant battle and one I am, unfortunately,
> losing. I have always had a dislike for
> myself, nurtured by parents unwilling to*

compliment, parents who did not know how to encourage talents (or help in the discovery of them), parents who were more tied up with one another than with me. Theirs was a generation of stalwart parenting, "Let the baby cry," the philosophy of their day. Now my self-hatred is virulent—I want to hold the baby, to soothe its crying (NEVER let it cry, for God's sakes!) but what did I do? I gave the baby away!

Before I met you and Wally, my friendships reflected self-loathing: I was bread legs, teased mercilessly, encouraged by supposed friends' taunting to despise myself. That was until I met you. You're so full of love for me, you encourage me to love myself. And, yet having this baby, giving it up, has been a huge set-back in this arena.

Suicide is a constant option—a dark companion. There are two reasons I want to live: the hope that someday I will meet the little girl I gave away, and a professor here who believes in me, loves my work, nurtures in me what I do not nurture in myself! Please do not fly here—I truly am okay—I just wish I did not have to make decisions—I feel so empty and alone without the baby. But I will survive, I promise!

Love,
Katrina

Katrina,

You've always valued my opinions, looked up to me, right? Then, value this: I love you! You're the greatest, Girl! Get it, Girl!!

You are a gift!!

Love,
Zan

"Katrina, your work is so full of expression," my favorite professor, Dr. Clara Hall, told me. "You've come a long way in such a short time. All your feelings must be revealed in your work as you are so quiet. You should go to Penland next year."

"Penland? What's that?" I was surprised at her description of me. No one had ever called me quiet before this last year. I had changed drastically, become isolated.

"It's not what, it's where. It's an arts community in North Carolina that has lots to offer. I'll write and see when they have openings and get a schedule of their classes. I'll help you choose an instructor who will complement your style. I think you'd do well to study under a Japanese artist—it would be stimulating for you, something new and different to broaden your perspective."

"I'm not sure I want to go," I felt pushed, insecure.

"You can't hibernate forever. I don't know what you are hiding from, but you have to spread your wings sometime. You have to fly. Or, you'll bury yourself in your depression, and your work will never go anywhere. It's in my best interest for your work to succeed—then I can say, 'I was one of her first instructors!'" She put her arms around me and hugged me close. I let myself be embraced in the hug, but did not hug back.

I thought about her suggestion, and truly, having nowhere else to go—Sarasota was no longer an option, I was too afraid I couldn't stop looking for my baby; Atlanta felt too big for my self-imposed isolation, so I applied.

Go! Go! Go! Zan wrote,

> *What else are you gonna do if you don't? Where else can you surround yourself with your passion? Thank Allah, you have a passion! If you didn't, you'd be dead or committed, know what I mean? Jelly Bean!*
> *Go! Go! Go!*
> *Oh, and one more thing—Go!*
>
> > *Love,*
> > *Zan Dora*

I went.

CHAPTER 4

*M*y roommate there was the brightest star that had shone my way since I'd spent the summer in Sarasota and met Zan and Wally. A nonstop talker, full of ideas, pushy, overwhelming; she was not going to leave me alone. She made me go with her everywhere.

"Flipping far out, woman," she exclaimed when I unpacked some of my work. "I've never seen pottery like this. You're good, you know that? I was so afraid I'd get a dippy roommate. You know, an untalented fruit loop."

"I don't think Penland takes untalented fruit loops, Gia. I was afraid I'd get a roommate like you," I said, causing Gia to laugh uproariously.

"Sure, girl, sure. I'm a holy terror, I know that. No one in their right mind would want me for a roommate. My mother would even agree with you!"

Gia was short, busty, built like a fire hydrant, and her pots reflected a comical self-image—squat, round cups, and big-breasted fertility goddesses were her primary subjects. Vanessa would love her work!

"We're coming up next weekend," Zan announced over the phone one night. "If you can't make yourself come to Sarasota, we'll come to you."

"You know why I can't come to Sarasota," I protested, but Zan silenced me. "Who's we?"

"Wally and I are driving up together. We want to come and check on you. And, he's moving to Georgia at the end of this month, so we want one more trip together."

"Why's he moving to Georgia? I thought he was committed to Florida?"

"Committed to Florida or in Florida! Oooh, he'd love that! He got a job in Columbus, Georgia. He's doing something with an agricultural agency. He loves dirt, the farm, and Florida hasn't given him an opportunity like this one. He will be applying his engineering degree to a rural community—this is right up his alley."

Wally and Gia liked each other from the start. I knew he liked her when he nicknamed her Gia Good Body. I saw little of them the rest of the weekend, and the only reason Wally left with Zan was so Zan would not have to drive home alone.

"I'm flying to Sarasota this weekend," Gia told me. "Ummm, I like that friend of yours. I want to meet his mom too," Gia said while painting her toenails.

"Vanessa? You'll love her. Take some of your pots. She has an art shop where she carries mostly women's work. Her shop, Mariposa, is on Anna Maria Island. Her customers will love your pieces. Particularly the fertility goddesses. Take plenty of those."

"I just hope she loves me. I think I'm moving to Georgia with that friend of yours."

"What friend?"

"Wally, goofball. Who else?"

"You just met him." I had not seen that one coming and was a bit overwhelmed with my reaction though I didn't let my face show. I found myself jealous—felt a loss so deep I had a major cramp in my stomach. How could this be? I had had my chance, my opportunity. How could I interfere with Wally's happiness when I had turned him down? I shook myself, straightened my shoulders, told myself to get over it! It wasn't as easy as it should have been, but I knew in my heart it was the right thing for both Gia and Wally. For some reason, once I thought it over, they did fit perfectly together. She was also the typical body type he found attractive: short and muscular with an engaging laugh. Besides, the reason I had turned down marriage to him was just so something like this could happen.

"Are you stuffy or what? I've always dreamed of living in Columbus, Georgia, haven't you?" Gia threw back her head and laughed, her eyes gleaming. She smelled of love. I envied her, felt a loss even though I'd had my chance.

While Gia was in Sarasota for the weekend, I realized Penland was different without her. She'd been a constant companion, pushing me, organizing my social calendar, talking. Without her, I sat in silence on the front porch, observing the goings-on, not participating.

"You've sat on your ass long enough." A tall black man approached me one evening, and I jumped.

"What's it to you?" I turned back to people-watching, ignoring him.

He stared at me until I was forced to look at him.

"I like your work." He sat down in the rocker next to me.

"That's strange," I said, "most men don't."

"I was raised by strong black Southern women, so maybe I understand your work while most men don't."

"Maybe you do," I conceded, warming up despite my resistance; his alarming appearance (any man who approached me would be alarming) but interesting conversation was penetrating my wall.

"I can't believe you talk and smile," he said, grinning at me.

Every night, he waited for me at the rocking chairs. After Gia returned, she was so dopey in love he was a relief. I saw little of her—she was always on the phone with Wally, no longer pushing social events on me. She would have left immediately but felt she had to finish her classes. "Besides," she told me, "I'm not moving to Sarasota then to Georgia. By the time this class is over, Wally will be settled in Columbus. Can you imagine me in Columbus? Are they ready for me?"

"I don't think so! Most places aren't ready for you! This could be funny!"

"Yeah, and the way I look, some dog will probably pee on me."

"What do you mean?"

"Mistake me for a fire hydrant! I'd better not wear red!"

"They probably don't have fire hydrants in Columbus, Georgia, so you won't have to worry. What are you going to do for a living?"

"Wally and I talked it over. He's going to find a place large enough for me to have a studio. I'll sell my pottery through Vanessa and do art shows. Weekends will be hell because I'll be traveling, but I'll be home all week. We are so in love we are getting married soon!"

"Isn't that a bit abrupt? You just met! How did you make these decisions so quickly?"

"You, Wally told me, are one of the most spontaneous people he knows! You moved to Sarasota, rented an apartment, and got a job without knowing a soul! How dare you act this straitlaced, this stiff with me? We are both in transition—he is moving to Georgia, where he knows no one; me, finishing Penland and not knowing what I was going to do next. So, we've decided to embrace the opportunity, move in together in Columbus, then if it is working, we'll get married by December in Columbus. I've always wanted a fairy-tale, Christmas wedding! Will you be one of my bridesmaids?"

Though stunned, reeling actually, I agreed. A Christmas wedding with all my friends there, and one of my best friends the groom; on second thought, it did sound magical! And it wasn't in Sarasota, so I did not yet have to face that fear—the resistance I had to going there.

"We've never formally introduced ourselves," my new friend said a few nights later. "My name's Clayton. Yours is Katrina, isn't it?" He had a straightforward way of taking charge of a conversation. "Nice Southern name." He always knew when to leave me alone, when it was okay to push. On nights I was depressed, he handled our conversations lightly; on nights I was happier, he bulldozed. We frequently talked late into the night.

"So, tell me, what is your definition of the artist as a young woman?" he asked me late one night.

"What the hell? What are you talking about?"

"I don't think one can truly be an artist until one defines it in personal terms. Wouldn't you agree?"

"Are you majoring in philosophy or art?" I asked sarcastically.

"Art. But I hold fast to my belief. If you can't define it, you can't be it, can't create it."

"Bullshit," I shouted, then realized he had riled my passion, made me respond.

"Bingo!" he exclaimed, "just what I was looking for!"

"What does your art express from your inner being, Clayton?" I challenged.

"I'm working on it. Black man's struggle in white man's world—that's too trite, too dull for me. Primitive art doesn't do it for me either. That's why I particularly wanted to study Japanese pottery—study under Shoji Muraoka. I think I'm focusing on the will of the black man to claim his power, to find his place in the art world. How many black artists can you name? Have you studied art history? There are damn few black people who've earned a place in art history books. Sure, we have our artists and our art, but they are yet to be recognized outside of 'black art.' I'm into recognition. It's something I need to do for me and for my people. What about you? You seem to have a deeper side—an artist's personae, so to speak. What's it all about, Alfie?"

I laughed and began to sing the popular song, diverting his attention as I sang fairly well. We ended up the evening without returning to his philosophical commentary, but Clayton was not to be stopped. He hit again the next evening, "So last night you copped out, you didn't answer me. What's your definition of an artist?"

I made an attempt to define what I thought comprised an artist. "Isn't an artist someone who functions primarily through their creative expression? More right-brained than logical, methodical? Does an artist have to make their money as an artist, or are artists all people who attempt creative expression in a wide variety of forms? It can be pottery, watercolor, theater, dance, right?"

"In my world, be it Utopia or perhaps make-believe, I like to think of an artist as someone who spends their vocation earning their livelihood making art. That's what I am aiming for. What about you?"

"That would be my ideal, my dream too, but I'm not sure how that will happen. Money, you know? That important fact of life."

"Your art is so expressive—so very female—has so much yearning. I get the feeling I'm missing something. Are you hiding something? It's as though you are trapped in your artwork. All the message just ain't there, girl. You know?"

I did not respond. I was almost hostile and turned back to people-watching, excluding Clayton, something I had not done in weeks.

"I hope you discover it or admit it, whichever is the truth for you. Your work is powerful, but it will be more so once you wrestle your enemy and win. And, from what I know of you, you will win, trust me, not the enemy."

I glared at him. He left the rocking chairs quickly that evening and did not show up for our conversations the next week. During that week, my pottery changed, due somewhat to Shoji Muraoka's Japanese influence. Delving further into the Japanese style, I incorporated bamboo, building a tripod stand with the bamboo to hold my work of thrusting slender vases. The vases were not quite phallic but almost. On the flat sides of the vases, I imprinted textures from burlap to knobby fleece, textures I had never used before. Some of the vases had the same texture on all sides, some had a different texture on each side. I said some of my changes were due to Mr. Muraoka, but not everything I did was from his influence. I was also reacting to Clayton's comment that my work expressed female energy to the exclusion of male energy. Mr. M. was the first to notice, saying, "Well, Katrina, you're finally exploring new possibilities, eh?" as Clayton snickered in the background. I glared at him while simultaneously smiling at Mr. M. "A big step for you—one I've been waiting for," Mr. M. continued. I turned bright red and heard Clayton agree under his breath.

"Damn him," I thought and continued to avoid him.

When I raged about Clayton, Gia laughed at me. "You let that intellectual bear get to you," she said. "He stimulates you, pushes you just as he means to. You need it."

"And, you don't?" I sneered, sarcastically. "You're content with large-breasted fertility goddesses and oversized cups?"

"For your information, smarty, I'm trying new ideas too. You've just never asked to see them."

She was right. I was jealous of her love life and had avoided her the past few weeks.

"I'm sorry, Gia. Let's go to the studio and see your stuff. I've been steering clear of you, but it's because you are so damn happy."

"I'll only go if you promise to meet Clayton tonight."

"What's it to you whether I see him or not?"

"Lots of reasons. One: he's driving me crazy—every night bugging me—where are you? What are you doing? What are you working on? Two: you are happier when you talk to him—you're more inspired, less depressed, calmer even. Three: I'd like to have my friend, you, back in my life."

After I promised to see Clayton later, we left our cabin and walked to the studios. Gia's work was outstanding—she had been exploring new dimensions, using new glazes and firings I'd never thought to use. "Mr. M. suggested these. It has an interesting effect, doesn't it?" as if there was any doubt. I agreed, wanting to try some of these ideas myself.

Most playful was her hand building—her "fire hydrant people"—again, comical self-portraits. But now her pieces looked like her, Wally, and other people at Penland. "I know Mr. M. didn't inspire these." I laughed.

"But he thinks they are wonderful—'American' art, he calls it. I'm giving the first two to Wally for a wedding present. No traditional bride and groom as cake toppers at our wedding!" She laughed.

"He'll love them! They're so—you!"

"So Wally too, eh? He'll know which one of these is him, won't he?" She laughed. The male was squat and pudgy; her figures looked remarkably like people in our classes. I spotted Clayton and Mr. M. but didn't see any that looked like me.

"You've got everyone here from class but me," I said, with a question in my expression.

"Observant, aren't you?" Where had I heard that before? Gia pulled back a piece of plastic from one of her unfinished works. I gasped.

"It's my masterpiece, my final," she said, revealing a clay figure so like me it was unmistakable. Yet this figure was so very sad I had a dramatic visceral response. It did represent me, the part of me I lost, left behind in Sarasota.

"I'm sorry," Gia whispered.

My eyes filled with tears. "It's amazing," I said, reaching to touch it when Gia's arm stopped me, reminding me it was wet clay, not yet complete, ruined if touched. I was no longer a potter and forgot basic technicalities but responding to the intensive sensitivity Gia's work provoked.

"You're not offended, are you?" she asked.

"No way. It's great. Masterpiece," I whispered, "all of them are." I kissed my hand to the wind.

"Now, go see Clayton. I told him you were coming, but he doesn't believe me. He knows how stubborn you are."

*****

"So, decided to come back for me?" he greeted me once I returned to our philosophical porch spot.

"I can take it. You were right, Clayton, but I'm not willing to talk about it…yet."

"I'd rather talk to you than push you away. I'll leave it alone for now, but talk once you're ready—if you ever are. It has something to do with what Gia's expressed in her portrait of you, doesn't it?"

"So, she's shown you that?"

"I've seen her working on it faithfully, every day, struggling to get it just right. It's one powerful piece, isn't it? She's captured something inside you we've both observed."

"Yep, she got it to a tee. I just may never be ready to talk about it, unfortunately."

"You can always trust me, you know that, don't you?"

I was beginning to, and it made me feel peaceful while it also frightened me.

The next night, we walked the grounds, stopping under a big oak tree and lying down on a blanket, looking at the stars.

"You are a dear friend, Katrina. You know that? Sometimes I think I'd lose my mind if I didn't find people in the world like you."

"What do you mean?"

"Artists—other deep people. I spend a lot of time dealing with dumb people, surface people, it seems. I love it when I can talk to someone the way I talk to you."

"I love you, Clayton—your mind, your art, your heart. You have a big soul."

"I'm getting married after these classes are over. If I wasn't, I'd propose to you."

"That'd be a trip, wouldn't it? People are hardly ready for a black man to marry a white woman yet. Maybe one day it'll happen, but not yet. Especially here in the South!" I responded warmly to his words; they made me feel internally happy. After never having any male friends, now I had two whom I loved dearly. Clayton was someone I valued greatly and loved talking to intelligently. But again, like with Wally, I was glad we were friends, not lovers. This time in my life was about new beginnings with men—men as friends, people I trusted and thoroughly enjoyed. A new dimension in my life, a depth I had always searched for and was welcoming in.

"I'll tell you my story if you promise not to pity me. I've never talked about it except to two other people, and it feels like it might overwhelm me to tell it, to revisit it."

"Like you're going to go crazy or something?"

"Or something. Yeah."

"I know about those feelings. I felt that way until I met Annabella. She keeps me sane. She believes in my work—in the importance of a black man making it in the art world. She promises to support us—she's a teacher—even if I struggle and never make enough money. Like Van Gogh—poor man, never sold but one painting during his life, and now look! She's even okay if I never succeed. I'm not, but she is."

"You're lucky to have someone like that." I paused, preparing for opening the emotional wound after concealing it over the past year.

"Well, here goes." I took a deep breath. "I got caught with my pants down—literally—and had a baby. I had the baby and gave it up for adoption. That's the reaching—the yearning you feel—see in my work. I long for that baby, my arms always feel empty."

"Shit, that's worse than I considered." I began to cry, and Clayton pulled me close. "My sister had a baby too—two or three years ago. My mom is keeping him and raising him while my sister goes on with her life. She's in college and hopes to take him back once she can support herself. I think that's a difference between blacks and whites. Whites have a different opinion about children out of wedlock, don't have the acceptance for that, that we have in our culture. We were forced to have so many while enslaved, all babies are precious to us."

"Yeah, my parents would rather die than know I was pregnant. I never told them the whole nine months."

"How'd you do that?"

"They left the country for a year. My father is a professor at Agnes Scott and had a sabbatical. Fortunately, it was the same year I was pregnant."

"I bet you will find someone someday and have more children. You're too good to pass up—like gold, like the girl next door that men wake up and always wish they'd married. You're like Annabella." He paused. "Don't mourn too much for the child you lost, or you'll never be true to your future children."

"You ought to major in philosophy. Either that or bullshit, I can't figure out which. I never really wanted children until I got pregnant. Now, children are what I want more than anything. Almost more than being an artist."

"As much. Only as much. You have to have a strong drive to make it in the art world, or you won't succeed. Don't ever give that up."

"But, I'm not sure I even want to make it. What does 'make it' mean?"

"You think that way because you're white, middle-class. You have the advantage of not thinking about money, about material needs." He brushed my hand aside as I objected. "Not really, not the kind that has experienced hunger, doesn't know if the rent will be paid. You've always had food, a roof over your head, I bet, bet you didn't question whether you were going to college or not, you were just going. And it was always only a matter of where you were going, not how you were going to pay for it. Am I right?"

"Yeah. You're right. I never had a choice. Never even thought about it. I was going to college. That was it. Finishing my degree too. No student loans either."

"I would have loved that advantage. I knew I was going—my mom was totally focused on it, but paying for it was another story. I had to keep a scholarship profile because, buddy, if I didn't, I didn't go. In my family, we had to do what Mama told us! So, I had to choose between an academic scholarship or an athletic one. I bet you don't have to help your parents out with money either."

"No, they help me," I admitted.

"I'm still helping mine, paying off my brothers' and sister's college tuitions. I send money home for my mom even if I have to go without. Sometimes it means I produce artwork for sale, not for the love of it. Money isn't always spent on what I consider my finest work."

"My parents support me, you're right. They pay for my time here at Penland, for my supplies and stuff. I work, I sell, but it's only a pittance so far."

"Money's a big part of my focus because it has to be. I don't want Annabella to support me even though she's willing. I'm willing to let her for a while on the hope, the dream, that I will succeed, that'll I make it and be able to pay her back."

"You're a deep man, Clayton."

"It gets me in trouble sometimes. I don't stay happy for long—my mind takes over, I start questioning the universe, the reason for everything. You need to recognize the advantages you have. You've had your trials, your shit. You are understandably drained and defensive. I believe you'll make it. You'll do well in art and in life."

"Thanks. It's been a long time since I've believed in me. I need your support. It means the world to me."

"I guess it's time to go to bed. Are you tired?"

"I guess, but I do love talking to you! I could talk all night."

"We'll continue tomorrow. Meet me here tomorrow night. I have a plan."

"What?" I folded my arms across my belly, almost as if guarding myself, protecting myself from what he might have in mind. I frowned, deep in thought, unable and unwilling to tell Clayton what I was thinking. What did he have planned for me? Would it strip me of my protective shell? Hurt me deeper than I already hurt?

"Trust me. Just trust me."

"That's a big request, but I'm learning."

He arrived early the next evening just as a full moon peaked over the oak tree. He was carrying a shoebox close to his chest.

"What's that?" I was suspicious.

"Miss Impatience. Just relax." Clayton spread the blanket down, and we sat, face-to-face. "My mom's a saint," he began as if he was a storyteller bound to tell his story, "she's tied to this world and to the world of her ancestors. She carries the knowledge of both worlds—she exists freely, matter of fact, in the South where she was raised, but she never lost sight of her oral history—the rituals, the beliefs of her ancestors. Her mother made sure of that.

"Here in my shoebox are the tools to lay your pain to rest—to soothe the trouble you carry within." As he opened the shoebox, he moved into the center of the blanket. "I have to move to continue my work," he said, then held up a sculptured piece of clay, an abstract work that looked like arms reaching for the sky. It was unlike anything I had ever seen. He sat it in the middle of the blanket and took a smooth white candle and a small penknife from his box. He began to carve and shape the wax until it looked remotely like me. I giggled nervously. "It's okay." He patted my hand gently, and I relaxed, taking a deep breath, knowing it was not time to ask questions.

He sat the white candle on the abstract art and then picked up a green candle. "This symbolizes your young daughter," he told me as he carved it too, again in my likeness. He picked the white candle back up, lit a match to both, and melted them into one piece. He set them on his sculpture, inside the arms, and set it down on the blanket between us. "As the green candle melts into the white, close your eyes and take a deep breath. Imagine accepting your daughter freely, with love, without guilt, without emotion." I closed my eyes as Clayton lit the candle, and I almost fell asleep, his voice so soothing, so peaceful.

"Release it, Katrina. Give up your grief. Receive love— from your baby for doing what was right for her. From yourself. Find within the deep love you've lost." As he spoke, a chill snaked up my spine into the back of my head, numbing my face, drying unshed tears of emotion, of deep pain. I took a gulp of air and opened my eyes, searching for Clayton's eyes, looking for reassurance. He sat as if in a trance, eyes shut, mouth pursed in thought. Slowly, finally, he opened his eyes without speaking and motioned for me to blow out the candle. Out of habit, as I blew, I made a wish, praying for a family—for new babies to replace the laughter I had lost in giving away my firstborn.

After ceremoniously burning the two candles into the sculptured artwork, Clayton whispered, "It's time."

Caught up in the ritual, I whispered back, "Time for what?"

"You need to bury the mother and child and, in doing so, free yourself of your guilt."

"I'll try," I promised and took the spade he handed me, digging a hole the size of the shoebox, two feet down. Neither of us spoke until I finished. As I lowered the pottery into the ground, Clayton sprinkled a yellow powder over it, whispering, "Ashes to ashes, dust to dust." Then he turned to me. "Repeat after me."

"Ashes to ashes, dust to dust," I noticed the reverent tone of my own whispered voice.

"Take this guilt and provide new life, you must."

"Take my guilt," I hardly noticed changing Clayton's words, claiming them for my own, "and provide new life, you must."

"What was done was done in the spirit of love."

Clayton acknowledged my whispered repetition of his words.

"Fly away, fly away, and bring the peace of the dove."

When we finished, he whispered, "Don't speak," and sealed my mouth with his gentle fingers. I put the last clumps of dirt on the hole as the tears streamed down my face. Our work complete, my unshed tears had finally come, and I cried in Clayton's arms, deep, sobbing gasps of unspent emotion. After a while, we walked back to my cabin, wordlessly.

Gia must have picked up on my mood as she said nothing but helped me into bed, tucking the blankets around me. "Sleep well," she whispered and turned out the light, shutting the door as she left me to my drifting images. I heard her shuffle down the hall to call Wally but never heard her return.

"How do you feel?" Clayton was playful the next morning, eager to see me.

"I do feel better. A bit groggy but better."

"That's a recipe straight from my mom. I have one more, but it'll keep."

That night, he met me at the rocking chairs. "You are beginning to trust me, eh? That's another repair job I'm working on."

"What do you mean?"

"Trust. Something else you need to rediscover. By not asking me—all day I might add—about my other recipe, I see you are learning to trust again—at least, trust me."

"That I am, that I am. It's a big step."

"I know," he said; and by the way he looked at me, I knew that he knew he was treading on my spirit while at the same time nurturing it.

"This is for you." He pulled out a flat piece of clay about the size of a fifty-cent piece. As I took it in my fingers, I felt, before seeing, the detail of his work. A woman was carved into the face of the clay with her arms outstretched; the background showed a faint outline of a child.

"Keep it in your pocket and rub it when you feel despair coming on," he told me. "It'll bring you peace, take away some of your pain." He didn't tell me then that as I rubbed it, I would rub off the carving in direct proportion to finding happiness in my life, putting some of my grief behind me.

"What was that witchcraft you performed?" I asked Clayton.

"Not witchcraft. Mama Power. My mama's one powerful black lady, and when she works spells, treats people, they get better. She taught her powers to me, made sure they were passed down to my generation. They work, don't they?"

"That they do." We sat in silence for a long time. I finally asked him a question I had dreaded asking, "Are you ready to leave Penland? I can't stand the thought. What are you doing next?"

"Annabella and I are getting married—December 8. Will you come?"

"Wouldn't miss it! Where's it going to be?"

"Charleston. Annabella's got a teaching job there, and I hope to get involved with the art festivals. I hear the city is planning a huge festival at the end of May, beginning of June. I'd like to get involved as an artist or in management. Probably both in order to earn a living."

I found leaving Penland difficult for many reasons: I hated saying goodbye to Gia and Clayton although we promised we'd write and visit. But worse was not knowing what I'd do next, where I'd live. I wanted to be an artist, but I also needed to support myself. I had graduated college; my parents' support would end soon.

"Move to Charleston with me and Annabella," Clayton offered, but I declined.

"A new marriage doesn't need a third person. Besides, you've helped me so much. I need to fly on my own to see if I can."

"You can! My mom's medicine is strong. It doesn't fail as long as there's love within the person receiving it."

"Come to Columbus," Gia and Wally both begged when Wally came to pick up Gia.

"Yeah, right. First, I can't see me in Columbus, Georgia. Second, you lovebirds would forget me as soon as you set up house. You'll make babies and all the stuff married folks do."

Although they protested, I told them honestly, "There's nothing in Columbus for me. I don't have someone to make me move there."

"But you will come for the wedding, right? It's going to be December 21. I've invited Clayton too and Zan. It'll be a great time. Don't forget: I want you as one of my bridesmaids."

"It's right after Clayton's! Two weddings in December…
at least it won't be too long before I see all of you again. I will
put it on my calendar right now," I promised Gia.

Sarasota, Zan wrote,

> *I need you! We can move into the art
> section, share an apartment. Today! Today!
> Come today!*
>
> *Zan*

> *I'm still avoiding Sarasota. I cannot
> bear to think that every dark-haired two-
> year-old girl might be mine! I'm better but
> haven't been cured that much. Maybe one
> day, I hope and pray.*
>
> *Katrina*

CHAPTER 5

I imagined the whole world was coupled but me. I moved back to Atlanta and stayed with my parents for two weeks. A man, someone I knew from high school, called when he heard I was back in town.

"We live in a big house on Briarcliff Road and have room for one more," Ed said when he called.

"Who's we?" I was interested but didn't know Ed well. We had only hung out in the same group but had not had much interaction, Ed and me.

"A group of artists needing a cheap place to live." His voice sounded eager to have me move in; he sounded more fun than I remembered.

"Such as? Anyone I know?"

"I'm not sure. Do you know a potter named Tricia Travis?"

"I might have met her at Callanwolde. Is she tall and thin with long brown hair?"

"Real pretty?"

"Yeah," I said, remembering her as a hard worker, a friendly woman who had not been one of the cutthroat, competitive potters but someone who shared ideas and supplies. I liked her.

"Same Tricia. She shares the house, and there are two women actors—Scottie and Ginny. They're together—lovers."

"Do they perform at Open City? I think I met them there. Were they in *Women behind Bars*?"

"Sure were. You've got a great memory. That's where they met. Open City's right around the corner, so they walk to work. Don't own a car. Callanwolde is just three blocks down from the house."

"Who else?"

"So, if there's somebody you don't like or don't know, you're not moving in?" He scoffed.

"That's not it. I'd like to know what I'm getting into. It sounds great. I think I'd like to share a house with you."

"There's another guy, Tony. A jazz musician from New Orleans, and we have room for one more. What about it? We have art events every month to help pay rent. The first weekend, Ginny and Scottie host theatrical events and sell tickets. The second weekend is music, and the third is an arts sale—pots you and Tricia offer and my paintings. All proceeds pay rent."

"How did you know I threw pots?"

"I saw your mom at the post office. She was telling me you were at Penland. Seemed proud of you." That was a first!

I told him, "I'll need a work space."

"I figured. There's a garage in the back. Tricia has a kiln and has room for another wheel." He knew how to convince me.

I moved in. Rent was so cheap with so many people living together, I didn't need a day job, reminding me happily of the discussions Clayton and I had had over what made an artist: maybe I would be a "real" artist one day. I certainly hoped to be considered an artist sooner rather than later. I was happy at the Briarcliff House. That was important too.

Zan wrote:

> *Vanessa and I are coming to Atlanta*
> *the weekend of your art sale. Vanessa has*
> *an unusual present for you. She also wants*
> *to make sure your work environment is*
> *stimulating. People are clamoring for your*
> *work down here and she's got to ensure your*
> *productivity. You KNOW what a mother hen*
> *she is!*
>
> *Zan*

The weekend turned into a surprise reunion with Gia and Wally, Clayton and Annabella coming too.

"We have blessed each other," Clayton told me. "Vanessa's taking some of my work to Sarasota, and you've found a house with a large porch and rocking chairs. I sure hope you think of me when you rock out here."

"I do." I was so serious Clayton laughed. "I'm not working another job, so I've been giving serious thought to your idea of what an artist is! Maybe I am one after all."

"You are, Katrina. That's what I was trying to tell you at Penland. We believe in you, now all you need is to believe in yourself."

"I'm working on it," I responded.

"Vanessa says we're at the forefront of a new or rather old art form that's just being recognized—something called folk art. She's amazed that you, Gia, and I all produce in that genre yet met at such a structured workshop with Mr. Muraoka. I guess that shows our range."

Now I laughed at him, his seriousness, his philosophical bent, which had not been diminished even after a move to Charleston. "Clayton, my philosopher." I hugged him close, drinking in his warm heat, a heat I had come to rely on and associate with getting well, burying some of the demons that haunted me.

"You are a gift," he said. "Ms. Folk Art. Nice ring to it, eh?"

"I do like the sound of it. Moving in here, I live with enough people that I don't need a day job—that's pretty folksy too, ain't it?" We both laughed. "Pottery pays my share of the rent. Am I lucky or what?"

"Ain't luck, girl! My mom calls it grace. That's what you've got—grace."

Vanessa's unusual present was an old station wagon with 110,000 miles on it. "This thing's for you," she told me. "Zan and I are flying home. It's too old to sell, and Gia and Wally don't want it. Besides, I think you can use it to haul your pottery stuff, keep Queenie clean, and keep low mileage on her."

I named the car Gracey, after Clayton's comment from his mother—I did have grace and appreciated it. I hung Mardi Gras beads on the rearview mirror and fluorescent stars on the ceiling. It *was* perfect for hauling—no worry about dirt, clay, bamboo, other trash I picked through and piled in the back. Most everything I salvaged fit, so I didn't need to rent a truck. I included a lot of found objects in my work.

While on this visit, Gia, Wally, and Vanessa spent a lot of time planning the wedding. It was to be in Columbus, held at the River Mill Event Center.

"I was not brought up religious," Gia told me. "Wally and Vanessa are fine with a neutral location. It will make my family more comfortable." I was getting excited—the wedding was only three months away!

The wedding was as wonderful and as different from Clayton's as it could possibly be. Clayton and Annabella married December 8, in a church with their reception in the fellowship hall; I did not know anyone else at the wedding and was one of the few white people there. I finally met his mother and found her a powerful presence; she smiled at me and looked at me as though she knew me through and through. Clayton must have told her a lot about me.

At Gia's wedding, everyone I cared about was there: Zan, Clayton, Annabella, and Vanessa. Gia was beautiful in a cream-colored dress, her flowers, daisies. Wally was radiant, wearing a cream-colored tuxedo with a daisy boutonniere. They each had two attendants: Zan and I stood up for Gia; Clayton and Mike, Zan's boyfriend from Sarasota, stood up for Wally. I wasn't surprised Wally did not follow tradition: his mother, Vanessa, was his best "person"; he chose her instead of a best man. We partied into the wee hours with endless champagne. At the end of the wedding, before the reception started, I noticed a tall, dark-haired man leave the premises. He looked vaguely like Jonathan.

"Did you see him?" I asked Wally. "What's he doing here?" I nearly came out of my skin in anxiety.

"Yes, I saw him, and yes, it was who you think it was," Wally answered as Zan walked up and chimed in.

"I thought I saw him too. What in the hell was he doing here?"

"Hell, if I know," Wally answered honestly, "but I chased after him and asked him that question. He said he was torn up that he wasn't my best man. Wasn't in my wedding."

"How did you respond?" I asked Wally.

"I told him he knew good and well why he didn't stand with me. He looked shocked like he didn't know what the hell I was talking about. He asked if that was you standing beside Gia."

"He asked about me?" I squeaked.

"I told him I didn't want to hear any of his lies, fabrications, bullshit! He looked so hurt I could hardly stand it, but it's my wedding. I didn't want him here. I think he got it and left soon after. I almost believed he didn't know what I was talking about, but I think it was just a bunch of shit."

Clayton walked up just then and put his arms around me, hugging me tight. "How'd he even get invited? How'd he know about your wedding?" Clayton asked. Not one of us had a clue and finally put the subject to rest. All except me; I tossed and turned all night, horrified I'd almost come face-to-face with him, horrified he had seen me and asked about me.

Wally and Gia left for the Bahamas the following morning. Wally never told me Mike was one of his attendants because he wouldn't ask Jonathan. He didn't consider Jonathan a friend anymore after what happened to me. I only found that out later. None of us knew if Jonathan had sneaked into the wedding and wasn't even invited. I never did find out.

*****

I met a wonderful man, Matt, months after I moved into the Briarcliff House—met him at the Laundromat. He was arguing with the attendant to turn off the television so he could study for exams, not caring that seven other people were watching *The Price Is Right*. Since he needed to study, he was vehement about turning off the TV. I watched his argument escalate knowing from the outset that he would win. I could tell by the way he stood, the way he intimidated the attendant. He noticed me watching the interaction and winked. "She needs the television off too," he said, bringing me into his cause. I nodded to encourage him, to gain his approval though I could care less whether the TV was on or off. The attendant finally turned it off, and the mindless audience dispersed, finishing their laundry in a hurry. The place was quiet except for the churning of the washers and dryers.

"Happy now?" the attendant glared at Matt. He smiled charmingly back at her, failing to win her over but captivating me entirely. Later I realized that was his point, his goal— he was performing for me. He was tall, over six feet, had a well-kept beard, wore jeans that fit his lean body perfectly with an Emory sweatshirt worn casually over a T-shirt.

We finished our clothes at the same time, and he took his nose out of his book. "My name's Matt," he said, grinning at me. "I'm studying for my finals at Emory." He waved at his books, then grinned and indicated his sweatshirt too.

"What's yours?"

"My what?" I was grumpy, disappointed yet determined not to flirt with a man I felt sure was younger than me. I had finished college already; dating rules had changed, but not for me.

"Your name?"

"Katrina."

"I hate to be forward, but can I have a ride home? The laundry's heavier on the way home for some unscientific reason." We stashed his bike in Gracey, and I drove him to his apartment. I hated to be rude by not giving him a ride home just because he was younger.

"What are you studying?"

"I'm getting my master's in research science," he said, and I hoped he didn't notice my sigh of relief. My attitude changed immediately when I realized he was older.

"How old are you?" I was blunt, and he laughed.

"I got a late start. I'm twenty-six."

"I'm glad you're not an undergraduate," I said and, now that I'd established his eligibility, invited him to my house for dinner.

The Briarcliff House was chaos when Matt and I arrived. (What was new about that?) It was actors' night to prepare dinner, and since they were both dramatic, Scottie and Ginny were arguing.

"No meat." Scottie stamped her foot with disapproval, herself vegetarian and determined to convert the household, particularly Ginny and particularly on their night to cook.

"That's unfair! I got a great price on this leg of lamb," Ginny said.

Just then the pan rose off the stove and clamored to the ground. Scottie became quiet, compliant. "Lamb it is," Scottie said, almost whimpering, lowering her voice to a whisper.

"What shut you up?" Matt asked Scottie; he didn't seem to miss anything.

"It's the ghost," she whispered. "We've all heard her— some of us have even seen her." She continued talking directly to Matt as if reassured by his presence.

"Just now, I bet she's the one who shoved the pan off the stove and, if you'll notice, turned on the oven, indicating it's leg of lamb we're having for dinner. Old-fashioned biddie—" With this, the lights flashed on and off. "Definitely not vegetarian." Scottie was still whispering.

Matt checked the oven. "Are you sure you didn't turn on the oven before you started arguing?"

"He's a research scientist," I explained to them, "he probably won't believe our ghost stories."

"A research scientist at the Briarcliff House?" Ginny began laughing, then asked Matt questions about his degree program. I helped finish cooking, and by then, everyone was home, ready to eat. The freaky atmosphere disappeared as quickly as it came on. I had learned almost as soon as I moved in that the two actresses were manic in their emotions, and I found it intriguing. It was part of the appeal of the Briarcliff House.

"I have a task for all of you," Ed held court once dinner was over and everyone sat around, drinking the last of our sweet tea, picking at leftovers.

"What?" I asked.

"What now?" Ginny picked on Ed, claiming he was a perfectionist—and retentive—she picked on him a lot because she was a slob. As long as the main house was clean and straight, Ed didn't care how Ginny kept her own room. He figured that was Ginny's problem. Or more probably Scottie's.

"Let's do something artistic to reveal what interactions we have had with the ghost. I'll paint what I think of her. You"—he pointed at me and Tricia—"sculpt her. And you"—he pointed at the theater people—"do something theatrical."

"Are you sure it's female?" Matt asked.

"That we are," Ed answered. "It's the only thing we all agree on."

"And, she's not vegetarian," Ginny contributed.

"And, she's suffered a great loss," Scottie added. "We've all heard her crying."

"I'll do a research study on your ghost." Matt was so serious we all laughed uneasily. "I'll gather data by asking each of you questions about your experiences with her and see what everyone has in common."

"You may even have an experience of your own," I said.

"I doubt it." He smiled hesitantly. "I'm neutral here."

Though an unbeliever, he was still a research scientist—he began his investigation that evening and took himself very seriously. He made a set of questions and scheduled a time to meet with each of us, coming over the next night to start.

"It's not just the ghost he's researching," Ed teased before Matt arrived the next night.

"What do you mean?" I asked, knowing full well exactly what he meant, the attraction between us obvious.

"He's interested in getting to know you better," Ed said. "This ghost research gave him the perfect opportunity."

"Knowing Matt as little as I do," I said, "I think he'd have found a reason to come over without the ghost."

"Yep, I agree." Ed raised his eyebrows and smiled.

Although Matt moved into courting slowly, he was persistent, determined in his research on the ghost. He didn't argue to get his way, he just assumed he was right, and generally he was. Reminded me of when I first met him and he was determined the television was going to be turned off. He was bright and funny, making it easy for me to fall in love with him. He moved slowly in his pursuit of me, so I suspected that he had figured out my reluctance and was loathe to experience rejection. He knew innately to proceed cautiously.

All of us were motivated by his research questions, agreeing that they helped us focus on our part of the assignment—the artistic expression of the ghost. I knew I'd have to balance my time between producing art for sale, work on my ghost assignment, and now I made time to be with Matt.

"When did you first observe the presence you later called a ghost?" he asked me the next evening. I was the first he interviewed.

"I was working late in my studio when I heard footsteps outside the garage. Since I thought it was Tricia, coming to work with me in the studio, I kept working. I was so intent, it was five or ten minutes before I realized Tricia never came in. By then I had reached a stopping place, so I opened the door. No one was outside, but there was a wailing and an eerie light. A gray sweater was left on the doorstep of the studio. I told Ed the next day, and he's the one who said I'd met the ghost. Ed says she always leaves something gray when she pays a visit. At first it freaked me out, but the others had found her kind, unthreatening. She's never been mean to any of us."

Matt interviewed Scottie next and went home at the end of the night, never asking to join me in bed. I knew the sparks between us were there, but it made me more interested because of his slow approach.

"Have you been dating Matt for long?" Scottie asked me after he left.

"No, as a matter of fact, I met him the same day you did. We're not even dating yet. He's just a bright, funny guy—someone to hang out with, you know?"

"I hope you won't fight with him like Ginny and I do. God, we fight about everything, don't we?"

"I think Ginny likes a good fight and a good fighter. That's one reason she likes you."

Scottie laughed. "She does like a good fight. She would argue with a Mac truck, I think. And, making up afterwards is worth it."

"She's spunky, all right."

We turned as we heard a sound at the back door. Ginny opened the door, her face pale, drained of all color.

"I've just experienced the ghost," she whispered, her eyes too bright, almost feverish.

"We all have," I said impatiently, anxious over her dramatic entrance.

Scottie hushed me, pulling out a chair and pouring a cold glass of water for Ginny.

"She touched me," Ginny stammered. "Stroked my hair. It was too weird. Then she put this"—Ginny indicated a gray shawl around her shoulder—"here."

"She touched you?" I stammered.

"Yeah. Cold, clammy fingers. Moist and sweaty." Ginny shuddered. Scottie steamed a hot rag at the sink and washed Ginny's face until some of her color began to return, her eyes lessened in intensity.

"She wailed the whole time, moving her lips like she was trying to tell me something."

"I wonder what her story is," I said. "We need a ritual to put her to rest. I'll write Clayton and see if he knows anything that will help."

"I think that's a good idea," Scottie said as the formidable Ginny cried and Scottie's face, full of anxiety, was weary with concern.

Gather whatever she's left each of you, Clayton wrote,

> *The gray items you wrote me about—I hope you kept some, preferably all of them. Make sure everyone who lives in the house is at home and participates in the ritual. That is important. Also, Ginny is instrumental from what you wrote in your letter since the ghost touched her. She must be the one to speak the words of the ceremony. Matt must be there, too, since he is conducting the research study. It doesn't matter that he's never met her. His detachment gives the ghost the freedom to leave the house. The others of you are too emotionally involved to let her go gently/easily.*

*Bring the artwork you made for her—
and, it should be finished (don't leave anything on earth incomplete or she won't be
able to depart). Matt must bring a written
survey and the theatre people must have
something tangible representing their work.*

Clayton's instructions were thorough, to be carried out at midnight underneath a full moon. Ginny was so anxious to be rid of the ghost that she insisted we all complete our work by the next full moon, just three weeks away.

During those three weeks, Ginny worried constantly that she could not stand the wait. Matt helped Ginny face her emotional upheaval by spending time with her, being logical about it. His scientific, no-nonsense approach kept Ginny from slipping over an emotional edge.

Matt set the table for dinner one night, and as he reached for the last dinner knife, he made a low sound. I looked up curiously as he took his hand out of the drawer, pulling out an old newspaper article stuck in the back of the drawer; he was careful not to rip it. The cabinet was built into the dining room wall, and he worked slowly to release the paper from the silverware shelf.

"What is it? What'd you find?" I asked as he slumped down on the bench around the dining room table.

"I think I know why we have a ghost," he whispered, waving me to join him on the bench. I peered over his shoulder, looking at the paper headline; the paper was dated January 14, 1886:

*As a fire ravaged the shed behind 766
Briarcliff Road, a young woman watched
the flames engulf her youngest brother.*

*A witness reported they heard her mother
scream, "It's your fault! All your fault! You
were in charge of the baby. Why'd you let
him go outside? Why'd you leave him out
there all alone?" When the young woman
could stand the blame no longer, she ran
into the shed herself—we think to rescue
the baby. As soon as she entered, the roof
collapsed, caving in on her, killing her and
her brother instantly.*

*All that was left of sister and brother,
boy and girl, were their hearts. A fireman
cleaning up their ashes located two hearts
that for some reason did not perish in the
fire.*

*He also found the young woman's
gray sweater. There were no bones, no other
clothing to indicate that two children died
last night at 766 Briarcliff Road. Just two
hearts.*

Ginny came in unnoticed as Matt read the article out
loud. "That makes sense," she whispered as Matt jumped at
her voice.

"What," I asked her, "what makes sense?"

"I think she was asking me 'Where is he? Where is he?'
She must have meant her brother."

"Call Clayton and see if this changes the ceremony,"
Matt suggested.

"Okay. I guess if anyone will know, he will." I called
him in Charleston. He picked up after four rings.

"Of course, it changes everything," Clayton answered.
"Matt's right about that. It will be best if you do the ceremony

on January 13—that's next week and not the full moon. Burning the gray items is even more important now that you know how she died and why the gray items are significant."

"Burn them? What do you mean?"

"Have a bonfire in the backyard as close to the shed as possible without setting it on fire again. Burn the gray things the ghost's left you."

"Anything else?"

"Yes, but let me speak to Matt. You won't like this, I know."

"No, tell me," I insisted, but when he did, I wished he hadn't.

"Get two hearts—chicken or lamb, something from a butcher. After burning her gray things, have everyone sit around the fire and burn the work you've made for her. Finally, you must burn the hearts, making sure they turn to ash. Then, she can go on to the other world. Do not change the order: gray things, artwork, hearts."

I hate to regress here, but I have to explain something. Eventually I married Matt, and I am still in love with him after twenty years. Why tell you now? I don't know. Even if it doesn't fit, I feel compelled to write, and I have lived my life long enough not to question intuition, especially mine. Now I go with my odd feelings, finding that the intuitions are right at least 99 percent of the time.

How can I explain my attraction to Matt after such disasters with other men? Maybe because Matt was friend first, lover second. Also, Matt is the only man I talked to before making love. Actually, he was the first and only man I ever made love to. Fucking is a more appropriate term for my previous relationships even though at the time, I thought Jonathan and I made love. Once all that transpired between us happened, I realized we really didn't. Matt and I talked for weeks before he asked to take me to bed. We courted in the old-world way—Matt vowed it was because he was a Scotts man, a man who loved tradition, but I think it was Matt, pure and simple. He asked me about changing our relationship from friendship to physical. Who does that? When I responded yes, we planned the event for the night we released the ghost. I will never forget the date: this particular day was Friday the Thirteenth, January 13. Now we celebrate that date as much as we celebrate our anniversary and our children's birthdays. Forever a lucky day for Matt and me also, so far, a forever date for us both.

We planned our union as thoroughly as we planned the ghost's goodbye.

Respect and equality are part of Matt's appeal, his DNA. We relate as equals; he asks my opinions and respects them even when they differ from his (which is often since I am the artist, he the scientist). I planned then to spend my life with Matt—to have his children and to create a home for all of us. I'd found a man who delighted in my creativity and my unusual lifestyle—in fact, his lifestyle was as unusual and interesting as mine (perhaps even more so?). He always allowed me to be a lightning bug, encouraging my light to shine. He never tried to imprison my light in a jar, capturing, injuring my spirit, cutting only a few air holes in the lid for me to breathe but no longer fly. I fly, and as I get older, I realize how unique this is—a valuable and rare commodity in a marriage. Many women are lightning bugs sealed in a jar; their light in place for their husbands, their families, but their own light shut off to the world and from themselves.

January 13 finally arrived. I was anticipating both our solemn ritual with the ghost and Matt's and my uniting with one another.

The morning was set aside for my rituals, my upcoming event with Matt. I cleaned my sheets and sprinkled rosemary on them for good luck in love. I placed candles around the room and picked fresh flowers. Matt was not coming until the afternoon when everyone in the house planned to get together.

We had anticipated the ghost celebration so much we were at the house as early as four that afternoon. Matt and I were more hypersensitive than the rest of the group since our evening promised another memorable event. The moments ticked by slowly before the light finally escaped and dusk crept in. We built a fire next to the shed just as Clayton directed—careful not to be too close to set fire to the studio but close enough to make sure we attracted the ghost.

Matt began: "As you know, each of you who live here has met the ghost. We're also aware that she has suffered a terrible tragedy, leaving her bound to the earth because of the guilt she feels over her brother's death."

As he made that remark, we heard an eerie groan and saw gray smoke rise behind Matt. The smoke began to encircle the fire, merging with its red-orange, producing a color I cannot describe. I was so frightened, my skin pimpled and shivered. As I looked around, my roommates' faces reflected the fear I felt.

I sank slowly down, sitting by the fire as Matt's words echoed in my head like a religious incantation. "Release your guilt, slip away to peace," Matt chanted over and over, pointing at each of my roommates to stand at his signal, join in his chant, then burn the gray items they had, and next dedicate their artwork to the ghost. Then our work was placed in the fire to burn to ash. Scottie and Ginny acted out a piece in a provoking dance designed to release and building up fear in the rest of us at the same time. The music was eerie yet hypnotic. They pulled a dark-gray scarf between them then placed it in the fire. It sparked and burned brightly, the smoke rising among the trees and swirling around until the scarf was nothing but ash.

Ed was next. He provided a painting that looked like the ghost most of us had encountered. He told stories about his encounters then put the small canvas in the fire where it smoldered and smoked, making an awful smell as only canvas can. I don't think any of us had ever smelled canvas burn, but now that we had, it was a smell we would never forget and hopefully never encounter again.

Tony played a sad, solo saxophone piece; his jazz so full of the blues we all shuddered. He placed the music, a piece he had written just for this, in the fire. Next, Trisha contributed a gray piece of pottery, and then it was my turn. I made an urn, one similar to what might house actual ashes from a funeral. I said, "This vessel is for you, ghost, to nestle in on your journey to the afterlife. I made this urn to contain and nurture your spirit in your passage to the unknown." I placed the urn by the fire, and as I did, a beautiful gray smoke swirled into the urn, seeming to snuggle deep inside. I was sure I was crazy and imagined it until I looked at everyone else. It was obvious they had seen it too. Since I was last of the Briarcliff roommates to contribute, Matt leaned down and sealed my urn with the decorative top I had made for it. We all sighed with relief as Matt placed two hearts into the fire. We sat around in silence for about an hour before one by one we rose and went inside, our first night in our home without the ghost (we hoped). None of us spoke a word as we left the fire.

We wandered back in the house slowly, solemnly, and sat together in the living room, silent once more. The atmosphere was meditative, so heavy you could almost see it. Without a word spoken, yet as if on cue, Ed stood, and the rest of us rose and went off to our separate rooms. Matt left briefly to return to the backyard, making sure the fire was totally out before we slowly went upstairs to my bedroom. We climbed onto my high, antique double bed and, sitting knee to knee, gazed into each other's eyes. I cannot say how long we sat this way as I was lost in the depth of security, experiencing feelings I had never before felt or imagined. Since then, I have never lived without being wrapped in his blanket of indescribable warmth and...how can I say it? Words are inadequate for what Matt does to and for me. I cannot describe what has made up our love of a lifetime.

Matt broke the silence eventually by reaching over and cupping my chin in his strong, long fingers. "Tell me what makes you so full of sadness and resistance," he whispered. This was not at all what I had expected to hear.

"What do you mean?" I asked as though I did not know what he was referring to.

"There's something very tragic in your eyes," he said. "As though you've lived far more than a mere twenty-four-years. What is it?"

I trusted Matt and yearned to tell him, but I was so afraid of his reaction I began to shiver violently. He opened his arms, and I collapsed into them.

"I will not judge you, I promise," he continued to whisper, "whatever it is," as he gathered me against his warm strength; he was encouraging but not pushing.

Something inside me broke as if I was backed up against a dam, and through an avalanche of tears, I poured out my story, looking up rarely but feeling Matt's body sob too, a jagging response to my sorrow as I told him about Brett's trickery and the baby I gave away.

"I've not been with a man since," I ended finally.

"I imagine not," Matt said, "so why don't we just start slow?" and he kissed the back of my neck so sweetly I nodded off to sleep. That evening was one of the first of many glimpses of true, complete intimacy, and our marriage has remained that way. A touch, a look, a kiss between us can be so powerful it overshadows everything else. Matt can look at me, and I understand more from one of his nonverbal glances than I have ever experienced in any other communication.

As we continued to move slowly towards consummation, it was only natural for Matt to move into the Briarcliff House, giving up his apartment in June. The Briarcliff House roommates were delighted.

"Someone sane!" Ginny said.

"Someone to keep us sane!" Ed said, hoping he could share some of the responsibility of running the house with Matt.

"I'm going to set up a compost system," Matt replied, and everyone laughed at his concrete response to everything.

Once Matt moved in, he wanted to share his goals with me—both personal and financial. He said, "I think we're long-term, so I want you to know I can take care of us," he told me.

"That's so sweet. But I have paid the rent for a while now, so don't worry about me."

"It's not sweet. It's realistic. When I was a freshman, another student dropped out of Emory to start a pizza business—at first just delivery. Have you ever heard of Feasta on Pizza?"

"That's my favorite! Best-tasting by far. What's that got to do with you?" I asked him.

"Well, he needed investors, so I helped him out. I own 49 percent of the company."

"That's amazing. Where'd you get funds like that?"

"I got a full ride to Emory, and my parents were so proud of me, they gave me the twenty-five thousand pounds [fifty thousand US dollars] they had in my college fund. I didn't want to fritter it away, so I went in with Lucas. I believed in him but knew I was taking a risk. So far, it's paid off. Now he's setting up storefronts, and they're so successful he's thinking of selling franchises. He has inquiries in Alabama and Florida as well as throughout Georgia. I'm going with him to meet with lawyers to define what we want from a franchise owner and then on appointments with potential buyers."

"I am impressed! I had no idea you were anything but a research scientist."

"There's more."

"More?"

"Yeah, I love to invent things—I consider myself a sort of Tom Terrific."

"You mean the cartoon character who wears a funnel as his thinking cap?"

"The very one."

"What have you invented?" I was intrigued; Matt was a lot deeper than I had imagined.

"I convinced Lucas to turn the pizza box into a yard sign—the outside of the box glows in the dark and says PIZZA DELIVERY HERE."

"Amazing! Briarcliff House is so far off the road we have to pick up our pizza because by the time the driver finds us, it's cold. I never get Feasta on Pizza unless I'm at someone else's house."

"I bet you didn't know the first time you order from Feasta on Pizza, you get the yard sign box to use for all future deliveries. His pizza deliveries are the fastest in town."

"Let's order one tonight. I want that box. That's genius, and everyone in Briarcliff House will love it! First time we'll have Feasta on Pizza delivered here!"

"Why, thank you."

CHAPTER 6

$\mathcal{W}$e got word that Wally died a year to the day after the ghost departed. Maybe that's the reason I will always remember the day he died—it was January 13, 1977, a year to the very day we held the ghost ceremony. The year before, 1976, we'd put the ghost of Briarcliff House to rest and Matt moved into the house. Now I faced another ghost, a ghost I was afraid I could never release, never bury.

Wally had a serious accident: he turned up the gas one long cold weekend, and his gas line malfunctioned. Gia did not find him until she came home from a festival Monday morning. His mother brought suit against the gas company for the gas line, but they retaliated by investigating his death as a suicide. Gia refused to have any part of the legal suit, calling any money from the gas company "blood money."

When my phone rang, when I received the news, it was Vanessa who called; I dropped the phone, falling to the floor, and began wailing. Matt ran to me and grabbed the phone; I was too distraught to talk. Matt listened carefully as she relayed the events that led up to Wally's death, realizing I could not comprehend anything. He hung up and, without another word, cuddled me and tucked me into bed. He knew not to talk; he did not tell me any more about Wally's death until the next morning. Still I was not ready but listened in agonizing stillness, realizing (but not wanting to) that I had lost one of the best friends I had ever had. I loved Wally deeply, and the world would be a different place without his presence.

I returned to Sarasota for the first time in five years to attend Wally's funeral. Despite Matt wanting to join me and take care of my dreaded trip to Sarasota, there was no way he could go. He was a teaching assistant at Emory and at the end of his term, with grades and finals due, so he could not hire a substitute. He called Zan and made arrangements for me to stay with her to get the emotional support I needed. As we walked to the entrance to the church, we became quiet, so overcome with grief we could not speak. Gia did not look at us; her eyes were black, ringed like an animal's. Vanessa was the only one who kept the ceremony on schedule, orchestrating the event as if a musical conductor. She wanted an artistic ceremony, a loving ceremony—not only for Wally, but was thinking of all of us, especially Gia. Vanessa had asked each person to say something special about Wally at the front of the church. After I said my piece, a carefully worded letter of love, I held up a piece of pottery and went to Vanessa, handing it to her. It was unlike anything I had ever made: a masculine, strong piece representing the feelings I had for Wally, my first male friend. It was straight, almost rigid clay, no swirls, no curls, as so often my work entailed. It was in a soft gray glaze with no other color. As Vanessa took it, Jonathan stepped out of the crowd, reaching for me, tears pouring down his face. I looked without seeing him, taking minutes before I knew who he was. I looked too to see if a young child was in the audience, a child who resembled him. Always looking, as I knew I would if I ever came to Sarasota. No wonder it had been five years!

Jonathan and I stood face-to-face, looking at one another so intensely minutes felt like hours. The color left my face, and I turned to ice, my bones felt frozen. I couldn't breathe. All I could think was ESCAPE—fast—so I ran out the front entrance of the church, stumbling down the stairs. I reached a trash can and threw up, missing my clothes but spewing all over the inside of the can. Zan followed close behind.

"I should have known he'd come," she said. "I've seen him around Sarasota the past few years, but I didn't think it was worth telling you. He has tried to approach me so many times I call it Jonathan sightings. Fortunately, I've always been able to flee. He loved Wally, like a brother." As she said this, we exchanged looks, remembering the actual brother he had. I shivered all over and almost threw up again. "They were great friends until Jonathan messed with you. I don't think Jonathan ever knew why their friendship ended so abruptly. He never knew how much Wally loved you and never forgave him for what happened. Several times he'd start to ask me about it, but I ran. I didn't want to fraternize with the enemy, so I avoided him. I haven't been thinking straight—Wally's death took me totally by surprise, it's all I've thought about. I never thought to tell you he'd probably be here."

I felt a strong pair of arms encircle me from behind, and someone kissed me on the neck. "I don't even have to ask who that was, do I?" Clayton whispered. "It's so damn tough, so damn tough. Hang in there, girl."

"Damn right, it's tough!" I cried, tears spilling down my face and heaving sobs escaping deep from within. "Tough to say goodbye to Wally then see that bastard. Tough to be here thinking I might run into a young girl who looks like him."

"If you see him again, you must confront him," Clayton said. "I know you can't do it yet, but someday…" He paused for a minute, took a deep breath, then went on, "I can't believe Wally's dead. Damn, that's heartbreaking!"

"Neither can I," I heard Zan whisper. We joined in a tight hug, holding each other, embracing for a long time.

"I cannot go back to Vanessa's house now," I told them, "I just can't. Can't take the risk he might be there." I couldn't bring myself to say his name. "She'll understand, won't she?"

"Vanessa or Gia?" Zan asked.

"Vanessa," I replied. "Gia doesn't even know what's going on. She doesn't care who's here, who's not."

"Vanessa will understand. She knows how much you loved Wally. And, poor Gia, she can't bear to talk to anyone, so it might be better for her." I also knew I could not bear Vanessa's house; the closeness to the ocean, the salty smell, the feelings of love surrounding her home where I had spent so much time with Wally and Zan. I immediately headed back to Atlanta, eager to see Matt, hold him close. Zan wrote me several times, revealing the struggle she was going through with losing Wally.

Katrina, she wrote,

> *It's as if I lost a brother! I took Wally for granted and will never do that again. Because Vanessa and I are so close, I knew I'd see him several times a year, so when it is the season, the time for him to visit, I still look forward to it, often forgetting that his visit is a mere figment of my imagination. I have to adjust to his being gone again and again as I often forget he is never coming back. The grief! I know you struggle, too, as we were the closest to family I have experienced in a long while. Bank Notes! I miss our innocence; the love for one another; our closeness. Thank God I have Vanessa.*

We hang out all the time now, needing one another, sharing our loss. If not for her, I don't know what I would do! I hope you find solace with Matt.

Zan

I testified against the gas company two months later, answering truthfully that Wally was the last person who'd think of suicide. He was too full of life, too full of high-shrilled laughter, playful giggles. Too full of love for Gia. Right after the funeral, we found out Gia was pregnant when Wally died, the baby due in April. Now Wally would never know his child. Wally was the last person who would have considered suicide; he would have wanted to live even more if he knew he was going to be a father.

Gia's grief was so deep she locked herself up in Columbus and never answered or returned calls and finally told Vanessa and me, "I need space. Space! When I'm ready, I'll call you. Don't call me. I can't handle anything, and I've got to. The baby's due in three months, and I have to get myself together. It's the only reason I want to live. I'll call you when I can, but it won't be anytime soon."

The day of the deposition, Vanessa joined me in the lawyer's office; we were in this fight together. When we met with the gas company lawyers, we were quickly overwhelmed by their aggression. All they cared about was winning the suit; they did not want to pay Vanessa any money. Once the deposition was over, I cried in Vanessa's arms outside their office.

"Thanks for testifying." She did not sob but stood solid, rock-faced. "You're one reason I think we'll win. They know I'll deny his suicide. But, from their perspective, why should you defend him? Why? No reason except that you're telling the truth. My lawyer says they'll settle out of court. They don't want you as a witness since you knew him so well. Particularly because he had a young wife with a baby on the way. That in itself defies suicide. Wally was not unhappy, and I think they know that. Know they fucked up."

I saw my testimony as a gift of friendship. When I met Wally, he had loved me more than I had loved myself; he was my first male friend. I could hardly bear my grief.

> *Dear Zan,*
>
> *Wally's dead. Dead. How can I write that? I know you know it, but, even so, I have to write it to take hold of it, to claim it as real. Thanks for letting me tell you no matter how hard it must be for you to face it (as if you don't think about it every day). I know, too, that it might be harder on you since you and Wally are the same age. And, you had the joy of seeing him regularly. You both lived in Sarasota longer than I did. How could it possibly be harder than what I'm going through? I feel stripped, empty, nauseated. I think of you, of Gia, and know it has to be harder but I cannot imagine! Wally fell asleep on a Friday night and never woke up. At least he never went through pain, that we know of. I imagine, I hope, he must have had sweet dreams of Gia and their life. Then I imagine Gia finding him Monday morning. When Vanessa called me, it shocked me, numbed me! The lines for his heater were installed improperly—he died of gas fumes without knowing*

there was danger. The saddest part is that he died alone; dead in his cottage, by himself, all week-end. I cannot bear the thought. He never knew about the baby. Gia was going to tell him Monday morning. Imagine how he would have felt! He so readily agreed to marry me when I needed a father for my child; how excited he would have been to find out he was going to be a dad! A little Wally! At least, if we get through to Gia, we will get to meet this little being and hopefully keep Wally's existence alive by embracing his child.

I am lonely knowing he is not in the world—someone who loved me unconditionally. He's the first man in my life who loved me like that. What a gift! Male friendships, though rare, have been so valuable to me. How will I recover? Maybe never will! Gia's distraught—pregnant, due in three months, alone in her pregnancy. I have tried to call but she asked me and Vanessa to give her space; said she'd call us when she's ready. I wonder if she'll ever call. I'm sure that you know this from Vanessa but it helps to write it to you, helps me vent through this letter. God, I miss you!

How do you like beach-side living? I envy you—I know you must love it! I hope your love, your relationship is improving. I am in love, too. The permanent kind.

He's one year older than I am—totally brilliant, opposite from me. While I'm an

*artist, this man is a research scientist. When
he talks, I act like I understand. He met
Wally and Gia a few times and they adored
him. I'll write the story of their meeting in
another letter—it's worth repeating. You'll
get a kick out of it!
Write!*

Katrina

Having never heard from Gia, and thinking I probably
never would, one weekend I drove to Columbus to visit her.
She had been so removed and unreachable I was worried and
knew I needed to spend time with her. I took a risk—didn't
even tell her I was coming. In my heart, I knew she'd tell me
no, not to bother. It was a risk for me too as Gia was now
seven months pregnant, and I was not sure how I felt about
that. What irony: Wally asked me to marry him so he could
give my baby a name, and now his own wife was going to be
a single mother, his child would never know him. He would
never hear his baby cry, never comfort his own child, just as
I never had any contact with my firstborn.

When I knocked, Gia flew the door open and glared at
me. "What are you doing here?"

"That's how you greet me? Your funky roommate? The
one you pulled out of the hole I was in when I arrived at
Penland? I'm here because whether you know it or not, you
need me."

"No, I don't." She turned to slam the door in my face,
but I stopped her, placing my foot on the threshold.

"I loved him too. Loved him more than I even knew.
Can't we cry together?"

"That's just what I'm afraid of—if I start crying, I won't stop…ever! I can't let you get to me. I feel like I'm buried alive."

"I can't say I know how you feel because I don't. But let me in. I want to help."

Reluctantly she opened the door, hesitating not only because of the emotional desert she was living in but physically she wasn't well either. Her home looked like a war zone; it was filthy, more of a disaster than a living space, a sure sign of the depression she was bogged down in. Trash overflowed, broken clay was shattered everywhere. I could only imagine she had thrown her work against the wall in a deep rage when she found Wally's body, but it looked like she'd been breaking things ever since. It even smelled; so did Gia.

I went to the kitchen and fixed chamomile tea—luckily, I had brought some. I pitched newspapers and magazines off of two chairs and gestured to Gia to sit. She couldn't. She paced the living room up and down, back and forth, edgy like a wild animal caged and broken. I didn't ask her to sit again, knowing it was not possible.

"Tell me, Gia, tell me—everything! Let it out, scream, rage, share with me."

"See, this is just what I was worried about—why I didn't want you here. I don't want to rage, cry. I want to shut down, shut up, shut off, shut, shut, shut—fuck, fuck, fuck!"

It was a long night, but finally I saw a kink in her armor and dove in to reach the tiny thread of hope I saw there. I unraveled the thread and spun a "Wally" tale in soothing tones until finally, finally, Gia sat. She shared; she talked without ceasing. I listened, never interrupted, asked no questions, just paid attention. That's what she needed. No judgment, no interrogation, no viewpoints, just an open mind, a listening ear.

At four that morning, I convinced Gia to shower and go to bed. She confessed she had not slept for months except in short spurts, maybe showered once a week. Once she fell asleep, she didn't wake up for two days except to eat and go to the bathroom. It was as if she was ill, but the illness was not physical; she was emotionally spent, exhausted.

For those two days, I cleaned, gathering up bags and bags of trash, filling at least four with shards of pottery. I shuddered to think what great work had been destroyed. I loaded the dishwasher and washing machine for more loads than I could count, thankful I was not a pioneer woman scrubbing everything by hand.

Finally, after the second day, Gia emerged from her bedroom and smiled at me with relief etched on her face, her eyes hinting at the imp I knew was under there somewhere.

"I have a surprise for you. Get dressed. We're going on a field trip," I told her.

"Where?"

"Pasaquan. Ever heard of Eddie Martin?"

"Pas-a-where? Eddie who?"

We drove to Buena Vista, Georgia, thirty-three miles from Columbus. Although such a short distance from Columbus, Pasaquan was not as well-known in the 1970s as it is now, so Gia had never heard of it.

It was a delight! Gia would later credit Pasaquan as changing her life—that trip for her was influential. Eddie Martin lived a complicated life (is any artist's life simple?) but finally returned home to his mother's cotton farm in 1957. He used cement to build huge totem poles; he decorated walls and buildings both inside and out with mirrors and house paint. You could stand on one side of a room and view a mandala then turn your head to see the mirror image behind you. He finished four acres of painted masonry concrete walls and had six major sculpture pieces. As time progressed, people began to call the complex a folk art palace, a visionary art environment. He made huge artwork—heads of men dressed in what he called antigravity power suits. This began in the 1950s, so I trust he never heard of the Power Rangers of today's fantasies. I am sure he was a visionary; he thought so too and made his living for many years giving readings to anyone who showed up at the gate to his place. If he wasn't interested in doing a reading that day, the gates to Pasaquan were closed. What an interesting being! The complex was equal parts mysticism, geometry, and creativity. Eddie lived at Pasaquan but travelled all over Georgia, so the particular day we went, he was not there. However, once we arrived, Gia looked thunderstruck and took off to view all parts of the complex. We did not meet again until closing time.

"Well?"

"I think I have found my next inspiration! Give me time on the ride back, and once we're home, I'll share my thoughts and feelings." I left Gia to ponder, think, explore, and begin visualizing her next creations.

"I am moving on to larger pieces," she told me. That was the end of her fire hydrant people.

"I want to make larger pieces, but I'm thinking more along the lines of puppets. I want to make them *and* perform. I have a friend in Savannah who is a puppet guru. Once the baby comes, I'm going to see if I can work for her. I'll call her this week."

Motivation—that's what Gia had needed, and Pasaquan provided. She flung herself into her ideas and hardly knew I was still there. That suited me as long as she was no longer stuck in her depressive, overwhelming funk.

"Whatever made you think to perform? Haven't you always been a potter?"

"I think after Wally died, something happened inside me. I feel this burst of the creative spirit begging to get out, and throwing pots is not at all what's on its mind. Eventually, I may tell the love story of me and Wally, even the story of finding him dead. It may even be cathartic. I hope so."

I finally returned home after two weeks, and by April, the baby, a girl, arrived—April 23, to be exact, the day after my own baby girl's birthday. Gia welcomed Vanessa's two-week visit to help her adjust to being a new mom. No hippie birthing room for Gia; she had her baby as I had had mine. Sterile hospital environment, drugs to reduce the pain, no midwives. "I'm taking no chances," she confided to me. "Wally is dead. I'm not losing his baby. Doctor, drugs all the way." Since Vanessa was old-school in that respect, she gave Gia total support. However, the doctor did allow one exception: he invited Vanessa into the delivery room.

"I couldn't have made it without her," Gia let me know. "I was too emotional. Vanessa kept me grounded. She cut the baby's cord, was the first to hold her. Her grandma."

"What's her name?"

"Katie. Not Kathryn, Catherine, or Kathleen. Just Katie. After you, Katrina. Other than me, Wally loved you more than anything in this world. He called you Kat—never Katrina. This baby's Katie—never Kathryn. She is named after you."

I wept.

"What's she calling Vanessa?"

"Vanessa wants to be called Lady V. Perfect for her, isn't it?"

It was.

While Vanessa was in Columbus, she bought Gia a VW hippie van—the kind you could sleep in. I was amazed Gia accepted it, but Gia loved it! She saw it as her gift of freedom. She named the car Harmony and was ready to live in that van, just her and Katie. She kept her house in Columbus, her home base, but her first stop in her puppetry quest (her words, not mine) was Savannah. Then she arrived in Atlanta to study at the newly organized Center for Puppetry Arts with Vince Anthony and parked Harmony in our backyard. We didn't care how long she stayed; we all wanted to spoil the baby!

The next field trip happened right after Gia had her baby. Clayton called. "I have a friend who goes to Mercer University. She was telling me about these incredible kaolin mines near there. They aren't even closed off to the public."

"Kaolin, as in clay?"

"The very same."

"Let's go!"

"I can come down with Annabella and the kids this weekend, and we can leave from Atlanta."

"I've never heard of it, so do you have directions?"

"Vaguely, but my friend says it's not hard to find."

Clayton arrived with his two children and Annabella. It was hard not to stay up all night Friday talking, but with the trip set for Saturday, we reluctantly went to bed. The whole Briarcliff House decided to come, looking forward to a break in routine. Clayton and I decided to ride together, and once we got going, we never stopped talking.

"Have you ever heard of Pasaquan?" I asked him.

"What is it?"

"It's a folk art palace in Buena Vista, Georgia, artwork created by Eddie Martin."

"I have heard of Eddie Martin. He's involved at Mercer too."

"What does he do at Mercer?"

"He takes students to visit some farm he owns. I bet it's Pasaquan. My friend's very involved with that program and knows him well. I'll ask her to set up a visit to Pasaquan, and we'll go with the kids."

"I bet Gia will meet you there. She says visiting there changed her life. The day we went, she didn't get to meet Eddie. I know she wants to meet him."

"How did Pasaquan change her?"

"She's no longer making small figures, only massive sculptures. They are performance pieces. She's studying puppetry! I think she's moving into our backyard as soon as she finishes her work in Savannah. Moving in, in her VW van and studying at Vince Anthony's new Center for Puppetry Arts."

"I think this trip is going to be much longer than I anticipated. I've heard of the Center for Puppetry Arts. It's the only one of its kind in the nation. We need to take the kids there too."

"It's not just for kids, they have adult puppet shows. Go with the kids then go back. I'll babysit, and you and Annabella can have a date night."

Clayton's trip did turn into a marathon; between visiting Mercer and various locations throughout Georgia, he and his family stayed with us off and on for over four months, even overlapping his stay with Gia's. It felt like Penland all over again.

When we started out for the mines, Clayton suggested we bring buckets to gather kaolin to bring home. We went back many times over the four months, each time bringing bucketloads of white kaolin back to my studio. The clay was such a mess we always took Gracey as we didn't care how dirty she got. It was about a year after we visited the mines that they were closed to the public, a reflection of the litigious society America was becoming. I was glad we had gathered the kaolin when we had. I developed a particularly interesting, innovative look, mixing kaolin and porcelain; never saw anyone else who used this in their work (except, of course, Clayton, who used it too). Even now, I greedily hoard the kaolin and have stretched it to last, but to do so, I use it sparingly.

The mines were like we had arrived on the moon. There were huge white hills made from clay, and in the center of the hills where they had dug out the kaolin was a huge lake. The blue/turquoise of the lake was unlike any color I had ever seen except for the turquoise blue of the ocean of Sarasota, the Gulf of Mexico. The only thing missing at the mines was the salty smell of the ocean that embraced me in Florida. If there was one thing I missed from that beach, it was the smell of the ocean and its turquoise-blue expanse. The blue here, at the mines, so vivid, was so like the Gulf of Mexico it brought a visceral response in my gut; I was glad I was here with my family, my artist friends. Here the lake was reflected in the kaolin hills, so it made an eerie picture unlike anything I had ever seen before. As soon as we climbed a hill and set down blankets and picnic supplies, Ginny stripped off her clothes and jumped in the lake. She screamed, "It's freezing," but none of us cared, so we followed right along behind her. Clayton's children turned their heads until we were immersed in the water, shuddering to see us old folk naked, but then they joined us, appropriately attired in their bathing suits.

Matt was a gift as he helped Clayton load the buckets full of kaolin. He was enjoying himself so much none of the rest of us interrupted him, but he said it was a good thing as it was quite strenuous work. For all future visits, he brought a shovel. Once we returned home, Clayton and I experimented for weeks until we finally hit upon the porcelain-kaolin equation. Our pieces were lovely, almost transparent. They were a bit fragile, but neither of us were known for utilitarian pieces, so when we sold them, our customers knew what to expect. It wasn't long until customers were clamoring for these particular items.

By spring, Gia had finished some of her work in Savannah and moved into our backyard in her van. Katie was almost a year old.

"Guess who is coming to Atlanta?" Gia exclaimed almost as soon as she arrived.

"I have no clue!"

"Bread and Puppet Theatre from Vermont. They do something entirely unique—they work with local groups, who get to take part in the crowd scenes of their show. I'm going to Kelly's Seed and Feed to practice with them. I want to be part of the crowd scenes."

There were a lot of babysitters for Gia, so she rehearsed with the theater group for well over a week. "They need people to let the puppeteers stay with them. Do you have any spare room?"

"Not with Clayton and his family here, and I know they will want to see the performance. I wish we did have room!"

"The performance is Thursday night. How many reservations do you need?"

"Make it ten…that should include all of us."

We went to the theater early, an old warehouse on North Avenue, on an unusually hot night for spring! We hired a teenage neighbor to stay home with Katie so all of us could go. The show was elaborate with full-size human puppets symbolizing the disciples, taking communion. The story centered on an Easter renaissance. We met Gia after the show was over.

"I was one of the disciples. They asked for volunteers from the local work group, so of course, I said yes."

"Man, I wish I'd known. I would have checked out your shoes!" I was teasing Gia, who was known for wearing funky shoes.

"I did have an unusual experience."

"Only you, Gia, only you. What happened?"

"The girl next to me was groaning, moaning. Her stomach was gurgling. I asked her if she was all right, and she answered vehemently that she was not. What was I to do? The show must go on...I couldn't strip off my puppet right before it was my time to take communion. I whispered to her how sorry I was but truly couldn't help her. Once we finished our piece, I tracked her down. Poor thing...she threw up all over the inside of the puppet. She was overheated. They'll have to make a new puppet for that disciple!"

We laughed all the way home. That could only happen to Gia. We had a blast that spring, but all too soon, everyone left, and it was back to the somewhat calmer just-us commune.

It wasn't long before I heard from Clayton. "It's the second year of the Spoleto Festival. Why don't you come to Charleston?"

"What's the Spoleto Festival?"

"It's something that started in Italy, and now we have one in Charleston. Gallery exhibitions, performances by the dozen. It occurs over several weeks."

"I'd love to come. I'll talk Matt into it. When is the best time, when are the most events?"

"Don't tell Gia, but I got her a time slot in Marion Square Park with her puppets. She thinks they called and booked her based on her reputation—doesn't know I had anything to do with it. She's doing two shows. She isn't part of the large Spoleto Festival but under a different performance group sponsored by RAWA, Renaissance Artists and Writers Association. I even got her a stipend!"

"Terrific! She's only been working with the puppets for a year. I know she's thrilled."

"Don't tell her I had anything to do with it, promise?"

"Promise."

"She performs the first week in June. Open City Children's Theatre is here too. Aren't Scottie and Ginny with them? I think they are performing the same day as Gia. Why don't you come up for that whole week? The Parisienne Ballet will be here, so I'll get us tickets. You've never been to visit me, so this will be fun."

When I told everyone at the Briarcliff House Matt and I were going to see Gia's puppet shows at the Spoleto Festival, Ginny and Scottie screamed. "We're going too! We're performing with Open City Children's Theatre at Marion Square Park."

"That's where Gia's performing." We decided to ride together and rented some rooms from the College of Charleston. We wouldn't have gotten space there if we hadn't signed up with Ginny and Scottie, who got their rooms because they were performing.

When we arrived in Marion Square Park for Gia's shows, I don't know why it caught me off guard when both of her shows dealt with death. She was perfection personified, and I'm not saying that because she's a dear friend of mine. The first show caused an uproar as most parents who had brought their children to a "puppet show" thought it was inappropriate. Being a mother without a child, I could hardly log in on the debate but felt that the show was harsh but real...death is something we can't protect our children from. Gia sat on a stool, just her. Her hands had on gloves—one was solid black, a formal glove reaching all the way to her elbow; the other was a beige glove, short, flirtatious with lacy edgings. As the show progressed, the black glove overtook the beige one. Nothing was said. It was a dance...the dance of death. None of the audience lost the significance as the black glove overtook and finally annihilated the beige one. As one, we gasped at the simplicity yet devastation of the show. Clayton's children were mesmerized. If I thought it was a show that was all right for children, they proved my point. That being said, they had always been raised with honesty and direct-ness; Annabella and Clayton never minimized them or clos-eted them from truth and reality. Their life had never been sugarcoated; I think many children in the audience's lives had been, hence their parents' horror, uproar.

The second show was completely opposite: one big, life-size puppet that struggled with a suitcase, packing all manner of items from food to gems to treasures. It took a while to figure out the puppet was packing a lifetime of experiences in her case, only to head up a pair of stairs that led to heaven. Arriving at heaven, the puppet was met by another puppet (here Gia borrowed from Bread and Puppet Theatre's ideas and asked for an audience volunteer—none of us volunteered because we didn't want to miss a minute of her show, but there were plenty of people for her to choose from). The vol-unteer puppet was taken through the items Gia's puppet had packed in her suitcase, each and every one evaluated and set aside, the point being that only the puppet would enter the gates of heaven, not the items from the suitcase. The show was also simplicity itself yet exquisite and poignant. I cried at the end of both.

Of course, Scottie and Ginny were more excited about Open City Children's Theatre's performances since they were performing. They were right after Gia's second performance, also doing a piece with suitcases, opening them to find faceless, life-size dolls. Then they did a takeoff on Snow White and the Seven Dwarves, with Ginny playing the jealous Snow Queen with a mean streak that tapped into her volatile personality. Typecasting? I'd never volunteer that comment!

That night we all went to see the Parisienne Ballet, who were performing outdoors. Katie and another toddler joined us, sitting in their strollers. We were in awe at the lightness on their feet. We were particularly taken with their leotards, nude in color and hardly there, showing off all the muscles of the dancers. When they finally turned around, everyone gasped (including Katie)! They were in the nude, wearing nothing at all! We kept our composure, and Charleston embraced it—I think wanting to show their European sophistication.

We had a blast with Clayton's family, and I was glad to see that Gia's energy was no longer wallowing in her grief but producing art from it!

CHAPTER 7

*O*nce again, I turned my attention to Zan and began to think about her. Right after Wally's funeral, Zan broke up with Mike and married a man she had fallen madly in love with after only three short months. Since I didn't know him, and because the wedding was in Sarasota, I couldn't bring myself to go. It was even harder to go to Sarasota because now Wally was gone. I dreamed that Zan and her new husband would ride off into the sunset. What did I know? I was wrong, wrong to think Zan would choose the most perfect man for the most perfect woman. Despite my love for Zan and admiration for her tough and wondrous spirit, in this particular love, she was blind. Hers was one marriage I never understood, and I think, in retrospect, neither did she. She loved the man passionately, but that was it. Passion. The rest of the marriage was hell.

Her judgment and instinct were dead wrong. I always liked to think it was because she had only known him three months, but once I found out the truth, I was surprised she had chosen so poorly. He was a drunk, and the drunker he got, the meaner he was. He used his intelligence, the thing she most loved about him, as a weapon. When Zan got pregnant, he used his fists as well. It took her a long time to tell me. She never wrote about it; later she said she couldn't write the cold hard truth. When I saw her on a trip she made to

Atlanta with Vanessa, I asked her about her husband, and she whispered, "He hits me, beats me black and blue. He's sneaky about it—gets me on the back of the head under the hairline so bruises won't show. I have bruises now, but you can't see them. I think he's mean because I got pregnant. Doesn't want children."

"Zan," I practically shouted at her, "I can't stand it. I'm coming to Sarasota and beat the hell out of him!"

"Please, lower your voice! Vanessa's in the next room. If she ever found out how mean he is, she'd murder him in his sleep. This is a secret I must keep. I alone must figure out what to do about it."

I was so surprised by her admission of his cruelty I made a reluctant, agonizing trip to Sarasota just to check on Zan. I hoped (wrongly) that while I was there, he would not be abusive. He had no shame; he wasn't just cruel to Zan, he was vicious to me. He lashed out at her at the top of his lungs, not caring that I overheard. After witnessing his verbal abuse, I asked why she stayed. She shrugged her shoulders and raised her eyebrows. "I love him. That's all. I know it's stupid, but he is the father of my child."

Before I returned to Atlanta, we went to a bar where he sat on the middle stool between us. Knowing she could not hear him, he asked me, "What are you like in bed?" He was drunk and leered at me, staring at my breasts. No pickup line had ever been that obvious or disgusting, especially with his pregnant wife on the other side of him. I got busy with my drink, began to flirt with the bartender, who came to my rescue and flirted back.

Later that night, we went to the beach, and he said, "My wife looks better in a bikini than you do! You're a fat little thing, aren't you?" Then he bragged, "She's three months pregnant! Funny, Zan never mentioned you were fat." I stormed up the beach by myself and kept my distance. Mean like I said.

On the other hand, visiting Sarasota was no better than I thought it would be when it came to looking for my first-born child. I got a crick in my neck from looking over my shoulder at every three-year-old girl, thinking she might be mine. I also had fantasy Jonathan sightings (Zan's words) and shuddered every time I saw a Native American man, even those who were short! I couldn't get home fast enough.

I'm so glad you're my friend, Zan wrote after my visit.

> *I can't tell anyone else the things I write you, not even my sisters. They'd think I was weird—you might think that, too, but we know you're just as weird as I am. We've been through some heavy things together. Amazing, isn't it, how much alike we are, yet so different! God, I wish you lived closer!*
>
> *I've been wrestling with the overwhelming complexity of death recently. Obsessed with it, I'll admit. Of course, part of my obsession is because of Wally. I can't grasp the finality of it. I keep waiting to see his smiling face, hear his giggle. I know you're thinking it's been a while, get over it. But, how? I can't seem to. No, I just reread my letter and it sounds so cold. How can I write you that? I know you of all people understand! I know you are someone who'll also never completely get over Wally. I know that of you.*
>
> *I never understood that place between you two, you and Wally, even though I lived*

around it; I was surrounded by it and will never forget the unspoken language you two shared. So, of course, you understand. Forgive my lack of sensitivity.

I undertook an experiment. I acted as though I had five days to live. Everything I did was based on the knowledge that I would die in 5 days (okay, I know what you're thinking—I've lost my mind but I promise, I haven't). It was a wonderful exercise and everyone should do it to get in touch with their spiritual side, the value of their life. I went to a funeral home and laid in a casket, choosing the one I would want. I decided then and there I prefer to be cremated. Please do not shudder at those words. Dealing with the knowledge, accepting the reality of our own death is part of life. If I die and have not written down my wish, I want you to carry it out.

My unborn baby is intricately involved with my thoughts on death. She or he's the reason I'm glad to be alive. I'm not suicidal and if you're contemplating visiting me again, I'm okay, I swear! I promise! Visit me but don't do it to check on me. In facing death, I choose to live! If one could always live in such a heightened state of awareness, of appreciation, of thankfulness, life would be transformed. My life was renewed the week I undertook this experiment. There were no more excuses not to do the things I'd been putting off. I embraced myself, my

*neighbor, everyone. God, you know me!
Heightened sensitivity is frightening, isn't
it, since I'm already in overdrive! I'm convinced life is a gift yet we ignore it. I know
I'll get out of this marriage—that's another
conclusion I reached in the midst of all this.
There is no life in it. The baby will do better without the tyrant I married. I will stay
until the baby comes…only until then. I'll
keep you informed.*

Zan

I wrote letters suggesting Zan leave him, find an apartment, and live in Atlanta, but I went long periods of time
without hearing from her.

Dear Katrina, she finally wrote,

*The baby has arrived! Now that she's
here, he's stopped hitting me. But, his drinking has increased and he's taken a job as a
bartender at the beach…that's one bad
thing about Florida, it's made for alcohol-
ics. Bars open at 6 a.m., close at 2 a.m.
His shift is 8 p.m. to close and he hangs
around drinking until the next shift, then
comes home, falls across the bed, slurring his
words, groping for me. He is too limp by the
time we try anything so, thank God, he falls
asleep. My only joy is my little girl, Jessica.
She is dark haired like me, bright eyed like
him. I pray she has his intelligence without
his complexity. I'll write again soon. I've*

enclosed photographs of my beautiful baby
girl.

Zan

A year later, she left him. I wept for joy. She who was so beautiful had no business being with a man who beat her, no matter how intelligent he was. She wrote to me of her fears. *How can I support this child?* She wrote.

> *I'm so terrified, my knees are shak-*
> *ing. Ka-Trin-A! Help! It's a big responsibil-*
> *ity but I'll do a better job on my own. He*
> *won't back down with Jessie. A 45-year old*
> *man battling wills against a 1-year old! I*
> *could not bear it. Of course, he always won.*
> *Had to win. If I stayed in this marriage, he*
> *would wound her spirit. She deserves bet-*
> *ter...so do I!*
>
> *Zan*

Right after Zan told me she was leaving her lousy marriage, ironically, Matt suggested we get married. As she planned her separation, Matt and I began to talk of a more serious commitment. I trusted Matt like I had learned to trust Wally and Clayton. When I talked of self-doubts, Matt talked of his too. He had never been in a relationship with a woman for longer than two or three months and was fright-ened but excited about a formal union. We resolved to solve our problems together, focusing on goals as a couple. He was soft and gentle but at the same time fierce, willing to fight for what he found important. I wanted him to be the father of my future children; I knew he'd love them with a loyalty so intent he'd kill anyone or anything if it ever came to that.

Why Matt? After years of revolt against men and sex, why did I soften? open up and accept Matt's overtures and imagine him fathering future children?

I've always felt that there are certain things that cannot be explained by words or rather the limitations of words. My feelings for Matt fell into this category. I can speculate—try to express what happened, however inadequate this explanation will be. Perhaps it was his delicate handling of me—his deliberate slowness in asking the sexual question, making the move. With so many roommates, the Briarcliff House did not lend itself easily to intimacy. So we became fast friends long before we went to bed. At first, our fascination with the ghost occupied every moment of our time together. Matt must have felt instinctively that what I needed most was the trust, support, and love a friend provides. And time. So that's what he gave me...that's what it took to capture my heart. Instinctively that's exactly what Matt did. We are still friends—best friends to this day. To me, it is the thing I value most in our relationship.

> *Zan,*
>
> *Matt's moved in with me. I will finally write the story of how Wally & Gia met him, the man I plan to marry, or "Redneck Couple (Gia/Wally) meet Hippie (Matt)." Wally and Gia were up for the weekend and Matt's car broke down (he is a true hippie fitting all stereotypes). I picked them up to spend the weekend and dropped Matt off at Georgia Tech to see Swami Mukti— an Indian guru speaking on peace and love. Wally and Gia thought that was great and, of course, wanted to go but I wouldn't so*

they didn't. I felt embarrassed by Matt's enthusiasm and was a bit threatened by something outside the Christian faith I have always believed in. Matt gets out of my car and moons us—drops his pants to his ankles, wiggling his hairy butt in the air. Wally and Gia roared, laughed about it all week-end. It left me with questions regarding Matt's sanity: his going to see such an unorthodox speaker and playfully mooning two of my friends. Now, after having been with him for over a year, I've found him to be one of the sanest men I know. However, he does have a playful and spontaneous side as well. He fits right in where we live—he is perfect for the area of town we live in—rampant with hippies, peaceniks, environmentalists, artists. We both fit in here. I think it's the first time I've found my place (except for that sweet summer in Sarasota). Since we still eat meat, I call us "closet meat eaters" since it seems everyone else is vegetarian. We live near Little Five Points, a mecca for new age thought, creativity; the SoHo of the south. Thank God I've found this address as well as this man. Who'd ever think I'd land in heaven?

That visit was the last time I saw Wally but I didn't know that. In a way, he told me good-bye:

God's on a sailboat in the middle of the ocean, he told me.

*Wally, my God's not on a sailboat. I
can't sail. God's here at the Briarcliff House.
Well, MY God's on a sailboat in the
middle of the ocean.*

*With that, he died, left this earth for
his sunset and his boat. I wonder if he still
thinks God's on a sailboat now that that's
where he is, leaving his wife and child still
on Earth. I think about that a lot and sometimes scream at God. I miss him so much!*
*Other times I feel as though Wally's
here, looking out for me. How can that
be? I know you're thinking I'm crazy, but
truly on a regular basis, redneck guys seem
to show up right when I need them, when
I need protection; redneck guys with a dis-
tinctive giggle. I know Wally hasn't totally
abandoned us to sail away into the sunset.*

Katrina

Matt and I went to dinner with my parents, who finally
made time to meet us months after we'd been living together.
I got a read on them immediately as they exchanged glances
then put on their "civil" faces. At the time, Matt was sport-
ing what I called the Little Five Points hippie look, and I
think my parents expected an Emory research scientist: but-
ton-down shirt, preferably white, thin tie, neat loafers. Matt
wore Converse sneakers. However, it didn't take him long
to impress my parents, not only with his incredible intelligence, but Matt's parents were Scottish: live in Scotland.
Matt conversed eagerly with Dad about Scottish literature.
My mom beamed; if Dad liked him, she did too. My parents

were going back to Scotland in two weeks, so Matt promised to call his parents and arrange for them to get together. Once he contacted his parents, they insisted Charlie and Joan, my parents, cancel their hotel reservations and stay with them in Edinburgh. What a risk, I thought, but Matt was all for the arrangement.

"What can possibly go wrong?" he asked. "They're all four educators, and they all play bridge."

My dad was so self-centered, I imagined a lot of possible casualties, but Matt grinned and welcomed the mingling of our families. It must have gone well as my parents extended their stay an additional four weeks, and when they got home, they began to pressure us to get married—seemingly changing their attitude and wanting Matt to be a permanent part of our family.

"I'm game if you are," Matt said.

"That's supposed to be my romantic proposal? What about kneeling down on one knee and the whole bit?" I asked.

Matt grinned and hollered to everyone in Briarcliff House, "Come to the living room for an incredible performance—one you'll never forget." Ed, Tony, and Ginny were home and joined us in the front room, my face scarlet.

"You are the first to witness my request of this magnificent woman to marry me." Matt even kneeled on one knee. Cheers erupted from the three of them, and Tony ran to his room for his electric guitar, playing "Here Comes the Bride" ad nauseam.

"Okay, okay. I appreciate the fanfare, but that's enough," I said.

"Nothing's too good for you, darling." Matt spewed all kinds of compliments, but oddly enough, he was sincere and remained that way throughout our married life.

When I married Matt, I realized I was marrying a scientist, years ahead of his time. His parents stayed with us at the Briarcliff House the night before the wedding. We had a hippie wedding with no minister, no rehearsal dinner, no attendants. A simple Quaker wedding: we stood before friends and exchanged vows. The clerk of the Quaker meeting signed an official marriage license and declared us married. We had a huge party afterwards at the Briarcliff House.

Zan couldn't come, but she called the night before the wedding. Our verbal exchange was strained, awkward; I imagined because her own marriage had been such a failure. Neither of us could bear to mention Wally, which separated us even further. She said she couldn't get away from work, but Vanessa called me privately and told me Zan was struggling with my newfound happiness. She could not bring herself to join our festivities when her own marriage had been such a failure. This was just as I thought, but I ached that we could not share in this, my celebration. I could only hope one day we would rekindle our relationship and Matt would meet Zan.

Vanessa also shared that there was a dark-haired young girl who often played with Jessica at Zan's house. I drew in my breath, not knowing if she was implying that this girl was my daughter. Gasping for breath, hardly able to breathe, I cut the conversation short, choosing to focus on my marriage, ignoring Vanessa's inference. It was not a time in my life that I could take a closer look at possibilities regarding my firstborn.

How could I describe Matt to Zan? He was shaggy haired, wore glasses, his head always buried in a book. Even if Zan met him, she would not know him until she spent time—lots of time—with him. He is a complex and deep man, a man of many talents, many faces. The night Wally and Gia met him, he had an impishness that bolted out of him; he calls it a "daft half hour." On the other hand, he's private, not nearly as sociable as I am. What was the attraction between us? Pure chemistry, an inexplicable jab in my stomach, a kinesthetic response so intense, so visceral it would start in my toes and work its way to the top of my head. That feeling has never left even after years of being together. Having lived it, I swear, opposites do attract. What he had, I didn't, and vice versa. It works well for us.

Despite the uncomfortable phone call, Zan knew me. Her wedding present was not silver or some china pattern. It was a stringed hammock we hung on the front porch and relaxed in during cool Atlanta weather. I was glad Vanessa took the risk to share with me the deep feelings Zan was experiencing so I could set aside my feeling of separation, knowing with our deep friendship the awkwardness would pass. I just didn't know how long that would take, but I trusted it would occur. It was shortly after this that I got a sweet note from Zan:

> *I can just picture Matt. Brilliant, funny, unusual. He'd have to be to marry you, my fine friend. Good luck in marriage—a luck I've yet to find but hope to have one day. May you befriend one another in your twilight years, rocking in rocking chairs on your front porch together. Or, swinging together in my hammock. That's why it's so big.*
>
> *Zan*

Two months later, I was pregnant; I remembered the feelings well, only this time I was quietly elated, eager to share the experience with a mate, someone who was as joyful about it as I was. No secrets. Matt was convinced he'd find a hospital that allowed both of us in the birthing room. One morning he called Grady Hospital. "We're pregnant," he told the woman who answered the phone. I could hear her laughing as she turned to someone else at the switchboard and relayed what Matt had said. But, indeed, we were. *We* were pregnant—not just me. There would be no empty arms; I could leave the hospital and take the baby with me. We didn't go to Grady as they would not guarantee that Matt could join me during the birth. We found a hospital outside of Atlanta that allowed fathers to join in the birthing ceremony—a hospital that primarily had midwives, not doctors, do the deliveries. It was at least twenty-five miles away from our house but set up that far from Atlanta, so the new birthing philosophies could be embraced without judgment or interference. We were part of the decision-making process, and no medical personnel took that away. It was just what we wanted.

Throughout the pregnancy, Matt understood the emotional withdrawals I went through, understood they were related to the "other" baby. He'd retreat from me for a few days, tiptoeing, leaving me to grieve on my own. I appreciated his gift of understanding. After a few days, I'd jump back into life, raring to go, eager for the new child's arrival. It was right when I found out I was pregnant I got a sad letter from Zan:

> *Please sit down when you read this, and once read, burn it with matches or throw it in the toilet. I will only say it once and never again. Do not refer to it as I cannot bear it. I only write you as you are my heart, the one I trust and love most in this*

world (other than Jessie, of course!). And, after what you and I have been through, I trust you'll understand and not judge me. I was caught off guard. Jessie's visiting her dad for the summer. When he came for her, she was curled into her nap and since it was a shame to wake her, her dad and I talked, laughed like we once did. He moved closer and his man smell drew me in, the scent so familiar, his touch I had responded to for so long. He drew me into his web and we reunited. Since our divorce, this has never happened and will never happen again! I swear!

That's not the worst of it. I got pregnant. I had no idea until I was two months gone and the morning trash made me gag. I gagged with Jessie, too, and became suspicious. My period did not come. Shit, what could I do? I do not really believe in abortion but I could not think of another alternative. I would not go back to living with him—he was most brutal when I was pregnant, remember? Unfortunately, I can barely afford one child so keeping another baby as a single mom was impossible. I have often wondered if the anti-abortion zealots have had to experience the personal tragedy that faces a woman who feels she has no other choice? Thank God abortions are now legal! Yet when you hear about my experience (it was ghastly!) you will wonder why I say that! Abortions are no better than adoption—no better than keeping an unwanted baby. There is no solution except not to be a fool, use birth control or HAVE NO SEX!! Or, perhaps being a lesbian isn't such a bad choice. Ever thought of that? I guess not since you are newly married...to a man you love.

My parents took Jessica for two weeks—the visit was already planned so I did not have to lie to anyone. Vanessa took me to the clinic—God I love and trust that woman! I laid on a sterile table and cried tears for a lost soul, a tiny spirit I already loved. The nurse who attended me had served time in an abortion clinic too long. I cried out in my stupor and I will never forget, she leaned over me and hissed, "Shut up, silly bitch. You'll be back! All of you are. It's just another form of birth control." After her comment, I got my tubes tied. That's my solution. Complicated problem—one you and I have both faced, resolved and will probably always regret. I cry, agonize, over how many other women must surely face this problem and hate the choice we make. Are there any good choices? Perhaps if you love the man who you got pregnant with and marry him or move in with him, keeping a wanted baby, sometimes there is happiness. Who the hell knows? Please do not tell anyone about this. Never mention it

to me either as I cannot bear it. I love you!
Pray for me!

Zan

It took time for me to write Zan that I was pregnant. I shivered, recoiling from both of our experiences: me, who had given one child up because of a savage conception experience; Zan having an abortion because of an equally harsh experience. Once I finally wrote, she sent me a package with two maternity dresses.

A beautiful mother makes beautiful babies. It's so hard to find anything to wear when you're pregnant—especially anything that makes you feel special, not huge! Try these. Let me know if they don't fit [they fit perfectly]. They will also do once the baby arrives. They have a drawstring at the top so you can pull the top down and nurse. You are going to nurse, aren't you?

Zan

Zan made the dresses, burnt reddish brown, matching my hair and eyes, making me feel soft and feminine when it was hard to feel that way. Matt loved them. "Who sent those? Your friend Zan? Have I ever met her?"

"No, she's never come to Atlanta since we got together, and I don't go to Sarasota. We spent a summer together years ago, but I haven't seen her in ages. She's an earth mother, a true gypsy."

"Those dresses look great on you. Come here," Matt nuzzled my ear and felt my bulging belly. He loved it when the baby kicked, responding to his warm touch.

Dear Katrina,

It's hard to earn a living when you're a single parent. I've expanded my personal career in two paths—both of which are proving lucrative; neither have a thing to do with my English degree. I read cards on the weekends at a tea room, tarot readings, predicting the future and seeing people's "auras." Have you ever had your aura read? I'll send a reading to you through the mail if you'd like. You have a beautiful aura. I'm also selling real estate. Down near Ringling School of Art. The psychic feelings help me sell. I place people in just the right house based on feeling tones. Sounds funny, doesn't it? It keeps me and Jessie fed and I have flexible hours so I can spend time with her. She's growing like a weed and will enter kindergarten next year. Can you believe it? She doesn't have many friends but has one special friend who she spends a lot of time with. An older girl, dark-haired, funny, sensitive.

Zan

Of course, I wondered once again about this special friend Jessie had but couldn't bring myself to ask any questions. Instead, I wrote to her:

Zan,

Reading cards and predicting the future—perfect for you! Do you wear colorful skirts and headbands? What a gypsy!

Send me a reading after the baby comes—
one for me and one for the baby. Jessie's
five?? Amazing!

Katrina

We still lived communally at the Briarcliff House but knew we'd need to move once the baby was born.

"Please don't," Ed begged; and just as we started looking for apartments, Tony, the jazz musician, moved out, leaving a room available for the baby.

"See"—Ed was nothing if not persistent—"it's meant to be. And, babysitters! You'll never lack for them here!"

It was light-years less complicated for me since the studio was so close; I could step out in the backyard and be at work. But what did Matt think?

"I like it here," he said. "Always have—it's where I met you, for God's sake! Ed's right about babysitters. We can still go dancing." We both laughed as we'd hardly ever gone dancing. We were more comfortable at the theater, eating out or going to friends' parties, and art openings.

Three weeks later at midnight, my water broke, and I began to shake in fear. "This is not like the last time," Matt whispered in my ear, drawing a warm sweater around my shoulders. "It's 1978 now, and they'll let me be in the delivery room," he continued, never losing his soft, soothing tone. "Besides, isn't that why we chose the hospital? We'll have midwives who are totally supportive of my being there in the birthing room. I won't leave for a moment, I promise. Unless I need to pee. That'll be okay, won't it?"

I laughed, trying to shake off my jitters. "It'll be just my luck the baby will arrive right when you do," I shuddered again, and Matt pulled me close.

"Put it behind you, if you can. This is entirely different. A nice baby girl or boy, whichever the case may be, dropped into our waiting arms? Going home with us? God, Katrina, I don't know if I can stand it, it's so exciting! Are you going to be all right?"

"If you're there, yes," I said, and we headed to the car, our headlights searching out the destination, the trip quiet and calm, the only sound our breathing. He was right—how did he do that? Still, it's disgusting. He's always right. The birthing experience was nothing like my first time, seven years ago. First off, the baby came home with us. I knew that going into labor just as the first time I knew I would leave without a baby. Secondly, Matt was there, and birthing had become more family friendly in the past seven years.

Liam was a large baby—well over eight and a half pounds yet not difficult to deliver, and once he arrived, Matt and I made every decision regarding his well-being. He was never taken from us—never left our side. We had him at 8:02 p.m., and the hospital moved us into our own room just the three of us. They shoved two single beds together, and we all slept there. Liam only woke up once, crying because he was so hot—Matt had him snuggled under his arm, tight. We were discharged the following day.

Two months after Liam was born, we bought the Briarcliff House cooperatively with Ed, Ginny, and Scottie and still had rooms to rent out. I have always known that communal living made Liam the young man he is today. He was handed around among single people who had no children of their own, checked out for weekends or even whole weeks at a time, like a library card giving access to marvelous materials borrowed then returned. The adults in Liam's life adored him and treated him to art history lessons, early exposure to theater, and an absence of prejudice towards alternative lifestyles. His open attitude towards life began the instant he was brought home from the hospital when Ed rushed to greet us, embraced the baby, and took him inside to an enormous party thrown in his honor. I didn't even see Liam for two hours as almost everyone we knew held and wooed him. He was a social being, so he loved it and has always been that way: gregarious and outgoing.

Clayton and Annabella came down from Charleston with their own two children and stayed all week, Clayton checking out galleries to carry his work. Liam was fascinated by Clayton's children: a boy and a girl. His eyes lit on the children as soon as they came downstairs every morning, and he'd laugh and chirp, intent on gaining their attention.

"He's going to be a charmer," Clayton predicted, watching Liam's intensity. "Just like his mom."

"He doesn't have a chance," Ginny said, "his dad's a charmer too." Matt laughed, relishing the compliments and attention his new son received.

"How are you holding up really?" Clayton asked one morning when he and I were alone in the kitchen.

"It's better than I ever thought possible. I still yearn for something—someone I may never know—but having another baby has been a great healer. I'm sort of beginning to close the void."

"I have something for you." Clayton handed me another clay medallion with three distinct figures—a male, a female, and a child.

"It's lovely," I whispered, pulling the other medallion out of my sweater pocket. By now the clay figures were almost unrecognizable.

"I didn't know if you'd still have it," Clayton said, then chuckled.

"You know me better than that."

"Well, I did not know you'd have it readily available." He laughed again at my stricken face.

"I carry it everywhere," I said intensely, almost defensively. "I think of it as my power surge, and it helps especially when I'm depressed. It's always helped. And now I have another one. I'll keep it close too. Thanks!" I hugged Clayton, drinking in his friendship like a fresh glass of spring water.

Although it was winter, Liam and Matt spent hours on the porch, Matt discovering quickly that the best way to get Liam to sleep was to wrap him up in blankets and swing him in Zan's hammock. So Matt, clever man, read books and glowed with the discovery that baby chores could be easy and enjoyable while relieving him of other duties that were more unpleasant or labor intensive.

I struggled with the ecstasy of a newborn and the guilt of his not being my first, but held my melancholy in check, not sharing it with Matt since Liam was his first, and such an obvious success. Once again Zan and I did not share this pivotal time in my life. Atlanta was so far from Sarasota, and she was alone raising her child. Her parents embraced Jessie but had turned their back on Zan because they did not approve of divorce and her lifestyle. Her ex-husband never wanted the child, so he did not participate. I understood Zan could not drive to Atlanta but missed her sorely.

Instead of taking a break from work, I was inspired, and my pottery became more playful, different in expression, even more colorful. Later I gave credit for this inspiration to Dr. Seuss, which I read aloud to Liam every day. I spent three or four hours a day in the studio, eager to work then even more eager to return to the baby once I had expressed my creative energy. There was never an absence of sitters for Liam, and he adapted easily surrounded by so many different people.

I made a series of teapots that sold rapidly in Vanessa's gallery with orders for more. Most of the teapots were not for tea but just artwork, and I switched from clay glazes to high-gloss acrylic paint. One teapot was designed like a fishbowl with the fish on the outside of the teapot, shaping the spout, the handle, and the lid, delighted in being outside the bowl, not trapped inside. Another was the shape of a stove with cooking pots boiling and overflowing goodies and grease down the sides; one a garden motif—the handle a carrot, the spout a squash, and the teapot itself a fat, juicy pumpkin.

My stellar piece was not sold but given to Zan as only she could understand and would know not to sell it. The teapot was carefully crafted as blown glass and was like the Easter eggs of spun sugar with one side open to view an inside scene. Because even my kaolin/porcelain clay was almost too dense, the teapot was open to the scene. I could not find anything like the spun sugar you look through, so I had to use the kaolin/porcelain. Even though it was almost transparent, it was as close as I could get to what I was searching for. The teapot spout was a young mother, breasts full to overflowing, arms outstretched in yearning with the young child out of reach inside the teapot, cradled and content but distant, ignoring its mother, totally unaware of her presence.

In order not to overwhelm Zan, I sent her two teapots—the one described above, and the second one a ceramic teapot perfectly suited to brew tea for her to use in her readings and her secret potions. The teapot handle, spout, and lid were replicas of the tarot characters she was so familiar with.

Your teapots are stunning, she wrote,

> *and I am too emotional to even express
> my reaction to the mother/child one. The
> workmanship is overwhelming and I feel*

blessed to be the recipient of such artistry. Thanks for being my friend, for sharing your life with me, and most of all, letting me be privy to your deepest emotions. It makes me humble as nothing ever has.

Zan Dora

Zan,

I'm naming my teapots and other display pots: dish-functional...what do you think? Too funny, huh?

Katrina

Love it! Love it! Love it! Especially in a world where everyone is dysfunctional—no one's functional. However, given that we are so dysfunctional, I don't know whether to laugh or cry!

Actually, you are clever! I'm proud to know you!

Zan

CHAPTER 8

*L*iam and I took long walks in Virginia Highlands, a trendy shopping district. We became familiar with many of the shopkeepers dedicated to running stores that were unique and offbeat. Several were art galleries and took my work on consignment, which was exciting as I finally began to sell in Atlanta beyond my living room sales, which we still ran to pay the mortgage.

My favorite shop, Devine Design, rapidly became the only place I bought clothes other than thrift stores. The woman who owned and ran the shop reminded me a lot of Zan even because her name was just as unusual, as spiritual as Zan's. Her name was Joy Devine and her presence larger than life. Joy herself was a tiny woman, no more than five feet tall, shoe size five, with tiny, tiny hands that never stopped moving. If you tied Joy's hands behind her back, she wouldn't be able to talk. Her artistry was a perfect expression of herself— she designed and made most of the clothes she sold, and that in itself kept her hands in perpetual motion. Ginny and Scottie knew Joy too because she often costumed the performances at Open City. "Leave Liam with me," she'd beg when I'd drop by, giving me ample time to visit the shops that carried my work, take care of being paid, and receive new orders while Liam flirted with the Devine Design customers.

During this time of new parenting, I often wondered about Liam's older sister and how she fared—was she an only child or an older or younger sibling? What were her introductions to prejudice/art/culture/heritage? I get ahead of my story if I answer those questions now, so I leave you to remain curious and hopeful I will tell my tale. I do promise you that—I will tell my tale soon enough, hoping to have pricked your curiosity to keep you glued to my pages, inspired you enough to keep reading and gain a glimmer into my life as unusual as it is.

By the time Liam was four months old, he joined Morningside Mother's Day Out, giving me mornings free to throw, fire, glaze, and sell; but I put him in the program more for his benefit than mine. He was so social he needed to be around other children, but often the hours away from him stretched endlessly for me, creeping slowly towards his two o'clock pickup, his release (or was it my release?). It was my second step towards empty nest, and he was only four months old! I saw 2:00 p.m. as my victory, my completion of probation rewarded by the return of what I wanted most, my baby.

Joy said she'd never heard anyone drive so fast as I did for my two o'clock pickup, and she was surprised I never got a ticket between Virginia Highlands and Morningside Drive. "I know it's you even when you leave home and not from here," she swore, but I was secretly convinced it was more the sound of Gracey's muffler she recognized than the sound of my speeding.

The letters that arrived from Zan always cheered me— they were never dull or ordinary just as Zan herself was never dull or ordinary. I shared her letters with Joy, who said she'd know Zan right away if she was to walk into her shop. They were cut from the same cloth.

Katrina,

Here's your reading and the baby's:

When I close my eyes and visualize, I see deep purple around you. It is a rich purple; your health is strong and you are doing well, recovering from birthing your baby. However, you do need to take more calcium and drink more milk.

Purple is a creative color and you should continue working in clay—it expresses your creativity. However, you need to work around other people, not alone. You brighten people up and make it fun to go to work. I should know! I see you working in some type of studio—with other artists around, some type of shared space or collective.

You need to wear more of the rich purple color I'm talking about; I'll make you a dress in that shade so you'll know the exact color I mean. Then, buy a blanket in that purple and surround yourself in it. You will have inspiring ideas when you do. I know you—don't get discouraged in the mother role; you are still a sensuous being, young, vivacious, talented. You love being a mother but will always have to have your own identity—something more...so, don't get depressed; you will succeed in both: being a good mother and *in doing your own thing, I promise (I see it in the cards, heh, heh).*

Now, the baby's reading:

He is an extremely powerful presence; will never have much self-doubt. Much of this is because he has chosen you as his mother and you will always affirm his creative expression. He will not be a child who does what the crowd suggests just because the crowd suggests it and he will have confidence in his differentness. As a matter of fact, he will be the one to establish the rules, make plans for the crowd. He will struggle with his leadership role, however, all of his life because if he had a choice for his own destiny, he would live a simple, quiet life in the hills, playing guitar and minding sheep. Unfortunately, there are few existences like that and his romantic soul will struggle with the complexities of his era. If he leaves the country, I think he will move to Ireland, perhaps.

Funny to say Ireland because his color is green, a rich green like the richness of the hillsides. He is both healer and comedian. You are gifted to be chosen as the mother of this child and through your guidance he will adjust to his calling.

Lots of Love,
Zan

She addressed my darkest fears without me having written to her about them. Although I had been eager to be pregnant again, I was confused and afraid. I did not want to strangle Liam in my eagerness to mother him, to satisfy the longing I'd pushed down deep inside for so long until I was overwhelmed. Yet at the same time, I wanted to be a potter *and* a good mother. I was driven by a passion for perfection in both. Even after I found the mother's-day-out program and had Liam in five mornings a week, I found I was always juggling schedules and was exhausted.

A year after Liam was born, my annual checkup was poor. "You have a compromised uterus," the doctor told me. "Have all the children you want, then come back to me for surgery." I was confused and asked the doctor what he meant. "You must have had a large baby and had some strain at birth. Your uterus is sagging. Do you have trouble with incontinence?" He had to have been accurate as I did have trouble; I didn't quite have to wear adult diapers, but I couldn't sneeze without it being a problem.

Zan immediately wrote back, responding to the letter I wrote, a letter full of fear and frustration, telling her about the doctor's prognosis.

> *A uterus is not something to be thrown away, discarded as we throw away dirty diapers, regardless of your symptoms. Seek a second opinion, try yoga exercises, DO NOT HAVE SURGERY unless it is the last resort! I'll send herbal recipes. Be sure you try them as soon as you get them! No surgery! No surgery!*
>
> *And, by the way, NO SURGERY!*
>
> *Zan*

I took Zan's advice seriously and began to study yoga, paying for private lessons that targeted specific exercises for me. A month after I began the lessons, I had a dream:

> *I was sound asleep and felt a loving presence spread throughout my body, beginning at the top of my head and warming me all the way to the bottom of my feet. As I slept, I cherished its warmth as it felt alive, like a spiritual being. All of a sudden, sounds began to fill my body—sounds of chanting and singing, heavenly sounds as if there were angels present, the OM chant predominate.*
>
> *The sound was so pervasive I woke up, but the singing did not stop even though I was awake.*

"Matt, Matt," I was almost desperate, a little afraid—mainly afraid I was losing my mind.

"What?" he slurred, waking from a heavy sleep.

"Do you hear it? Do you hear the singing?"

"What are you talking about?"

He rolled over, instantly going back to sleep. The singing stopped. Maybe once I brought someone else into the magic, it had to end.

I went back to the doctor a week later, a new doctor since I had not liked the first one's diagnosis or the flip manner in which he delivered it.

"What are you concerned about?" the new doctor inquired after her examination. "You are in fine shape—I don't know what kind of surgery the other doctor was referring to, but you don't appear to have a problem."

I never knew if it was the angels' chant, yoga, or Zan's tea that cured me, but perhaps it was all three.

*****

Two months after Joy and I met, she began dropping by the Briarcliff House every evening. It took me a while before I realized it was not me or Liam, Ginny or Scottie she came to see.

"Something's hot and heavy, I gather, between Joy and Ed," I whispered to Matt late one night, and he agreed.

"The funny thing is I always figured Ed was gay, didn't you?" Matt asked.

"Yeah, I did. Fooled us, didn't he?" And weeks later, Joy moved in, adding her playful costumes and clothing to our monthly sales to pay the mortgage. She also babysat Liam at the house as well as at her shop.

"I'm pregnant," Joy confided to me three weeks after she moved in. "Gives me new perspective on things. Did you experience that too?" she asked in a conspiratorial tone I recognized existed between pregnant women, separating us from the uninitiated, the unpregnant woman or the never-fortunate-enough-to-be-pregnant man.

"That it does," I said, laughing, relishing my role as the experienced mom even though Liam was only a year old. "Wasn't that quick, Joy?" I asked, unabashedly.

"Yep. When you know what you want, you gotta go for it!" She laughed. "I'm going to start a line of clothes for pregnant women and call it Movin' Mamas. What do you think?"

"I wish I'd had something fun to wear when I was pregnant. My friend Zan sent me two dresses she custom-made, but everything else made me look like a mobile home. Yuck!"

"Where do you think I got the idea for my new line? Now that I'm pregnant, I find I don't like anything out there. I only like what I make and those two cute dresses you wore—are those the ones Zan made for you?"

"Yep, and they have a drawstring top, so I wear them while I nurse too."

"I'd like to take a look at them. Also, I'll make professional clothes. Now when women go to work when they are pregnant, they either look like candy canes or fruit baskets. I know there will be a market for pregnant fashion. I'll also start something for dads—call it Devine Dads—with pockets big enough for diapers, diaper pens, baby stuff. This is going to be fun."

"I'm looking forward to another baby in the house. It'll be good for Liam to share the attention."

Tricia moved out, leaving me the pottery studio on my own as well as opening up a bedroom for Joy's baby. Zan had been right again—I did not like working in the studio alone and felt creepy outside late at night without Tricia coming and going. Tricia and I had the same schedules, so we frequently worked late on the same nights. Even in our frequent silence, the togetherness took the edge off, and work was more productive.

"Get someone else to share the space with you," Matt suggested. "I'm sure other potters would be interested. It wouldn't cost them much, and you already have an extra wheel and the kilns."

"Either that or take classes at Callanwolde," I replied. "That might be fun."

"I like you at home in the backyard. What do you say we expand the studio and add space for another wheel and lease to two or three other potters, not just one?"

How did Zan and Matt do that—come up with the right answers at just the right time? We expanded then advertised at Callanwolde. Two potters wanted space right away, and I liked them. I was particularly pleased that neither one had styles anything like mine.

"I never thought I'd find anyone to share my life with," Ed talked to me late one night about Joy while she was still working. "I'm so picky, I've never dated much. I am totally anal. But Joy keeps things in perspective and laughs at me when I get neurotic."

Once Ed and Joy's baby arrived, Liam's true nature was revealed. Eric Dunbar-Devine, their baby girl, was a tiny thing compared to Liam. She weighed barely six pounds at birth while Liam arrived well over eight pounds. Liam softened around Eric—unbelievably gentle and patient, seeming to know instinctively what she could and could not do. At first, I thought he did not display sibling rivalry because she wasn't his actual sister. I figured he somehow knew that her parents were different from his. However, later after the birth of his own sister, my daughter, Sera, I learned that this was just Liam's nature. With his own sister, he was solicitous, devoted, gentle, and affectionate. He never hit her; he fought with Matt and me instead, begging us to turn the other cheek when she needed discipline. He created a child who had three parental figures (not just two) as he became her supervisor too. However, once again, I get ahead of my story, so keep reading (please).

Zan's letters continued to arrive on an irregular basis, and though we lived different lives, we both lived outside the mainstream and enjoyed the stories we shared.

Katrina, she wrote,

have I got a story for you! You will never believe it as I'm convinced it could only happen to me. I'm having my ten-year high school reunion this year so I called my high school in Parrish, Alabama. They gave me the reunion coordinator's number so I called her, asking why I hadn't been con-tacted. I know it sounds stupid for someone like me to attend my reunion but even the most airhead gypsy (me) likes to reexperi-ence her roots occasionally. Anyway, she checked her records and said she had me down as deceased. Deceased! Oh my god! How did you get that? I asked.

Your best friend from high school, Sandy Johnston, told us you died in 1977. God, Katrina—that's the year I went nuts about death and tried out my coffin, remem-ber? And that was the year they had down that I died. Maybe part of me died trying to live through that awful marriage! Anyway, Sandy saw a Suzanne Duncan—that's my real name—in the Birmingham obituaries and, thinking I had died, caught the plane from Boulder to attend my funeral. When she went to the funeral it was closed cas-ket so she never found out it wasn't actually me. She did wonder where my parents were! By then I had changed my name to Zan Dora so there was no trace of me, Suzanne Duncan, anywhere.

Everyone thought I had died—zip— gone. What an experience to find out more than one hundred people thought I've been dead for years! Needless to say, I got my reunion invitation and I'm going! I hope I look drop dead (tee hee) gorgeous as I want them to fall all over themselves when they see me "back from the dead!" What a stitch!
Worlds of love,
Zan Dora

It could only happen to Zan, I thought, laughing, rereading her letter. From having gone with Zan to Parrish, Alabama, I realized Zan Dora was her gypsy name—but I never realized her real name was Suzanne Duncan. Zan Dora—did I really think her name was Suzanne Dora? Was I naïve enough not to know she had created her whole name— she who created everything else about herself? It was then I thought to ask Joy if she had changed her name too.

"Of course! No one—leastwise my dear mother— would name a child Joy Devine! I was born *Cathy Smith*— dull as dirt, me? Cathy Smith? I was fortunate in that my first husband's last name was Devine—only good thing about that man! I took my middle name, *Joy*, and voila! Here I am! Theatrical, isn't it? And, no one ever forgets my name or my business—you can count on that! Don't you just love it?" She giggled wildly and twirled around, collapsing in a chair and laughing even more when I read her Zan's letter.

"I'd love Zan, I just know it!" Joy said, reminding me that other people we knew changed their names: Dirgi Darshi, Moktaranda, Verilyisaytoyou. "How about *Movin Mamas* and *Devine Dads*?" I was laughing so hard tears were rolling down my face.

"Hey"—Joy attempted to look stern, not wanting me to make fun of her business names—"no worse than *dishfunctional* or *fysh dishes!*" I got the hiccups laughing so hard, and Joy wet her pants.

During this time, Matt went to Georgia Tech to get his PhD, hoping to return to Emory as a full professor once his studies were complete. Since Briarcliff House was on the bus line, he took the bus to school. We still only had Gracey (for my work) and Queenie, my VW. Even though Matt had plenty of money, he was frugal. He spent the next six years between Tech and Emory, thriving as a teacher at both universities and a student at Tech.

He came in hepped up one night, and I could tell he had something bursting to share.

"One of my students gave me this as a present." And he spread out a camouflage blanket on our bed.

"Not the most attractive bedspread," I said, hating to dash his enthusiasm.

"Not a problem. It's not for the bed."

"What's it for then?" I asked him.

"It's made of parachute material so nothing sticks to it."

"Sticks to it?" I was confused.

"Nothing—not leaves if you are raking the yard, not sand as in it's a perfect beach blanket."

"You're kidding! That's the only thing I don't like about the beach is sand all over everything."

"I want to make them out of bright-colored parachute material…ripstop nylon, with colorful ribbons on them."

"Joy is the best person to talk to about production and supplies," I said.

"What a great idea!" Matt left to talk to Joy immediately. She did have great ideas, so it wasn't long until Matt and Joy bought a warehouse in the Old Fourth Ward and began production. Joy insisted on a catchy name, so we took a vote with everyone at the Briarcliff House. The choices were:

> Easy Spread—nixed because it sounded too much like cheese or mayonnaise,
> Sun Spread—again, like butter or cheese,
> Beach Impeach—a close second, but we all remembered Richard Nixon and his impeachment process,
> Quilted Southern—the winner!

Matt shipped the blankets to Vanessa and Zan, who were thrilled with them. They sold them around Sarasota, Bradenton, and Anna Maria Island. It wasn't long before Joy used all the warehouse space for Quilted Southern; she had another space for her clothing line. Orders came in from Charleston too through Clayton. Quilted Southern blankets became a must-have for the beach. Joy and Matt hired a business manager and a bookkeeper, and Joy had a floor manager so she didn't have to stop production of her clothing. The materials and production were so expensive they sold for $45 wholesale, but that didn't stop stores or people from buying them since they lasted forever. Matt now had loads going on: Feasta on Pizza, student at Tech, professor at Emory and Tech, and now Quilted Southern. He was thriving.

CHAPTER 9

*S*ix months later, Zan sent another letter on a much more serious note:

> *Katrina,*
>
> *Sorry I haven't written in a while. I've been given a lesson in local politics, good ole boys, plain old rednecks. And, it has been eye-opening! I experienced the unbridled power of the mayor and it's been a shitty ride! I slapped him one night when he came on to me inappropriately and since then the bastard has made my life hell. "No one rejects me!" he shouted, puffed up, full of bloated self-importance. I'd laugh if he wasn't so fucking powerful! None of my real estate has sold since "the incident," as I've come to call it, and the tea room had to stop my readings. It suddenly became an issue that I had no business license even though the tea room had one. Whoever heard of getting a business license for reading cards? And, of course, my request was denied. Ha—what did I expect? The mayor has direct pull in those decisions.*

How do I fight this attack on my survival? I refuse to be pushed into a corner and forced to have sex with someone I despise. But then I got scared. I couldn't pay my rent.

Jessie and I need a break anyway so we are moving to Anna Maria Island. Fight or flight, I guess. This time I chose flight. You know me! I'd fight, but Jess cannot suffer. I know you understand. I can't put a child in the middle of such a vicious battle. What's your take on this? I'd love to talk to you. And, you'll never guess who adopted me? Wally's mother, Vanessa! She's 70 and though spry as a goat, loathe to grow old alone. She was divorced before Wally was born and when Wally passed away, there went her family. Gia visits on a regular basis but still lives in Columbus, Georgia. And, Gia still struggles with her grief, overwhelming Vanessa.

Her house is to die for—like I arrived in nature's heaven—the Garden of Eden. Jessie walks to school and I'm official caretaker of the house and grounds. In her own way, Vanessa's a gypsy, too, so I give readings from her house. Ask and you shall receive, seek and you shall find: I'm keeping my faith and my chin up!

Zan Dora

Zan,

> *I'm glad your problem was solved for your benefit. God, I love Vanessa! She'll be fun to live with. You two will raise some hell, I know!*
>
> *Please send me recipes for fertility. I'm ready for another child (so is Liam), and each month my damn period comes. Joy just looks at Ed, and they have another. I'm so frustrated!*
>
> *Katrina*

Matt and I never knew why it took us five years to have another baby, but it did. We never used birth control after Liam was born, but Sera did not arrive until one month before Liam turned five, exactly nine months after Zan sent fertility potions. I should have turned to her sooner!

Joy and Ed did not use birth control either, but they had two more children before Sera was on the way. After five years, the Briarcliff House was no longer a commune but two families sharing a home. I outgrew the backyard studio and had been working next door to Matt and Joy's warehouse in the Old Fourth Ward. When another piece of property became available, Matt bought it, realizing one day I would outgrow our backyard studio. The kids took over the backyard studio and turned it into a playhouse.

Our kids never lived like other children of the 1980s. They had more freedom because there were so many of them. They played outside the same as children of the 1950s and never got drawn in by television or video games. For one thing, we never bought a television no matter how much they begged. "Use your imaginations," was the constant cry from all the adults, and use their imaginations, they did! They all had their own distinct personalities—it was impossible not to, growing up as they did.

I don't know why, but it never drove Matt and Liam crazy like it did me that it took me five years to have another child. Liam never realized he was sibling-less as his interaction with Joy and Ed's kids, Eric, her sister, Corinth, and brother, Phillipe, was as if they were his brothers and sisters. With Matt's full schedule, he didn't care that we only had one child. Me? I agonized! Did I have female "problems" as one doctor had said, was I being punished for giving one child up for adoption? I thought about it every day once Liam turned three. It was hard to live with Joy as she was always pregnant. After years of watching her wear Movin' Mamas, I was tickled when I finally had to buy them. I had two thoughts that consumed me: I wanted a girl. God! How I wanted a girl! And I prayed for the baby's safe arrival. I did not care that I grew enormous. I gained fifty pounds while pregnant with Sera, proud of every pound.

It was pure heaven when a baby girl was finally laid in my arms after eight short hours of labor. *Sera*, short for *Seraphim*, my angel. She was also a huge baby, weighing nine pounds one ounce. She held court from the moment she arrived, holding her head erect and surveying the birthing room as if to approve of us! The first person she opened her eyes to was Liam as he was held up to see her; he yelled, "I love her already!" Once he shouted his approval, she seemed to relax and snuggle into my neck. The other children were ready for a new baby too. When I look back on Sera's childhood, I have to work hard to remember it. She was in the thick of things from the moment we took her home, raised by the other children almost as much as by Matt and me. She was never overwhelmed by the commotion of the household or the four other children. She was the center of their imag-

inative play even before she could sit up. Liam hauled her
in her infant seat or in the wagon to the middle of wherever
they were, and they would play around her, making her a
central character. I got in serious trouble when I came to
bathe or feed her. Liam would charge, "Annie Oakley's getting kidnapped! Kidnapped! Stop that woman's retreat!" as
I took her, running so I would not be waylaid by the other
children. I needed my baby time, so I risked life and limb,
combing her beautiful dark hair.

Although we lived close to downtown, our kids were not
tied to the safety issues most children their age were. There
were several reasons they had freedom while the rest of the
world lived behind closed doors. First, an adult was always
home or close by. Ed worked at home; Joy and I worked only
a few blocks away. Matt dropped in and out all the time with
his flexible schedule. Second, there was strength in numbers.
The kids moved as a unit of five with Liam the leader and
Sera bringing up the rear, included, coddled, in the ever-con-
scious desire to ensure each one of them was protected. They
roamed the neighborhood so much that the shopkeepers
knew them all by name. Every day was like trick or treat for
them as they dropped by certain shops to pay homage to
their adult friends and collect treats of all kinds.

Our backyard was close to being a junkyard, so we
dubbed it a treasure trove to give a more positive name to
near disaster. When Gracey, my station wagon from Vanessa,
finally died, the kids insisted we not bury her but install her
permanently in the backyard for their adventures and "driving lessons." Once Gracey was in the backyard as a permanent playscape, we hung a long rope swing so they could
stand on top of her and swing across the yard, landing in a
huge pile of leaves where Matt composted our yard clippings.
At least once a week, I'd swing across the yard, often yelling at

the top of my lungs, feeling young and free. Many afternoons I'd climb Gracey again and again, until finally exhausted, I'd go inside to take a long hot bath, pulling leaves and grass out of my hair the rest of the night.

Surrounded by artists and without television, our children were resourceful. They'd play for days with old refrigerator boxes, turning them into all sorts of things—robots, huts, grocery stores, sleds. We had a mudroom long before such rooms were common—we had one out of necessity since Ed never lost his compulsive mood for cleanliness despite coexisting with five children and three other adults, one of whom was a potter (me!).

Every Tuesday was the children's night to cook, and despite being the baby, Sera spearheaded the operation by the time she turned four, telling everyone, including Liam, what to do. They were whizzes at spaghetti, taco salads, even veggie lasagna. Phillipe and Sera were excellent at the stove and later expanded their interest to baking, keeping the family supplied in cookies, and, as they grew older, fresh bread and pies.

We had an enormous garden in the front yard, keeping the pets confined to the backyard. With so many children, each demanding a different pet, our backyard looked like a zoo—three dogs of varying sizes, a hutch full of rabbits, four cats of our own, plus a variety who dropped by knowing a free ride, an open door, when they saw one. Every child and adult had a row of garden to take care of. Everyone except Matt. He was chief composter and took his job seriously so that his compost provided us with the best soil (and therefore best garden) in northeast Atlanta. At least that's what we claimed.

We did not homeschool even though Joy wanted to. No one had the time or the energy to put in the effort it took. We also felt the children needed to cope with structure within society since most of the time we lived by our own rules. During their early years, the children thrived. Later, now that it's behind me, I see that their adolescence was no more than typical rebellion though it was hard to see that when it was *my* household in emotional chaos, *my* children straining to pulverize me. I often felt like chopped liver.

There are several instances from their unique childhood I'll never forget:

"You'll never believe what we saw today, Mom. Never!" Liam was almost shouting as the kids burst through the door one sunny afternoon when I happened to be home early.

"We were glad every one of us was there, or we'd swear we were hallu—hallo…"

"Hallucinating," Liam finished for Eric, and the rest of the kids fell over themselves laughing.

"A lady—an old lady—completely naked, walking down—"

"Not completely naked. She had on a shower cap."

"You saw what?" I was not prepared. "Where on earth?"

"Right across from Open City."

"She went into the ice cream store."

"Come on, kids, let's go for a drive. Pile in. I have to find out about this." We drove to the ice cream store.

"What on earth went on here today—" Before I could even finish my sentence, the clerk knew what I was talking about.

"If the kids told you, they were right. An older woman— not a stitch on—walked in and got in line for an ice cream, nice as you please."

"What'd you do?"

"I told her—no shirt, no shoes, no service. She stalked out."

"Well, let me know if she comes back. I can't let these kids run loose if those types of things go on."

"Ah, Mom, really...," Liam said.

"Yeah, maybe next time, it'll be a young girl!" Phillipe punched Liam in the shoulder, and they both laughed.

I smacked them both on the heads as we finished our ice cream and piled back in the car.

Then:

"It was not Spiderman, it was Superman."

"What are you talking about?" I asked another day.

"We were walking home from school and saw Spiderman in Fleeman's Drug Store."

"Not Spiderman. I'm telling you it was Superman."

"No, he wasn't either of those," Sera cleared it up, "he was his own superhero, couldn't you tell?"

Superhero, as they came to call him, made several appearances in the Virginia Highlands area, but Joy knew him well. She made his costumes.

"He's harmless. I swear. Modern-day Robin Hood."

*****

My two best friends, Joy and Zan, were alike in many ways yet, in other ways, as different as a hurricane is to a calm sea. Which one of them was the hurricane? On a daily basis, I'd say Joy. Joy was wispy, ethereal, stirring up adventures as soon as she closed up shop for the evening. She bought a convertible when Liam was seven and Eric five, and that was the only kind of car she ever drove after that. She cavorted around town every day it was sunny, which is frequent in Atlanta. Even Liam and Phillipe enjoyed sitting atop the back and waving at passersby as if homecoming celebrities; seatbelts were mere suggestions back then, not law. After an hour, they'd roar to a stop at Fleeman's to sit on the barstools at the soda fountain, slurping malted milk and eating burgers for supper.

Joy always said later as her children became adolescents that her struggle came from them thinking of her as their friend, as one of them, not their mother, not an authority figure. Eventually all of her children grew to be creative and contributing members of our culture but not without adventures, near misses, and many tears/hurts/anxieties on Joy's part.

Zan was more like the eye of the storm, the calm center creating mushrooms of activity around her like a magnet attracts metal. For one thing, being a single mother, she knew she must stand firm or lose Jessie irrevocably. For another, for all her gypsy ways, she emanated a power so profound she could be unapproachable. As far as I knew, her ex-husband and the mayor were the only two men to take her on. Though the mayor never "got" her, he did run her out of town because of her responsibility to her daughter. Otherwise, my bets would have been on Zan.

Zan and I both created supportive environments for ourselves, surrounded by artists and free spirits. Zan earned her way as Vanessa's gardener. And I'm sure you wonder how our household survived, paid our bills? Despite her antennae for high adventure, Joy ran a lucrative business that grew in profit as Atlanta prospered. Matt was always a hard worker, a professor at Emory or Georgia Tech (whichever could schedule him first), and good provider; he had investments in some early Atlanta businesses that were very successful, and my pottery business contributed to our communal resources. Other factors helped: we bought our large house before Atlanta's real estate boomed, and Ed managed a large portfolio he inherited when his parents died. It was during this time that Vanessa contacted Matt. "The land beside me is for sale. An old couple need to unload it—they are moving into a retirement community and want to sell their property."

"Well, you know how Katrina feels about the Sarasota area, and you probably know why."

"This would be an investment venture primarily," Vanessa explained. "And, you never know what might change her mind."

"How much is it?" They got into details.

"I'll buy it through a blind trust," Vanessa said, "and you can buy it from me at 0 percent interest."

"Why don't you just buy it?" Matt asked.

"First, I think of you two as my children, especially after what Katrina did for me with the gas company," Vanessa said. "Second, I don't want anyone to think I'm taking over this part of the beach. It'll be better if there's a separate owner."

"How about I pay you 1–2 percent?" Matt asked.

"Don't look a gift horse in the mouth," was Vanessa's response. "Zero percent is fine with me."

"Wow, it's a deal," Matt said. He flew down to Sarasota a few weeks later and sealed the deal, meeting with Vanessa, visiting with Zan. That's how we became landowners on Anna Maria Island.

*****

As the children grew, the adolescent years were not nearly as peaceful—or fun—as the childhood adventures had been. I always thought their childhood was much like my favorite movie *Goonies*, and I looked back at their childhood as idyllic—until Liam turned fourteen and Eric thirteen. They seemed to transform right in front of our eyes. I was not the only one who thought that. Joy agreed.

When Liam turned fourteen, I struggled with him; he was such a loving baby to be such a holy monster! The second year he was in high school was his albatross. And I was at a loss as to how to handle him. I wondered if my Sarasota child's parents struggled with her during her formative years? Was she a fiery spirit? A storm to be reckoned with? Perhaps she was also rebellious. In some ways, I hoped she rebelled if just for a little while—I hoped she had spunk and vitality demanding direction, boundaries. On the other hand, I was not sure I would survive Liam's protests. How could I live through it?

"What do you mean?" he sneered to all my questions, one day backing me into the refrigerator and pushing me. Who was this child? I did not recognize him. I knew I must not let him get away with stalking me; he was a foot taller than I was, and if it came to a physical battle, he would win—easily.

"What the hell do you think you're doing?" I followed him to his room and confronted him. "You cannot threaten me. It doesn't work! Understand?" He cringed before the hard-core teen personae slipped right back into place.

"I don't know what you're talking about!" he responded innocently, slamming his door in my face. Matt remained asleep on the couch during the whole interaction, knowing that this had nothing to do with him, everything to do with me.

"If you don't know what I mean, then I'm worried about you!" I shouted, opening his door. "You were threatening me."

"I was not. I merely questioned your right to tell me what to do."

"Well, that's my job. I have other jobs, but guess what? My main priority, my number one job is you and Sera—I'm responsible in seeing that you have integrity, that you don't pick on people. If you turn out lousy, I want to say I did my best."

At the time, he was on steroids because he had constant earaches; and later, on reflection, I realized the drugs changed his personality, gave him an unfamiliar aggression that had to be reckoned with. But that afternoon he did finally back down.

"I'm sorry, Mom. I just get so frustrated. Sometimes I know what I want, but most of the time I'm so confused. I'm too old to go everywhere with you and too young to drive. It's not fair!"

I tried to respond quietly to his dilemma, responding as much as allowed before the wall returned.

I wrote Zan, thankful she had an older daughter and hoping she could help me understand what was going on:

> *Zan,*
>
> *How did you survive Jessica as a teenager? Liam's gone off the deep end—the trigger appears to be the transition from middle school to high school. He's always been practically perfect so it is probably good for him though I'm not sure I'll live through it.*
>
> *He has never studied and has maintained a 4.0 average so now his study habits are non-existent while the stakes are higher. He made an F in Latin, a D in science and several Cs. We're totally worried and overly involved—worried about college scholarships which he must get in order to go to college. What's his reaction? He blows it off.*

He's so angry, enraged even, that he doesn't give a damn. So, we're pulling our hair out—HAIR—another battle entirely.

God, I thought sure I'd have a Republican child with a long, skinny tie and a white shirt yet we have a child who is so liberal he finds us reactionary. When Matt insists he comb his hair and get rid of the dreadlocks, Liam runs for the photographs of Matt's curly Afro, screaming, "How dare you? I win this case! Look at YOU!"

And, he has a point. It got so bad, Matt challenged Liam to a fight and I thought I would throw up. Liam went to his room and painted his body from head to toe in acrylic paint—a primitive aborigine ready to duel his father and claim his manhood.

Fortunately, Matt took responsibility for things getting out of hand and apologized before they came to blows.

How can we live communally and go through such battles, I bet you're asking. Why don't Joy and Ed call Human Services to come arrest us for child abuse? They don't say a word, can't say a word as their battleground is far more serious than ours. Eric, their firstborn, struggles and fights/ resists far more than Liam ever dreams of. She has run away from home already (she's only 13) at least twice when they thought they'd never find her. She runs away, living in drug-infested houses (what else can I call

*them?) shacking up with questionable char-
acters. A man of twenty who lives with a
thirteen-year-old has got to be suspect, don't
you think?*

*So, they keep quiet when Liam and
Matt go at it. Ironically, our house is just
one block away from one of the best teenage treatment centers in Atlanta so all of
us have considered "enrolling" our children
there. I am sure that will be Ed and Joy's
next step if Eric runs away again. Joy has
resigned herself to thinking that she cannot
answer the depth of despair that surrounds
young Eric.*

*Other tragedies have affected us: two
friends of Liam and Eric's recently came to
rough endings. One young boy (Eric's age
and one of her best friends) went out drinking with friends and never came home. He
got so drunk he leaned out of a car window
to throw up. Unfortunately, the driver was
drunk as well and at that very moment ran
over a curb, into a ravine and deep into a
gully. The young boy was tossed out the window; he died on impact. We cried bushels
over that one and it shook Eric up tremen-
dously. She is now (finally) attending school
regularly and has greatly reduced her sneaking out, the drugs, the drinking. She would
have been in that car if she had had her way
but Joy slept that night in front of her door
so she could not leave through the doorway
without physically challenging her mother.*

She could not leave through the window because it was nailed shut. Thank God Joy had an instinct about that particular night. Before that when she "jailed" Eric, she gave herself shit about doing it.

Then a friend of Liam's committed suicide. All hell broke loose—total chaos.

The young boy rode off on his bike to a forest nearby but first he dropped by the bike shop where Liam works before he took off so Liam knows he was one of the last people to see him alive. Does that fill Liam with remorse? Oh, God, it's awful! The boy stood under a tree, attached a rope to it, kicked the bike out from under him. All the teenagers are shell-shocked—they wonder if they could have done anything to have stopped him. Over and over they ask that question. I know that Liam has such a strong personality he does not contemplate suicide, no matter how unhappy he is. Thank God for that! He has told us he cannot comprehend such an act, which is why this friend's death knocked him to his knees.

Sorry to share such depressing news.

I love you!

Write!

Katrina

Katrina,

First off, sleep has become the number one thing I look forward to, need in my older age. I don't know if this is good

*or bad—I'm sorry if my words don't soothe
but it's true—boring, too, I know—and I
know you never think of me as boring. Well,
I am. Aging is a struggle—a battleground
of its own, not necessarily full of peace and
goodwill. Isn't that unfortunate? We work
this hard to get here and then it is as much
a struggle as every other age we've passed
through. Damn! I want serenity in my elder
years!*

*So, what has that got to do with
your letter??? It points out that I am at the
other end of the spectrum from you. I've
lived through it and have now passed on
to the boring side, the lackadaisical side of
life. Jessie's at University of the South in
Sewanee, Tennessee. She is totally ready to
leave me. She pretends she has no mother
unless she needs something: money, cookies,
clothes. She removed my name and address
from the mailing list so I never know about
parent's day, etc. This is exactly what she
had in mind (not me, I hate it!)*

*You'll never believe it but I'd almost
rather relive the hell of rebellion than live
with isolation—indifference—there is
no contact unless she initiates it (and it is
always when she needs something). Being in
the middle of the Rebel Hell as I called it,
I'm sure those words stun you but it is true, I
swear! It's like people telling us that teenage
years are worse than the Terrible Twos and
we could not imagine.*

We couldn't imagine anything worse than the Terrible Twos! But, it's true, I promise!

In the book The Road Less Traveled, *M. Scott Peck says that all children MUST rebel or they remain pansy asses (I interpret him loosely) and know that you of all people could never raise a pansy ass. Agree? You're damn right! I know you do even if your heart hurts with confusion.*

Love,
Zan

It was years of tears, outbursts, hormone overloads. Liam always took his frustration out on me, never turning his rage on Sera or Matt. He felt safer with me, so I became the one who felt unsafe—riddled with bullets—walking around with huge empty holes I tried not to turn into festering wounds.

"You're always at that damn studio," he'd scream at me one moment, then later the same evening, "Leave me alone! No one else's mother is so damn nosy!" I'd retreat.

He reached in, tapping my own sense of despair as a teenager, reminding me of the confusion I found when facing the world. His popularity did not seem to help. The phone rang for him constantly, yet he would not answer it, choosing instead to storm out the door, walk the dogs. Long walks. The dogs loved the long walks, their energy satiated for the first time. I could not say the same for Liam. His rage became a deep internal fire.

"What's there to look forward to if I have to go to work when I'm out of school? I hate school. It's a waste of time!"

Sera listened to his rages but fortunately found her fourth-grade projects interesting enough to remain motivated. And Sera had always found peace in physical activity: anything to do with exercise such as gymnastics or dance, she excelled. She started movement classes at the young age of three and never lost her love of physical expression. She starred in many roles before she even turned eight; she was chosen to dance in *The Nutcracker* every year from the age of five. And it was easy for her to participate as her elementary school offered after-school dance classes; she took movement classes at Callanwolde, and soon we enrolled her in gymnastics. She was busy, busy—three dance classes a week, gymnastics, and she was a serious student too. She loved academics almost as much as she loved dance...almost.

With Liam, it all came to a head when Matt and I told Liam he could not go to Florida with his best friend. He went any way and called us from Sarasota once he arrived. "Mom, I'm in Sarasota. Bryan and Maria came to pick me up, so I couldn't say no. Don't blame them. They thought it was okay with you." I sat by the phone, gripping it until my knuckles turned white.

"It's been twelve fucking hours since we've heard from you." I was so angry I used words I never used in front of him. "What do you think we've been through for the last twelve hours?"

Matt took the phone from me, talking calmly, almost soothingly. Sometimes he overwhelmed me with his approach. "Liam, this is serious. You were told you could not go. When are you returning?"

"We'll be back Sunday night," I heard him say as I listened quietly on the extension. "I didn't agree with your decision that I couldn't come."

"But that was not your decision to make. Our reasons were clear—if your grades were better, the trip would have been okay. You've been told that the last three weeks. What is there about that that you didn't understand?"

"I understood, I just didn't agree."

"Agree or not, you are down there. When you come home, we'll let you know what your punishment is. Believe me, you are not off the hook. Now, go ahead and have fun. We'll talk once you get home." I envied Matt's quiet simplicity, his directness; he always seemed in control of situations, no matter what. On the other hand, I was awash in guilt and grief, thought myself responsible somehow for Liam's disastrous year. Even though I knew intellectually it wasn't true, I felt his agony. I remained deeply absorbed by his turmoil.

There comes a point in mothers' lives when they should join Al-Anon, even if their children/spouses do not drink, just to hear the philosophy, just to learn the twelve-step viewpoint and try to live by the philosophy. It helps keep a lid (hard as it is) on codependency, which seems to thrive in families. It is crucial for survival. On the advice of friends, Joy and I both began attending meetings.

When Liam returned, he was tan, happier than I'd seen him in months. He was afraid of his punishment, so he was very pleasant when he came through the door.

"What do you think your punishment should be?" Matt met Liam in his room as I hovered outside the door.

"I needed the trip, so I don't know what to say. I know I was wrong, but I think you were too."

"That doesn't matter. That wasn't your choice. You did not obey us. That's pretty serious."

"Dad, I promise I'll work hard the rest of the school year and bring up my grades for a start."

"Damn right. Conduct grades included. One of the reasons you're not making good grades is all those Fs in conduct. What else?"

"I think that's enough."

"That's light punishment. You have violated our family by disobeying us and worrying your mother like you did. She went through hell, and think what a shitty role model you showed the younger children in the house. Eric has stopped running away, but since she sees you as a leader, what will she do now? What about Sera?"

"I never thought about that. How about if I take a night to cook every week and help clean up around the house. I'm sure Ed would like that. Is that enough?"

"I'll reevaluate when the report card comes in. If you don't pull those grades up, we'll take more severe action, you can bet your life on that." His grades improved as he said they would—he went from a 2.4 to a 3.0 by the end of the semester with Bs and Cs in conduct. Once the heat from his disobedience died down, he told me, "I met your friend Zan Dora. She's so cool!"

"You met her?" I had so many questions, but the simplicity of his declaration left me speechless. I hadn't seen Zan for years; she'd never met either of my children, and now Liam went to her house, met her, spent time with her, and I never even knew it. I was surprised I hadn't suspected that this would occur—even more surprised I hadn't sensed them meeting since I was so spiritually connected with them both.

"I found her address on an old letter and called her when we got to Sarasota. Her roommate, Vanessa, is cool too. They loved me—thought I was cute and funny. They also showed me next door—land you and Dad own. I didn't know we owned land on the beach. Why didn't you tell me? Why haven't we ever visited? Zan gave me a personal tour of our land, and I pitched a tent and spent a few nights there." I heard an accusation in his tone but didn't want to tell him why I had not shared much about Sarasota or Zan with him, didn't want to explain why I couldn't bring myself to go there. Didn't want him to know he had a half sister who lived in Florida.

Matt saved me. "That's investment property for now, Liam. We rent out the house, and Vanessa and Zan do the upkeep. We wouldn't have anywhere to stay if we went there."

"What about staying with Vanessa and Zan? They have a huge house."

"Sounds like something we might do. I'm glad you had a good time. I'll keep my eye on your grades, and a trip like that might happen."

Now, I was in a conundrum. I wanted his grades to improve, but I didn't want to go to Sarasota, and I could never tell him why. I kept my mouth shut, at least for now.

CHAPTER 10

an lived with Vanessa until she died at eighty. She died the summer after Liam met them, passing away peacefully in the night. She had not been sick. It was a shock for Zan. She called me right away.

"I'd love for you to come down, but I don't think I could handle it. Do you understand?"

Not really, I quietly told myself, but to Zan, I said, "Sure. How are you? Are you holding up?"

"No, that's why I can't see you yet. I need to hibernate, sort through things. I'm going crazy with grief. God! I'm planning a small memorial service. You know Vanessa—she knew everyone in Sarasota, and I don't want to turn this into a circus!"

"I'll come if you want," I offered, just to make sure she did not want me there.

"I'll call soon. I'd like you to visit, just not yet. I'm too tender."

Zan wrote me a few weeks later,

> Katrina,
>   It's worse than losing my own mother.
> Vanessa and I never finished a sentence, we
> knew what the other person was thinking.

Jessica is sick over it, grieving, crying. How can I reach out to her when I have my own sadness, my own sense of loss?

Vanessa has been too generous. As I wrote earlier, there's only me and Jessica, Gia and Katie, Wally's daughter. Vanessa was already rich when she got the settlement from the gas company. A huge settlement— she says you were responsible for her getting it. She never touched it, never needed to. She invested it and has let it grow.

She's left most of it to us since Gia won't touch that money. Calls it "blood money." It is enough to pay for Jessie's college and for me to live well.

Vanessa loved Liam when he came to visit—saw a lot of you in him and was touched he came without your approval. You know Vanessa, always cheering the underdog, the independent spirit. In her will, she left Liam $15,000 for college. Mariposa, her house and its grounds she willed to me. She left most of the rest of her money for Katie. She was so rich, Gia has plenty and we inherited a lot, too! I don't have to trudge the streets seeking work. Thank God—now I'm a rich gypsy—sounds funny, doesn't it? Oxymoron, eh?

She did have a request—she has two guest houses and wants them to be let to artists for moderate or no rent. She wants them dedicated in Wally's memory. So, I'll be the Grand Dame of an artist collective.

Will you be my first visitor? That's what she wanted; she specified in her will that your visits as well as Gia's will always be top priority. Wouldn't that be a blast for you and Gia to come at the same time? Vanessa always felt you had such integrity in Wally's battle that she wanted to make sure I honored you (which, of course, I will!) and she also wanted you here because she knew you'd inspire me, love me; and in her absence, in her death, she needed to know someone would.

Zan

Vanessa was an elf of a woman; her very spirit twinkled brightly. I cherished our deep friendship and would miss her even though we saw one another rarely. When I met Vanessa, we connected immediately. At least when she was on earth, I always knew she was near, a phone call away, selling my work. Without her love and support, I probably never would have become a potter. She influenced my life, and I knew that was not a rare talent of hers—she invested herself in many people she chose as family.

When we went through the deposition, she shared secrets of Wally and her life she never told anyone else. I wondered if Zan knew how close she and Vanessa were to being true sisters? All three of us had secret hells we shared. Since I'd pledged secrecy to both, I could not ask Zan if she knew Vanessa's story. Years ago, Vanessa told me:

She married a wealthy though cruel doctor in a time when such a marriage was fortuitous, never questioned despite

his personality flaws. Women at that
time did not question; if they rebelled,
they suffered. They rarely refused to live
the life society told them to live. She
said it was just as if she had accepted an
arranged marriage.

Once a man asked for her hand,
she was forced to say yes. She told me
she loved him modestly, without sparkle
or passion. This was hard to understand
as I saw her life as nothing but sparkle
and passion. Yes, she agreed, that was
why her marriage was like a tomb. He
killed her love quickly—overnight, not a
slow, painful death as many marriages are
destroyed. They'd only been married two
years when she got pregnant. His fury
had no boundaries, he wanted no children, never had. He married her with his
demands known—no children—ever—
so he blamed her entirely for this "mis-
fortune" as he called it.

In the fifth month of her pregnancy,
he insisted she abort the baby. Although
at the time abortions were illegal, he
was a doctor, so one of his professional
friends undertook the procedure because
Vanessa's husband had helped his teenage daughter when she had needed one.
Vanessa told me that was often the way in
the medical community before abortions
were legalized.

To Vanessa's horror, the baby was
fully developed and weighed at least five
pounds. Her husband had miscalculated,
and the baby boy was seven months old,
not five.

Vanessa felt as though someone had reached inside her,
pulling the essence of her being out of her body. She threw
up several days after the abortion and could not look her husband in the eye. Her hatred for him grew; she had hated him
before, but now her loathing was pervasive. As she shared
her story, she told me how difficult it had been years later to
watch me struggle with a different choice, the choice to give
my baby up for adoption. "Neither choice is pleasant," she
said. "Both are life-changing even when you think it won't
be. When there's an unwanted pregnancy, all decisions are
hell unless you are old enough or fortunate enough to love
the man you share the baby with. Then, you can end up marrying the man and keep the baby. Or, in today's age, a single
woman can choose to keep a baby without scorn or reprisals.
But when you and I got pregnant, any decision other than
marriage, a happy one, was hell."

Once Vanessa's baby arrived, sucked into distortion by
the abortion tool, it was her husband's hands that wielded the
death permanent; he killed the baby because the abortion had
only started the process. Vanessa blamed herself—she would
have fought for the baby's survival, even in its deformed state,
had she been stronger. She was weakened from the surgery
and the horror she faced at the baby's arrival. She was also
weakened by a marriage that was vicious, hateful, unloving.
Three months later, she was pregnant again. This time she
left Wally's father, choosing to have Wally instead of a pas-
sionless marriage with a man she considered a murderer. She

had only gone back to him, slept with him once more, to get pregnant. She explained that he repulsed her, but she wanted another child badly enough to use him as a sperm donor.

I wrote Zan:

> *Zan,*
>
> *I'm fighting a rash or I'd arrive in Florida tomorrow. God, I can't believe Vanessa's dead. She seemed the one person who'd live forever! She practically did, didn't she? I long to be with you in your sorrow but this rash is awful. Itch? God, I itch—makes me want to peel my skin away in sheets. I wear cotton gloves so I can't scratch myself raw. Matt calls it the Itch Bitch—I'm not the bitch (so he says), the itch is. I think he might be saying Go Itch, You Bitch, but he swears that's not what he means. I'll come as soon as I can.*
>
>

Katrina

Katrina, Zan wrote back,

> *I wish you could help me set up the art studios. I dream you are here, whispering ideas, challenging me, demanding creativity as only you do. We're buying six sailboats—small ones—for Wally's dream of heaven—so the artists can sail the ocean looking for inspiration. Jessica is quite a water spirit and thrives on the ocean. She loves the sailboats! Maybe part of Wally's spirit lives in her. Vanessa never named the*

*studios and I am waiting for you until I do.
Remember when we named our Sarasota
Summer group "Bank Notes"? I think you
came up with that clever name so I want
you in on the consecration of this collective!!
I leave it to you to remember we need to
do this: I AM older than you if you recall,
and since I am so much older, I may forget.
Most likely not, though, since this is my new
life and I will need a name for the space!
Also, a wonderful new sign leading in to the
art collective!*

*I am putting in a pottery studio so you
and Gia have work space when you visit.*

*Hurry! Get well! Come! Be with me!
Laugh! Waltz on the beach! I'd say make
love to me but that's not in the cards for us,
is it? I do love you—not physically (don't get
scared—I'm only teasing) but I do love you
completely. Maybe another lifetime for us to
share physical love? I have something to say
on this topic but it will wait until later.*

*It's pretty scary to be the Queen of an
Art Collective when I'm not even artistic!*

*Does landscaping count? I await your
arrival. Can you stay the summer? Bring
your kids! When you get here, we'll name the
Art Collective something creative!*

Zan Dora

Her letter aroused my curiosity. I wrote and asked several times what she was not telling me, but her answer was slow in coming. I admonished her too—Zan, who always believed in herself, should not be questioning her creativity. Not only landscaping but fortune-telling, people reading—her whole being was creative. She herself was creativity defined in my mind.

She finally wrote:

> *Katrina,*
>
> *I must share with you from my soul— we've always been honest, haven't we? I've never mentioned this as I thought too much explaining would be needed. Now, in my grief, I realize I must write and to hell with explanations. How do I begin to tell you about the last seven years of my life? Approach—avoid—plus—minus—I'll plunge in and trust you'll understand.*
>
> *Vanessa and I have been in love for many years. More than platonic love, a passionate physical love—we were a couple. Shocked? I'm sorry but it's never been the right moment to tell you. We were a quiet, sheltered couple—lesbians, the world calls us—not a choice of words I'd use to describe our intense, spiritual and physical relationship but the "tag," the "label" society gives us.*
>
> *We spent over ten years together—the first two years spent getting up the nerve to ask the question of a physical relationship. We tap-danced, tiptoed around each other for two years. Now that she's gone, I scream in frustration that we lost those two years. We didn't really lose them as they were two years of wonderment and discovery. We*

flirted, daydreamed, teased, everything but the deep relationship that did, fortunately, finally happen. Two years of wet dream heaven then over eight years of reality—which was even better than our fantasies. How many folks can say that about their lives, their marriages? Not many, I know. You—lucky girl—happily married for years—how many of your friends can say the same? And, like me, you love your work, your husband, your kids, your life. God! Have we been blessed! Did the angels kiss your forehead when you were born? I think so, tootsie, beautiful friend of mine! You've been a gift to me and I'm so glad I have someone like you to talk to. How many times have we said that to one another in our letters? We have shared—my God, have we shared! So many times, the only reason I'm sane is because of you.

Vanessa and I had a great giggle over our two years of flirtation once we took the plunge and found we felt physical about one another. How loved I've felt—stomach queasy, jittery even, whenever Vanessa entered the room. The only words I can begin to use to describe us might be:

> *Maternal*
> *Passion-filled*
> *Rich*
> *Intense*
> *Overwhelmed*

We were so much a couple yet so private (sometimes because of who we were but also, remember, I had Jessie). We never counted the years we have lived together in a relationship, never have we celebrated any anniversaries, but I do know that we have lived and loved for over 10 years. Oh, how I now grieve!! I cannot stop crying since she died. I ache all over. That's why I am finally telling you—so I can share from my heart. Thanks for listening!

Zan

I was caught by surprise. Throughout the years, I had never suspected—never read between the lines in anything Zan had written.

Her timing was crucial too! I had just hired an apprentice to help me in my business—a twenty-year-old girl. Her name was Reagan, and she was exactly twenty-four years younger than me. The odd stirrings I had when she arrived at work scared the shit out of me. What was it? Her youth? The loss of my infant daughter who would be a few years older than she was? Was Reagan my midlife crisis? Zan's truthfulness struck chords. Was I interested in Reagan that way? Was I gay?

Reagan's laughter embraced me, buoyed me to greater creations with clay. An artist falls in love with their muse, I rationalized in my anxiety over the depth of feelings she aroused within me. Zan's letter opened doors I never wanted to open. Pandora's box. Zan Dora's box?

For the first time in my life, I understood men of my age leaving wives they had been married to for twenty years, marrying younger women, girls really, and starting families all over again. The thought appealed to me. I wished I had seven children, not just two (I'd raised)!

When Reagan's hands brushed mine in our tactile world of clay, I shuddered, my body trembled. Thank God when I arrived home at night, I still had an urgent physical response to Matt. Was I losing my mind? Also, her name—an affront to my liberal sensibilities, so I began to call her ReaGun—as if she was a zap from a sci-fi world. She was alien to me, to my world. That's how I felt—my world was entering other realities, unexplored realities, places I did not want to go.

"No one's ever given me a nickname," she exclaimed the first morning I tried it out, shooting her with a bubble gun, zapping her with the ball. I remembered I had thought the same thing when Wally nicknamed me Kat; her pleasure was equal to what I had felt then. She squealed with laughter. "I love it! ReaGun—fits me well, doesn't it?" And she twirled around, her short dress skimming her upper thighs. How did she work in such outfits? But then I found her equally as sexy in filthy overalls. Me? I still wore Movin' Mamas because I was only comfortable working in them. God, I hated aging! Feeling old! Though my body was tired, my hair listless, my boobs saggy, mentally I felt twenty—what a strange complexity. I'd look in the mirror and gasp at who I saw—was that really me? The lightness of youth, the excitement of sharing my life—albeit work life—was that my attraction? Was my response a spinoff to the inevitability of empty nest? If my children no longer needed me, would I fill the void by being a mentor to Rea? Was it more deep-rooted than that—rooted in a cold hospital room, years ago, when Ilana made me sign paperwork that changed my life forever? Though I had moved on, established a new life, in giving away my first baby, I was always a member of the walking wounded. I had a hole within me—in my very center—as large as if a cannonball had been shot through me, making a gaping wound that never healed.

I was confronting empty nest, more intense perhaps since it was the second time I had made this confrontation. I frequently thought longingly of my children as infants while they screamed for independence. What were my choices? What internal confusion—I was too old to be a baby's mother, too young to be a grandmother. Yet perhaps I was a grandmother and just didn't know it—maybe my firstborn had a child. My children screamed, "Don't be so loud! Don't talk to my friends! Don't ask so many questions! Don't!" So I screamed at myself too: a scream of loneliness, a scream of emptiness while their battle cry was freedom! Where was my place? I had been so willing to have a baby I could keep I never once looked back, never regretted parenting my children. My children, the single most essential ingredient of my life, wanted me out of their lives now. Although I did not want to, I knew I had to let them go. I wanted my children to fly, to find their space, but at the same time, I did not want my nest empty. It was not a winning situation.

Maybe that was why there was something so totally captivating about working with Rea. It was as though she and I were mother and child without my being her birth mother, as though we were alone in a dark tunnel of energy—filled with laughter, fragrance, creative flow. What was so damn inspiring about her? She laughed, deep bursting laughter that drew me in; later when I found myself thinking of her, I waltzed in the meat department of the grocery store. At least I didn't leave my world but danced within it. The groceries were still purchased, dinners cooked, dishwasher loaded— all the things my family expected. But while I went through these tasks on automatic pilot, my mind was millions of miles away, cavorting with Rea. Did anyone notice? I don't know. I brought her name up in conversation whenever I could just to hear it spoken out loud—Rea—Rea—Rea. I thought my heart would burst with the song of it.

My mind was at war. I had everything I wanted except my firstborn child. Did Rea offer a torturous glimpse that reminded me daily I had a daughter just a little older than she was? That was part of it—she released energy like a steam of a teakettle—hard to see, yet potent enough to scald! The only time my internal war retreated was when I threw pots. I produced work like never before. And I sold. Lots of pots. At least I had that to pull me out of my reverie. New customers discovered me—old customers bought more—I sold everything I spun out. Why not? The work was richer, more passionate than anything I had ever produced.

Matt was a comfort—rock-solid beside me, cuddling, hugging, endlessly caressing, appreciating. If he noticed any difference, he never let on. He held me tight yet loose enough to allow me to mentally fly away. He encouraged me to spend as much time at the studio as I wanted.

For years I had worked in isolation, next door to other artists but spending hours by myself, stopping every now and then to talk to the other artists but alone most of the time. I finally hired Reagan because my volume of business demanded an assistant, an apprentice. Would I have hired her had I known the fireworks she'd ignite? Probably. She was so much fun. Yet she chafed at the paperwork and was interested in the art, not the business side of it, much as I had been at her age and Vanessa had done most of the business for me. We spent hours working together—I had an extra wheel she used. I could not ask her to do paperwork because she hated it so. Yet wasn't it valid to work as we did since my work had never been so expressive? Had never sold so well? No monetary value could be assigned to the creative process—could it? I asked myself over and over, needing to justify having her help me in the business (not the paperwork part), trying to justify paying her. There would be no question had I used her to do the paperwork or if I didn't feel so guilty whenever she was around. Pottery—clay—requires a lot of physical labor, and she did that willingly, eagerly as only the young do, relieving me to produce and create as quickly as I got orders. We were an efficient team, but I did not relax with it. I did not truly enjoy the break she provided. Why not? I was mentally overfull when she was around—my thinking muggy, unclear.

Muse—amuse—God, did she amuse! She was a muse, my muse! I needed someone to talk to, and the only one I could think of was Zan—she would understand. She was distant and would not judge.

I ran—escaped. I chose flight. Do women always choose flight? I wondered as I booked a flight to Sarasota. I planned a three-month sabbatical at Zan's artistic community, leaving Rea to run my business over the summer. A risk, yes, but it became a question of stability—mine. Several factors led to my demise: first, on her way into the studio every morning, Reagan stopped to put out her cigarette—stopped right in front of the glass windows where I worked on paperwork first thing. I'd gasp as I looked into her pretty face. Second, the cigarettes, smoking, became an integral association with her. I returned to smoking after twenty years of abstinence. We smoked cigarettes, pot, hiding in my studio, avoiding my teenage children, who were at the brink of their own decisions about addictions. Fortunately, they weren't interested in smoking; they were never drawn into the sensuality of it as I had been. I always found smoking appealing. I began to salivate as soon as Rea arrived at work, wanting a cigarette before she'd even parked her car. I had to get away to Sarasota; I needed to end this addiction, give up cigarettes…again. I was forty-four after all; smoking was far more serious for me than for twenty-year-old Reagan. I also needed to end my fascination with her. I needed to deal with my midlife crisis, and part of that quest meant returning to Sarasota, returning to the birthplace of my firstborn. Whether I found that child or not was not the point; I had to face the place that spawned my deepest grief, my greatest sadness. The point when I felt I split from myself—splintered in two, leaving part of my emotional well-being behind.

Today's world is so different from when I was a teenager. My kids are more confident, more outspoken; they are not afraid to speak out against injustice. They rage against the horror my generation has created, through protests, through their music, oftentimes through their lives. They are free spirits, and as a result, most of my nineteen-year-old son's friends are girls; most of Reagan's friends, males. Is that part of my fascination? I was not like that. Liam—confident, self-assured, creative, bright—willing to express his opinion even when not asked. That is his appeal. I am sure the girls wish he was not stuck in friendship—he is oblivious to the attention that centers on him, the attention he generates.

I, on the other hand, as a teenager, yearned for attention, the looks my son gets but doesn't see. Because he is ignorant and I was hungry, we received what we didn't want—he gets attention, I got none for a long time. Remember, Wally was my first male friend!

Maybe because he is a product of an Aids-fearing generation, his crowd runs as that—a crowd—they do not date, do not partner off. Matt and I laugh at our son's inhibitions, his chaste approach to life. How did he come from our union, two old hippies well versed in nudity, openness, spontaneity? Sera, on the other hand, is more like us—sensuous, uninhibited. Liam is uninterested, unattached, unavailable, private. It's amazing he survived our communal living, but he was the first child there, the heir apparent, he remains above reproach. The other children never tease him about not fitting into the communal heap; they accept him—not only do they accept him; he is revered. He exudes a power—a presence I yearn for but have never found.

*****

As soon as I arrived in Sarasota and saw Zan waiting for me in her flowing skirt and long black hair, I noticed a resemblance to the freedom and exuberance Reagan exudes. I hadn't seen Zan in years, and although her letters were wonderful, I had forgotten the intense physical presence she exudes, the way she spreads light all around her. How could I forget that? Twenty-five years ago, Zan had been instrumental in my self-discovery; she encouraged the nurturing of my self-love. Maybe she could help now. Both Zan and Reagan were spiritual as well as having tough, creative energy sparkling around them.

Zan enveloped me in an enormous hug then grinned. "We're going to the circus! Come on!" It was as though twenty-five years had never passed as we jumped in her little car and tore down the highway. We arrived at circus headquarters and watched the trapeze artists try new stunts.

"That's her," Zan leaned over and whispered to me, pointing to a slim young woman of no more than thirty.

"What's her?" I groaned, knowing what was coming.

"I think I'm in love again!" Zan laughed out loud. The performers laughed too, even though they had no clue what we were laughing at.

"Isn't she marvelous? I come here twice a week to watch them practice, and I think she notices me, too."

"Is she interested?"

"Who the hell knows? I'm only looking for a fantasy fuck right now. It's too soon for anything else."

I had not yearned for a fantasy fuck for years, so I was surprised and perplexed with Zan's interest. I tried to understand, but having my lover in my life and not suffering such a loss, I just didn't. Rea was a distraction but nothing else. I had not yet figured out how she fit into my life. I was sure it was a complex relationship, but it was not yearning for a fantasy fuck.

Even though Rea had been inspiring, I found my work more productive at Zan's without her constant distraction. I spent every day in the studio beginning at six and finally taking a break around three. Zan's pottery studio was state-of-the-art, more than I had dreamed possible. After working, I showered; filthy, hot, tired but replenished. After dinner, Zan and I walked on the beach, long walks, sometimes silent, sometimes full of conversation, always full of laughter.

"So, what's your take on what you're going through with Reagan? What's it all about?" Zan asked me on our first walk.

"I honestly don't know. I am so confused. I know it's somehow connected to her youth. Or to that *big* event in my life twenty-four years ago—you know, my firstborn child, my dark-haired baby girl. Also, my aging—growing old—menopause—that shit. I think some of the reason I had to return to Sarasota is to deal with my loss—the baby I gave up. I can't face aging without putting some of my demons to rest."

"I thought that might be. But, honey, don't take yourself so seriously," she advised. "Menopause is a beast you live through. It was hell on me. Vanessa and I both lost babies, so

I know some of what you're going through. Not the total hell of it but some of it."

"So, you did know about Vanessa?"

"It was one of the first things she told me. We cried together, hugged and shared. I think that's when we first noticed a physical attraction. Vanessa had thought about the gay lifestyle for years, but I'd never given it a single thought until we shared on that emotional level."

"God, she was good for you, wasn't she?"

"You'll never know how good. My mentor! My love! I get so lonely. I may find another love, but I will never get over her. She helped me through menopause. I swear, if she hadn't been there, I might have jumped in front of a train— tied myself to the tracks, anything to get out of prolonged overbitchy PMS."

"How long does it last? I can hardly stand it—the night sweats, the mood swings, the bloated feeling. It's as though I'm pregnant, but there's no nine months deadline, no baby. Pregnancy was hell, but then a baby is given to you, and you forget all the shit you've just been through."

"Are you taking anything for it?"

"I started hormone therapy a month ago. I think it's helping. I was in denial for six months. Somehow I thought I'd miss menopause. I'm only forty-four for God's sakes!"

"Everyone's different. Women are starting menopause earlier than ever. When'd you start your period?"

"At eleven. Strange. Most people who start their periods early usually have menopause later, but that's not been my case. Menopause has got to be what's going on. I've never been like this. I've never been depressed—hyperactive, driven, I work too hard to achieve perfection, but never depressed. For the last month, I've felt like a black veil is covering me. I called the doctor as soon as I started the hormones, and he said it's a side effect. I was so pissed! Why didn't he warn me? He says the blackness will go away, and I'm beginning to feel somewhat better. You couldn't have stood me otherwise."

"I hardly think that's so." Zan was offended. "Friendship's not just about the good times. I love you." We hugged tight. "Also, I have some herbs that help. Let's try some different things and perhaps a different diet while you are here. That should help." As we walked home in silence, we felt the warm beach breeze on our faces. There was an unspoken trust, an ease between us. I had forgotten how much I thought of the ocean smell, the sea breeze, the pull of Anna Maria Island. I was glad I was here.

"Are you having fun?" Matt called on Wednesday. "Is this like a midlife crisis? You go to Florida for three months, and I buy a Toyota Supra for my midlife adventure?"

"As long as you don't trade me in for a twenty-year-old model," I said. We both laughed. "Speaking of twenty-year-olds, how's Rea-Gun? Are you keeping up with the business?"

"I've stopped by a few times. She's always working. You'd be proud of her. You're keeping in touch too, aren't you?"

"Of course. I've called three times already."

"She's doing a good job—business is progressing, she's very busy, getting a lot of orders. She wants to hire Liam as a go-for this summer. What about it?"

"How can I pay him a salary?" I grumbled then realized it was a good solution to the constant manpower problem. It would not be an option if I was around. "Actually, it's a good idea. He can help with the lifting and packing."

"Reagan has him doing most of the wedging too—getting the clay ready for her to throw. He comes home at night exhausted, filthy, but for once, he's up early the next morning, raring to go."

"God, I can't believe I never thought of that. What a great job for him! It's just what he needs."

"I don't think that's all that's physical about the job."

"What the hell do you mean?" I bristled.

"Well, Katrina, you have to admit Reagan is a beautiful woman. I think Liam is taken with her. He gets up two hours early for work—Liam! Can you believe it? Combs his hair. I've never seen him like this. They spend hours together after work. It's great!"

I was jealous—it wasn't what I wanted. I changed the subject quickly. "How are you guys? Is living without me okay?" Part of me wanted him to say come home even though I knew I wouldn't. Couldn't yet.

"We're doing well. I'm writing a research article—you know me—my face is in the books and magazines—I'm always at the computer." He sounded so interested in his studies I was jealous of that too. I longed for his back, his arms to hold me. I'd only been gone four days, but it felt like four months. "Sera misses her mama. She's at a loss without you. Too old for camp, too young for a job. It's tough," reminding me of how I felt—too old to be a new mother, too young to be a grandmother.

"Send her and Brooke down here. There's lots to do. I'd enjoy them, and it wouldn't invade my R&R." Brooke was Sera's best friend.

"I was going to buy plane tickets today but thought I'd better ask you first. How about a Saturday arrival?"

"Great!" Send ReaGun and Liam too, I thought, but when I pictured Reagan and Liam together—down here—I knew that was not what I wanted. At all. I needed space from both of them.

Sera: mirror image of me in many ways; deft with her hands, her artistic ability already apparent; her bread legs unnoticed; she was brilliantly pretty and funny, a joy to be around. She was confused, though, often finding herself threatening to boys her own age. She was fifteen but looked nineteen—and smart enough that people thought she was nineteen. Everyone—adults and kids—related to her as an older teen, not the fifteen-year-old she was. Although we babied her, she was strongly independent.

I was ready for her arrival, and we fell into each other's arms as though it'd been months since we'd seen each other. Sera and Brooke provided endless diversions in the pottery studio too, spending mornings with me, asking millions of questions about techniques, appealing to my mentor side. They were productive too, creating pots I thought worthy of selling at art shows, beautiful in their simplicity. They spent the afternoons with Jessie at the ocean—cavorting in the sunshine. Jessie was intrigued by their adulation. She was home for the summer planning a huge wedding to a man Zan adored. The girls were thrilled by the wedding plans, providing a captive audience for Jessie, asking the right questions, making suggestions Jessie loved. They were more suited than Zan or I since neither of us had experienced a traditional wedding, and neither of us were interested. Jessie quit confiding in us and turned to Brooke and Sera. Sera grew more mature (was that possible?) through the trust and confidences disclosed with Jessie at the beach in the afternoons.

I had been at Zan's for several weeks when I finally brought up the name issue. "When and, most importantly, what are we going to name your complex?" I asked.

"Oh god! I was hoping you'd forget. I have absolutely no idea. No clue! There's landscaping, pottery studios, I'm thinking of building a black box theater. There's cottages for beginning writers—how do you name something so progressive?"

"And, preserve the spirit of the one who thought of it all?" I mentioned, thinking of Vanessa, her fairy-self, her mentorship of others, her exuberant love. "I guess that's why I have referred to it as a complex all this time. There are hardly words to describe it sufficiently, don't you think?"

"Yea. What would Vanessa have named it? Would she want it named after her?"

"The name *Vanessa* means 'butterfly' in Spanish. I have been doing some research since you asked me to help."

"That fits with what I've been thinking—I have been thinking of the name *Incubation*—a time to incubate new ideas."

"Oh! I love that! I think Vanessa would love it too. That's in the very spirit of what she was seeking when she started this place, wasn't it? Her shop is called Mariposa—butterfly/flower, also a Spanish name. It will keep up her tradition."

"Love it! I have a friend who makes beautiful signs out of driftwood. I'll call him and get him started with the name *Incubation* and the whole butterfly theme."

"Do you think *Incubation* fits or *Metamorphosis*? *Metamorphosis* is more butterfly-ie."

"No, I like the idea of incubating…being here to think, absorb, even procrastinate. *Incubation*—that just describes what I want people to do here."

"Going with the butterfly idea, have you ever thought of designing a butterfly house—a butterfly garden? It's a new thing in Europe I've been reading about, and it would be lovely here."

"See, I knew you needed to be here to create the name. A butterfly house fits into what I do creatively—landscaping! I'll start planning that too."

The third week in June, Matt called early one morning. "This might be bad news, Katrina. You've been summoned to jury duty starting next Tuesday. I don't think an artistic sabbatical will eliminate you. Duty calls." He laughed.

"I've been what?" I screeched, nearly laughing but realizing he was serious. "I guess I need to fly home. I'll come home Thursday and have a long weekend. What do you think?"

"That'd be great. Come home, woman! I can't wait to see you! Call and let me know when you're arriving."

Jessie would not hear of the girls returning to Atlanta with me, insisting they were too valuable for her wedding plans and offering to supervise them in my absence. It made my return easier—only packing for one, planning one flight. It also gave Sera more taste of the freedom she so eagerly wanted.

Matt picked me up at the airport, and Liam spent the night away from home. "I asked Liam to get lost so we could be alone," Matt told me. "Didn't even tell him you were coming. I wanted you all to myself. He probably thinks I'm having an affair. At least once he knows you are home, he'll understand. Until then, it'll just give him something to think about." We laughed.

We hugged tight, quickly slipping out of our clothes, walking around the house as we had done before the kids were born. I was sweaty from the trip and slipped into the shower. As I leaned over to retrieve my towel, Matt snuck up behind me, grabbing my breasts and whispering in my ear, "God, I didn't realize how much I've missed you!" He kissed me and edged me into the bedroom without closing the door. I think it was the first time in over ten years we hadn't bothered to close the door. Joy and Ed and family were on vacation, so Matt and I were the only ones home. A rare pleasure.

I waited until Friday afternoon to go by the studio, not wanting to descend on Reagan the moment I returned, not wanting to look like I was checking up on her. The studio was eerily quiet, empty as I opened the door, expecting Liam to be wedging and Reagan to be throwing pots. I stood a moment, confused, when I heard giggling from my office. I opened the office door cautiously. Reagan and Liam were on my office couch completely naked, Liam's head buried in her breasts with Reagan's legs thrown over his back in abandon. The look on her face was ecstatic. I stood dumbfounded when she opened her eyes and saw me. "Oh my god!" she whispered, barely audible. Liam sluggishly drew his head up from her breasts and gasped in strangled agony.

I ran out of the room, finding the nearest trash can and threw up. Everything I'd eaten for breakfast rose in my throat, sour. What the hell was going on?

Five minutes later, Liam and Reagan entered the studio, fully clothed, hair hastily brushed, both red-faced. "Son of a bitch, what the hell's going on?" I couldn't help myself, so I was screaming in rage. "You want to throw pots—I'll show you how to throw pots!" I picked up the nearest pot and threw it against the wall, shattering it into shards of glazed ceramic.

"My god, Katrina, that was a commissioned piece."

"Well, you'll just have to do it again, won't you?" I hissed nastily and glared at Liam before leaving, slamming the door so hard it rattled in its frame.

I could not tell Matt what had happened but grabbed him when I got home, kissed him violently, and pulled off his T-shirt roughly.

"Hey, what the hell is going on?"

"Let's make love, Matt. Right here, on the floor." I finished pulling off his shirt and made for his pants. I gen-

tly reached in and began to massage him; as always, he was
ready. I stripped quickly out of my clothes and was working
up to a frenzy when the front door opened.

"What the fuck?" Liam and Reagan stood in the door.
Matt jumped up, pulling his pants on and looked at them,
red-faced.

"What are you doing home?"

"Why don't you ask her?" Liam pointed an accusing finger at me.

I grabbed my clothes and ran into the bedroom, slamming and locking the door.

"Kat, what is going on?" Matt knocked gently on the
door. "Reagan and Liam look like death. Want to clue me
in?"

"Ask them."

"Yeah, ask us, Dad, it's obvious she's going to hide."
Liam sounded like he was sneering at me, and it was almost
more than I could bear. I remained behind the locked door.

"Can I come in?" Reagan knocked, asking softly. I
unlocked the door and opened it just enough to let her in.

"I'm so sorry! You surprised us. We've been meaning
to tell you about us, but you went to Sarasota by the time
we discovered that we liked each other. It's the most wonderful thing that's happened to either of us, but we didn't
mean for you to find out the way you did." Reagan talked
rapidly, barely breathing. She finally inhaled, a deep gulping
wail, and choked out, "You don't think I'm good enough for
him, do you? That's why you're so pissed off, isn't it?" Reagan
began to cry, deep, gulping sobs as I reluctantly wrapped my
arms around her, finding it amazingly hard to touch her.

God, I thought, she did not get it—didn't have a clue. It
did not have much to do with her and Liam. No one but Zan
would understand my jealous rage. I loved Reagan! Loved

her! She filled an empty space inside me that had ached for over twenty-four years. The pain was unceasing despite the sacrificial burial Clayton performed with me at Penland. Though the ceremony helped me move on, I was still left with a dull aching emptiness. I began to shudder.

"It's not that," I whispered, "it was the shock. I was not prepared. I would have been that way with Liam and any-one." I wiped away the tears streaming from her eyes, then cleared my own, reaching for a tissue. "I think of Liam as my little boy, I don't think of him as a man. It's my fault. I just wasn't ready. I'm not prepared to parent a man, a boy who is now an adult. I never thought you'd date one another. Not really, the way you are together."

"I thought that was it. We're having trouble keeping our hands off one another at work, but I know that's got to stop. We'll keep it professional, keep our hands to ourselves. I promise. I am so sorry!" Reagan began crying harder, wailing sounds as her body heaved with tears. I leaned over and drew her close, holding her tight. It was an emotional moment; I had always wanted to hold her, but not this way, not as a mother. My own body shook.

"What the hell is going on in there? Don't leave us out here." Liam's tone had lost some of its sneer, and we wiped our faces and opened the door. Matt and Liam stood looking at us with curiosity; obviously Liam had filled Matt in on the afternoon tryst. Matt's face was grim.

"Let's go to dinner. Wash your faces, and we'll check out that new restaurant in Little Five Points. I've heard it's good," Matt said.

"What an afternoon!" Matt whispered to me as we dressed for dinner. "I don't know if I could have handled walking in on them myself. You're doing pretty well." His honesty and support strengthened me. My nerves were still scattered; I couldn't remember what I wanted to wear, couldn't remember if I'd brushed my teeth, where I'd put my purse. Matt squeezed me tight. "Our children are growing up, aren't they? A whole new frontier, isn't it?"

At dinner, Matt brought up the topic we had talked around but not mentioned. "You know, Liam, if you keep working for Reagan at the studio, you've got to have a little more presence of mind. If one customer walks in on you and Reagan, your mom loses that customer, rumor spreads, and she'll lose more than one. That's a pretty high risk you are taking."

"I told Katrina that's the way it'll be from now on," Reagan said. "I promise...no more horseplay at the studio." I noticed she did not promise no horseplay at all, just at the studio.

After dinner, Matt and I strolled through Little Five Points while Liam and Rea went out dancing.

Fortunately, the next week, jury duty occupied me mentally and physically, giving me little time to think about Liam and Reagan. I was selected for a trial even though I thought they'd never consider me: airy-fairy artist and all. The case was a young fellow charged with orchestrating a drug deal. He was Liam's age, accused of selling over five grams of cocaine. The prosecutor sought to convict him of drug trafficking with a minimum of ten years. The accused was obviously bright, leaning over several times to confer with his lawyer, assisting with the presentation of his case. I was caught up in it, overwhelmed by the responsibility of making a decision that would affect someone's life. If we as a jury convicted the young boy of trafficking with a minimum sentence of ten years, would we produce an even harder criminal? Or did we convict him of the lesser charge of possession and hope he'd redeem himself after spending just a little time in jail? It was complex and exhausting, mentally draining. We finally convicted the young man of possession—the only thing we felt the prosecutor actually proved.

The judge asked to see us after the trial. "That was a difficult case. You did very well because of the complexity of the evidence or lack thereof. I could tell you were considering every aspect. But now, you've left me with the hard part. This young man is heavily involved in the drug trade, yet he's bright—he's attended two years of college and is working on a degree. I will pray for guidance with my decision, but it'll be a tough one. You were a great group! Thanks for your hard work."

I was ready to go back to Sarasota. I wanted things simple, I wanted vacation time; I did not want to think about anything but my art—my pottery.

Matt took me to the airport Friday morning. "I'll miss you, sweetheart," he whispered in my ear, kissing me gently but firmly. "Have a great time. You need this vacation, don't you?"

"Hell, yes! I'm exhausted. Must be because I'm getting old."

"Call me when you get there." Matt made me promise him as he kissed me goodbye.

"I'll call. Take care of yourself. Don't bury your nose in a book so much you don't keep your eyes on Liam and Rea, okay? We don't need any unwanted pregnancies, you know."

"I won't. I know it's serious. I'm not a complete bookworm, you know." We were so fond of one another, our relationship so comfortable. Not only were we both hippies but we were nerds too.

On the plane back to Sarasota, I realized there was something about being away that made me value my life in Atlanta even with Liam and Reagan "a couple." So much for thinking Liam was a virgin, had never partnered with any-one. I could not have lived through the last two weeks at home without Matt's quiet strength, his unwavering support. We were a couple despite my midlife crisis. Matt had a mid-life crisis too—he had bought a Supra, a fast, sleek-looking sports car he tooled around Little Five Points in. It was the first car he'd ever owned.

When Zan and the girls, Sera and Brooke, picked me up at the airport, Sera was wired, talking nonstop. "Jess said," "Jess did," her sentences began until Brooke interrupted, finally able to wiggle in the conversation. "Tell her about Addie. You forgot the most important part, Sera." Brooke was so frustrated with her forced silence she was now accu-satory, whining.

"Addie? Who is Addie?" I asked. "And why don't you tell me?" I encouraged Brooke since Sera had been center stage so far.

"Addie's so much fun, you won't believe her!" Brooke began. "She's living at Zan's, says she's going to be a writer."

"A writer?"

"She's Jessie's best friend and maid of honor at the wedding—she's so smart, you know, she has to use her time wisely—help Jess with the wedding and make sure she has time to write."

Good for Addie, I thought, strong-minded enough to set boundaries with these girls and focus on her work. Hopefully I could do the same.

"She says we wouldn't be interested in what she writes. It's for adults. Boring!"

As we drove into the carport, Jess ran out and greeted us in the driveway. "You get to meet my best friend! You'll love her!"

"That's what I hear. The girls told me. When do I get to meet the writer-in-residence?"

"She's walking on the beach now, looking for inspiration, but she'll be back for dinner."

When I met Addie, I knew instantly why the girls liked her. Addie wore a traditional braid down her back, coarse black hair, shiny and lustrous. She had firm, solid shoulders, large, well-shaped hands. She wore a long flowing skirt, a shaggy blouse, and shawl; and even with no makeup or other ornamentation, she was striking. She spoke rarely, drinking in the conversation as if gathering material for her writing. The girls thrived on it, vying for both her and Jessie's attention by seeing who could tell the funniest (or grossest or scariest) story.

"Do you ever let anyone read your writing?" I asked her at dinner.

"Not until I'm finished with it," she said. "I'm afraid it'll jinx it."

"What do you write about? Can you tell me that much?"

"I'll think it over," she said, then giggled embarrassingly like a schoolgirl, self-conscious. "I'm not used to being asked about my writing. I don't even tell many people that I write," she explained, apologetically. "Writing's a private affair until you finally send it off to a publisher or agent, and I'm not even close to that."

She was right—pottery was a task of solitude only in its creation then becomes public as soon as you sell it, try to sell it, or give it away.

More artists had moved in during my two weeks' absence, and Incubation was at maximum occupancy. Rose was another potter, my age, and we worked in the studio every morning. In my absence, the girls had gotten used to helping Jess or sailing with her, so they did not return to the studio after I came back. Jess assured me she valued their company and wouldn't want it any other way.

"I've known of your work for a while," Rose told me. "You're known for weird configurations, interesting glazes and paints. What are you working on here?"

"I'm not really sure," I confided, but when I got back into the routine of full days spent in the studio, I realized my work had returned to abstract pieces—not functional pots. The late Anna Maria stage, as I later dubbed it, was remarkably like Penland: pieces of mothers reaching to the sky, only now it was male/female figures reaching for one another. I spent more time hand building than on the wheel, and I realized the work was intricately tied to Reagan's discovery of Liam (and her lack of discovery of me). Also, I was discovering a depth inside I had previously been unaware of. How did life do that? Keep opening new insights just when you thought you were all grown up, over it all. Now there were abstract pieces that expressed solitude/search/sometimes discovery. At least I hoped that was the message they conveyed.

"Your work has such a piercing quality," Rose commented. "If I didn't know you personally, I'd think you were complex, almost hostile in your worldview."

"That sounds more like philosophy than pottery." Addie stood at the door of our studio, her face flushed.

"When'd you come in?" I smiled, noticing Addie's eyes were bright from her own concentration, the residuals of her work session.

"I needed a break. My muse seems to have flown away for the day."

"Ah," Rose said, "muse—that's what your work reflects, Katrina. The definite influence of a muse."

How right you are, I thought to myself. You'd be surprised to know my son's girlfriend is my muse. My release of her, my need to let her go the inspiration for my work.

Addie came in and perched on one of the work stools. "Teach me to throw," she asked me, and I looked up at her, interested.

"Why?" Rose asked.

"I need a break, something different. I get too serious for my own good—too lost in my work, and then it loses its flavor, its direction."

"Jess's wedding's not enough of a diversion, then?"

"It helps, and so do your girls, but I'm feeling stale."

"But, at your age," I pushed, "are you old enough to undertake serious writing? Have you lived enough to capture the human experience?" I gasped after I spoke, aware that I had gone through more serious shit by age twenty than at any other time of my life. How dare I accuse Addie of innocence when I knew so little about her? I was resting on my menopausal laurels—smug in my middle age. It was the first time I'd felt anything positive about aging.

"I like to think so," she replied. I noticed she always maintained a respectful conversational tone whether she was speaking to me, Jess, or the younger girls. "It's not even that I've lived so richly," she went on, "but I listen well. I have a wealth of other people's stories to share."

I had noticed that about her. "Yeah, I'll teach you to throw," I answered her earlier question. Although she didn't elicit the strong attraction Reagan had, there was something pleasurable about this woman, something that drew my curiosity, causing me to want to spend time with her. "Mornings are best, then we can both work on our own stuff in the afternoons, okay?"

"Okay."

Teaching Addie to throw was not only fun but productive. She asked basic questions I hadn't thought about in years, and Rose and I both enjoyed her presence in the studio. She was a natural, her strong work hands at ease with clay from the start.

Our work relationship—Rose, Addie, and myself—was manic-depressive: we'd talk incessantly for an hour then work in silence the rest of the morning or vice versa. With the energy of the three of us filling the studio, we all produced a variety of pieces—Addie's new and tentative, mine continuing a yearning search for identity, Rose's lovely but functional.

Of the three of us, Addie talked the least, and I could see how she collected information about people for her writing. It wasn't that she didn't have anything to say or was overwhelmed by me or Rose; it was that she was an exquisite listener, a collector of people, not interested in other hobbies such as collecting seashells or buttons. Yet she did open up and share, "I like Jess's fiancé," she said one morning, bringing up a topic Zan and I rarely discussed. I was sure Jess talked about him a lot but not to me; perhaps to Brooke, Sera, and Addie, intent, inquisitive, rapt listeners.

"What made you think of him?" I asked.

"Don't know," she replied. "I've been feeling the desire for a relationship likes hers for myself. I am twenty-four years old, you know, two years older than Jess. I have no idea what I want to do with my life. Marriage would be interesting, enjoyable even," she said wistfully.

"Don't you want to write?"

"Yes, but that's an interest, not a profession. Besides, I can write and be married—look at you, a full-time potter. It's not mutually exclusive, you know. Also, writing doesn't pay the rent. I can't live here forever."

"Why not? Zan wouldn't mind. With Jess moving out, Zan would appreciate you being here, staying here. I think I'd live here if I were your age."

"No, you wouldn't. Think about it—you're too full of life, too open and inquisitive to hole yourself up for any length of time. You're just doing it now to be with Zan and to get away from Atlanta. I haven't figured out what you're running from because you haven't shared, but I know it's not your husband. Besides, this is Utopia, and Utopia only lasts a little while."

I was shocked into silence. How did she gather such insight from our few days of working together? I had never said a thing to provoke these conclusions. It was uncanny, unnerving, and I wasn't sure I liked it. I liked her, but her gift of observation felt invasive, a little too close for comfort.

It wasn't until days before Jess's wedding that my suspicions began, my questions about Addie bloomed. When I met Addie's parents at Jess's shower, I realized something was amiss in her family tree.

Addie had grown up in Sarasota just a few years older than Jess. When I reflected back, I realized Addie had the chiseled features of a Native American while her mom was pale, freckled, petite. Her father was no different from her mom; although tall and well-built, his hair was red and curly; his complexion the ruddy complexion of the Irish. It was obvious they adored Addie and made it clear in the first five minutes I met them that she was their only child, the star of their sky.

"Why didn't you tell me?" I hissed at Zan later after the shower was over and Addie's parents had gone.

"Tell you what?" Zan asked with an innocence I immediately saw through. Her response was so calculated, my suspicions grew in intensity, and I became agitated.

"How long have you known Addie? God forbid I ask you this question, but she's adopted, isn't she?"

"I've been friends with Addie and her parents for years." Zan tried to deflect my anger, my questioning, my train of thought, but I was not going to be diverted.

"Something stinks here. Her parents aren't even your type of people. There's no circus to them, no mystery. Except the mystery of the elephant in the room!"

"Hold on a damn minute," Zan bristled. "All my friends aren't artists or lesbians. I do have straight friendships, you know. Married couple friends. Even some dull friends, thank you very much." Zan was hissing right back at me.

"You're not going to distract me. How'd you meet Addie and her parents?"

"Calm down. Addie will hear you, you're screaming, for God's sakes. Do you want to wake up Sera?"

"Don't start with me, damn it," I lowered my voice and spoke through clenched teeth. "She's mine, isn't she?"

"Sera? Yes, she's you to the core. Laughs like you, tells stories like you, she even walks like you. I think she may even be an artist when she grows up. She already has the gift. But I think she'll go in a different direction from you. Have you seen her dancing on the beach? She is exquisite!"

"Goddamn it, you know very well that is not who I'm talking about. Would you stop your shit, please? Please?" I sat down at her table and burst into tears, sobbing deep from within, my heart aching in wrenching pain. Zan came up and caressed me lightly on my shoulders.

"I'm sorry. I didn't mean to make you cry. I am not in any place to respond to your questions. I don't know the answers."

"What do you mean?"

"I've had my suspicions for a long time, but I don't know anything, not really. That's why I've never said anything to you. Truly, I did not know how you would respond. Would you clam up and never write me again or dash down to Sarasota as soon as I wrote that I thought maybe I'd met your daughter? Would that be fair to a little seven-year-old girl I'd just met, living with the only family she'd ever known? No, I truly can't say whether or not Ilana handed Addie over to Mr. and Mrs. Woodbridge, but I have always had strong feelings that might have been exactly what happened. I have always wondered if she was yours."

I could not stop crying. I shuddered, and my shoulders shook with sobs. "Tell me everything—everything from the beginning. How'd you meet her? When'd you start thinking that she might be my daughter? Everything!"

We talked—Zan talked, I listened, long into the night; occasionally I interrupted her for more details, to ask questions, but only occasionally.

"Jess loved Addie from the beginning. For one thing, she loved her traditional family, needed their solidarity in the absence of ours. There Addie fulfilled Jessie's needs only too well. They met at Sunday school at Christ Episcopal Church—met at a time when Sunday school was terribly important to Jess. Even now, church means everything to Jess. She's getting married in a traditional high church wedding, for God's sakes! At the church where she grew up! She's marrying a youth minister—my daughter! So very different from me, and though I do love it, I have never truly understood. I do respect it, it's just not me. It's no wonder she needs help with her wedding from Addie, Sera, and Brooke. I know nothing about those traditions. Nothing!

"Mr. and Mrs. Woodbridge and Addie went every Sunday, rain or shine, so Jess began to spend the night with them on Saturday nights so she wouldn't miss church or have to go alone. I was too hippie, too gypsy as you call me, to attend church. Finally, after years of trying to fit in and especially after the incident with the Sarasota mayor, I just quit going. Instead, I went to beach gatherings on Sunday mornings or even walks with Vanessa, both of us silent, reflecting on our own spirituality. Eventually, slowly, with Jess spending every Saturday night with the Woodbridges, I began to spend those nights with Vanessa. It was the beginning of our curiosity about one another, a welcome time for me to relax from being a single mom and begin sharing my life with someone I loved, even if it only happened once a week.

"Jessie loved church! Always went once the routine was established. I met Addie when she was seven, at first just a friend of Jessie's, a friend who was a good influence, someone Jessie loved. Then, I met her parents, and I had a knee-jerk reaction—all kinds of questions arose. Was Addie adopted? If she was, was she yours and Brett's? She certainly looked Native American while her parents were redheads, obviously of a different heritage. Who knew? I'd be damned if I'd ask Ilana—you remember, I'm sure, how much she hated me, absolutely despised me. I'd also be damned if I ask Mr. and Mrs. Woodbridge. Remember, this was the traditional family my own Jessie chose for herself, people she clung to. What if I asked and found out she was yours? I would then infiltrate Jessie's family, the family she needed. I could possibly disrupt what she so eagerly sought. I was not exactly the best candidate to make inquiries into a closed adoption. I felt I had no right to begin asking questions of Mr. and Mrs. Woodbridge or Addie. Plus, I never knew—not really—if you wanted to find the baby you had released. You were always confused about this—not clear, like you are about everything else."

At this, I looked at Zan through foggy, glazed eyes. She was more concerned by this than by my previous hysteria; she got in my face and shouted at me, talking nonstop, shaking me. I could not hear a word she said. I felt as though I was on a subway watching a conversation take place on the platform outside the train while I was inside the train moving rapidly away, moving away from a conversation I was clearly involved in—one of utmost importance to me. Finally, I realized the conversation was right in front of me; Zan was talking, embracing me, loving me as I slowly came out of my deep, intense reverie, a deep, internal shock.

"I've got to go to bed." I stood up shakily, nearly pitching forward on legs too traumatized to hold my weight. I felt bone-weary, aged, bleary-eyed.

"I've never asked Addie if she's adopted," Zan confessed, "but I bet money on it, she is." Zan reached to hug me as I passed, but I could not stand the thought of anyone touching me right at that moment, so I shrugged her off.

"I cannot be touched right now. I'm sorry. I love you, Zan...you've got to understand!"

"When Vanessa died, my brother tried to put his arm around me all during the memorial service, and that one gentle gesture affected me more than anything else. I could not stand it. His touch seemed to solidify her passing—if he hugged me gently, then she really was dead, gone. Finished. Complete. Over. Is that how you feel?"

"That's about it. Maybe questions I've had for the last twenty-four years are coming closer to being answered, and I don't know if I can handle it. God! You're the greatest friend! Thanks for understanding! I do love you!"

"Love you too," Zan whispered quietly in my ear as I shot her a look of complete despair. As I left for my room, I felt as though I couldn't stand up, felt as though I was crawling to my bedroom. I actually made it there somehow on both legs, but once in my room, I was too adrift to pull down the covers or change into my nightgown. I tried to sleep but lay across the bed instead, staring at the ceiling. "What the hell do I do now?" I asked myself. "What the hell do I do?"

I stayed in bed for three days—longer than I had ever hibernated before. Sera did not even notice as she was spreading her wings and flying on the beach with her new friends, Jessie and Addie. Zan did not bother me either—just opened my door slightly, sliding in food and basic supplies. I assumed Matt or Reagan never called because Zan never brought me a telephone.

On the third day, I finally got up long enough to take a hot bath. I turned pruney-skinned because I stayed in the water too long. After my long soak, I went in the kitchen, checking around the corner first to make sure no one was there, and made some steamed tea with milk and honey. I went back to my room and, for the first time in days, raised the bamboo blinds to let some light in. There on top of my covers was a sheaf of papers neatly stacked with a note on top.

> *Katrina,*
> *You've given so willingly of your art I'll take the risk of sharing mine with you.*
> *I never appreciated your love and patience in teaching me how to throw until your absence these last three days. Rose is a great potter—but not here to teach me and loses patience with my stupid—silly questions, my curiosity in learning your trade.*
> *So, here it is—the story of my life— or my fictionalized life as you'll read in my search for identity and rightful place in this*

world. The reason I'm reluctant to share it—as you'll readily see—is that it is not fictionalized enough at this stage; it's too much of my self-rendering to plunge, break into the competitive world of fiction—so feel free with your comments and criticisms. I'll welcome them—anything will be an improvement, I'm sure!

Read and weep—at its primitiveness and lack of "art" but despite the apologies, it is mine—all mine—written and created by me!

Addie

It was entitled *Addie in Search of Self*, as she had told me earlier her favorite book was *Dibs in Search of Self*.

ADDIE IN SEARCH OF SELF

How can I say when it first occurred to me that I did not fit in—in my family, into average society, or the slow sunburned Florida coastal life I was born into? Was it when I was three and my mom caught me in a department store, looking up the skirt of a mannequin, squealing, "I see you bottom!" or even earlier when my dad told me of my first trip to the beach? I chased the waves so quickly he almost lost me, barely kept up with my free spirit embracing the waves recklessly? As soon as I got there, I immediately stripped off my swimsuit and ran into the surf, naked as a jay bird.

I have always related to the nature of Florida—the grasslands, the shoreline, the wetlands—far more than to its people. Despite my fearlessness of mannequins and waves, I never had a friend until I was seven years old and in the second grade. I think it was because I could not partake in the delicacy of small talk. Didn't know how to have conversations. I have always listened, absorbed, rarely talked unless spoken to, a part of me other children found suspicious. They would meet me and immediately back away, returning wildly to their parents to embrace the normal fold where every child speaks over the next one, desperately trying to win the attention of all adults present. In this arena, I did not compete, could not compete, didn't even know how.

Because another thing separated me—I am an only child, an only ADORED child—I always had too much attention from my parents. Once I escaped them, the last thing I wanted was more attention from grown-ups. So, I stood out— tall, large boned, silent, uncomfortable, looking in on other children, never able to open the social door and join their chit chat, their small talk.

I let out a loud sigh and stood up so quickly the blood rushed to my head and I saw spots in front of my eyes. I backed into my bed—my safe haven of the past week, and once again, it embraced me.

I put the notebook down, needing a break from its intensity, the depth of Addie it told. I fell asleep. Deep sleep, without dreams. When I woke up, the need to keep reading was thick. As I read, I made a visual picture of every scene, allowing daydreams of myself in her young life and as Super Mom, rescuing her from isolation/separation/awkwardness. Oh, the powers and benefits of daydreams—always outdoing and overdoing the true picture—the "real" life story. Maybe that's what heaven is—the fruition of our daydreams.

> Maybe this is not yet the writing I think I have inside but rather something preliminary, something I must do before I can write the Great American Novel. My cleansing, my purification. It may be true for all adopted children that we must wrench inside ourselves, deep inside, before getting on with our lives. Is there something irrevocable about knowing we were given away—given up perhaps as easily as handing a ticket to a train conductor?

At this I stood again, my stomach heaving furiously. It was all I could do to make it to the bathroom before pitching the whole contents of my stomach into the toilet. Easy? That's what she thought? How little she knew of the actual experience, her limited version—half the story. Her half. How could I explain? Could I explain? It was anything but easy. I knew she would steel herself against my version, never listen to my side. I must hold my counsel or lose what trust had grown between us. She had shared her writing with me after all, so I could not violate the trust she had extended to me.

The puzzle came closer to being solved when I was ten years old. I met a man, a man old enough to be my father and dark enough to be the Native American I always imagined was my real father. In meeting him, I closed gaps in my anguish. How has he helped? It is hard to explain; I cannot put the solution into words. He does not put much into words either. Never has much to say. The only person I have ever met who was so like me. Yet, in my anguish, in my search for myself, I claim to be a woman of letters. Read on and hopefully I will unlock the mystery but I cannot promise I will. I can only hope.

He is silent, close to himself, unrevealing yet present. There. A powerful look, a carefully chosen word or two make him an incredible presence. He looks like I wish I looked—like I hope I will look someday.

Is that something unique to Native Americans? A powerful silence. I think the silence, the power, is unique yet unacknowledged (oftentimes even by those individuals who hold the power), a product of our insecurity in trying to fit in today's white world. Our strength is often denied, overlooked, even negated.

I, an adopted child, do not say "our" lightly as in the time I have come to know this man, I am convinced that I am part of his culture. I feel that I am perhaps Native American by birth. But, because of adoption, I do not know, may never know.

This man does not fit into society but I don't think he cares. I, too, do not remember fitting in, but, unlike him, I have always cared. Again, a product of my adopted origin? I think very much so. Our world—the Native American Florida, at least, has vanished, gone with the thrill of the hunt—no, thrill is the wrong word; rather, the need for the hunt; gone once no one needed to live off the land. We became a vanishing people, invisible even to ourselves. I often wonder if that's why I was put up for adoption. Am I Native American? Was I given away because of my skin color? My differentness?

A slow bubbling sob escaped my lips, but I kept reading, riveted by Addie's words.

We remain silent. Locked in our silence. Yet we share this silence. At least there is power in that.

I never truly understood the nature of my being until I happened upon this man. Met him at his gift shop full of what once was Florida, what is central to the Seminole, the Indian Floridian. Once I found him, I visited his store often and sat with him, silent, unquestioning, grateful my adopted parents did not prohibit our unusual friendship. At first, they were so confused by my need they went with me to his store. Either my mother or my father always accompanied me, sat with us, listened to our quiet discussions without contributing. Finally, they realized this was a need I had and they respected that I had to be with this man. They did not read something into it, did not forbid a relationship that nurtured me in a way they knew they had not, could not. I was fortunate they took the time to nurture me in ways other parents may not have. I was lucky they seemed to understand this unusual friendship and came to accept it; let me go visit him.

Finally, after we had been friends for well over a year, he spoke of loss—his loss of a friend not only through death but through an emotional crisis that remained unresolved. His friend withdrew without ever telling my friend why.

Why did this man strike chords within me, produce harmonies I'd been searching for throughout my life? I think—truly believe—it is his origin. Though uncertain of my own parentage—my lineage—I am almost certain this man is what I might have found if I discovered my own birth father. He lives as I want to live/expresses what I want to express. Yet, he is not like this to everyone. As I sat in his store on many Saturdays, I watched him interact with customers; often it did not come easily. Yet the two of us relate easily, deeply, harmonize with few words, sincere silences, trusting glances.

I have decided to adopt Jonathan as my spirit father of this earth,

I gasped. I was so mesmerized, I had to keep on reading:

to bury my desire to discover my birth parents by performing a ritual taking Jonathan as my Ancestor.

Was this man the same Jonathan I knew? His mother owned a Native American gift shop when I dated him. I'm sure his friendship with Wally ended abruptly once I got pregnant. Wally was too loyal, too much in love with me to remain friends with Jonathan once we made our devastating trip to Oklahoma. Wally had, after all, offered to "father" my child as his own. I would never ask Addie who her characters were; I could not violate the trust she offered in allowing me to read her private musings. I swallowed deeply and kept reading:

> He told me of losses he experienced and though I could not identify, I felt the intensity his sparse words revealed:
>
>> ...he never was able to settle down until late in life, finally finding one woman to hold his interest/fire his passion;
>> ...he lost the one true friend he had and was never quite sure why the friendship collapsed.
>
> Recently, we shared an intense experience that rocked us both to the soles of our feet, changing our lives irrevocably, much as finding one another had ten years earlier. The experience made us closer. Was that possible? We were already close but afterwards, more so.
>
> This experience began when Jonathan asked me to accompany him to his twenty-five-year high school reunion.
>
> "I have no family, no wife. I need someone to go with me and I love you like a daughter. Will you go?"
>
> I couldn't look directly at him, his voice was so full of emotion; my hands shook as I hugged him and said, "Of

course, it'll be fun!" Later, I was glad I had the insight to know that his request was important, dear to him.

We arrived at the high school gymnasium, the same high school gymnasium where only years earlier I had suffered my own adolescent traumas, and an attractive woman bore down on Jonathan as soon as we arrived.

"Remember me?" she asked, her voice high pitched, grating, incongruent with her exterior beauty. I realized later (not immediately) that she was nervous, keyed up, raw.

"How could I forget you, Randi? How the hell have you been?" Jonathan was smiling as he embraced the woman and his face was softer than I had ever seen it. "Addie, this is my high school sweetheart, Randi Hall. Addie Woodbridge."

"Is this your daughter?"

A natural question for her to ask at a twenty-five-year reunion, I later remember thinking. Though no one before had ever commented, Jonathan and I did share a sharp resemblance.

"Almost. Adopted daughter." When Jonathan said that, I shuddered involuntarily, but he did not notice; his attention riveted on Randi.

"Well, this is your son," Randi stepped back to introduce a tall, thin young man about my age. Jonathan gasped, coiling over as if someone had punched him full on in the stomach. I had an instant physical reaction myself as I stared at a man who looked so much like me, I might as well have been looking in a mirror.

"What do you mean?" Jonathan finally managed to strangle out, his eyes looking like they would surely burst from the sockets. Barely able to recover his voice, he spoke almost inaudibly. I moved closer to hear.

"I got pregnant right before we graduated."

"And never told me?"

"Yes, that's it. Abortions weren't legal then, remember? You broke up with me the week before graduation so you could see the world without me tagging along. I knew then that I was pregnant but I was too proud to tell you. I didn't want you to marry me out of pity."

As Randi and Jonathan continued their conversation, I grabbed the young man's sleeve and edged him toward the food table, sure we were better off not listening to their conversation.

"What's your name?" I asked as we moved away, leaving Jonathan and Randi without them noticing our departure.

"Dibs. Yours?"

"Addie Woodbridge. So, how'd you get a name like that?"

"Book my mom read."

"*Dibs in Search of Self?*"

"God, I can't believe you've heard of
that book. I thought my mom was the
only one who read it. She wanted me to
know even if I didn't have a father; she
had her 'dibs' on me, I was her choice."

"How long have you known
Jonathan was your dad?"

"Not until recently. My mother was
never open about my father until the last
six months and then it seemed as if the
flood gates opened and she told me everything. She checked my schedule, made
sure I could come on this trip. Says it's
important I finally meet—confront my
father. I don't know what's come over her
recently. She's never been like this before.
Out of the blue, I know my father, my
mother's hometown, more than I've ever
really wanted to know. This is the first
time we've ever been to Florida—I guess
she never wanted to take the risk of running into him."

"She's awful pretty," I said and then
it hit me that she looked a lot like my
adopted mother: small, thin, beautiful red curly hair, handsome carriage. It
made me love Jonathan more, feel like
running back to their conversation to
protect him, as if there was anything I
could do.

Dibs was an interesting young man. He told me a lot about himself that evening, made me wonder how he trusted me so completely in such a short time to reveal so much.

Later, Jonathan and I made up a name for this event: we called it the Infiltration. Though he was reeling from discovering he had a son, he did tell Randi he'd always loved her, had always regretted his stupidity as a high school senior when he'd let her go. She, in turn, still had strong feelings for him; after all, she'd kept his child, raised his son. They began a courtship shortly after the reunion and Randi moved in with Jonathan a year later. Dibs, a recreation coach, got a job at the YMCA in Sarasota and moved here, too.

So, how did meeting these two people shake ME up? They—Jonathan now with Randi and Dibs—became my adopted (chosen) family, my moral support, the final piece of the jigsaw puzzle completing the landscape that is me. Addie Woodbridge.

Addie in Search of Self? I've found her whether I discover my birth parents or not. I've put the search for them on hold because of Jonathan's new family. Randi, for some reason, gives me the fulfillment Jonathan has given me over the last ten years. He's become my chosen birth-father and she is rapidly becoming my selected "birth-mother." She kept the unwanted—no, more unexpected, child of her youth while, for whatever reason—who will ever know—my birth mother relinquished me—released me to the universe. I finally realize I did not land badly. My adopted parents, I know now, love me unconditionally. They know I am different, unique. They never expected me—pushed me—to dance to their drumbeat. They always supported my search for my own rhythm and they love that I have finally found it. What more can any child ask of their parents?

I have finally come to the realization that I may never want to know who my real parents are. Addie in search of self? I found her, sister! I found her! Amen!

I closed my eyes, breathing in deeply, silent tears streaming down my face. I heard a soft knock at my door, and Addie poked her head into my room.

Without a word, I stood, circled her in my arms, and squeezed tight. Finally, whispering, I said, "Outstanding! Simply fantastic!" as Addie squeezed me back in return.

I wrestled with my own decision…did I tell Addie everything? How could I? As Jessie's wedding was rapidly approaching and everyone at Incubation was involved, the wedding overshadowed my confusion, my own search of self. I tabled any decision about what to tell (or not tell) Addie for now.

Only three bridesmaids—Addie, Sera, and Brooke—
were in the wedding; and since two were my responsibility,
I got caught up in plans, dresses, parties, choices for gifts,
everything. I finally met Jeff, Jessie's choice of a loving husband. He was a catch, most importantly because he loved Jess
so. Thursday evening before the Saturday wedding, Matt,
Liam, and Reagan flew down, and I picked them up at the
airport. I noticed how significant Reagan was becoming to
my family since she accompanied Liam on a family vacation!
Since Incubation was full to overflowing, we all stayed in a
hotel on the Island: Reagan had her own room; Liam had
a room; and of course, Matt and I shared. I had to ignore
whether or not Reagan and Liam slipped in to sleep together
after we went to bed and made it none of my business. Of
course, Sera did not stay at the hotel with us. She was central to the wedding (at least so she thought), so she stayed at
Incubation to be near Jessie. Sera and Brooke were sure Jessie
needed them both intricately, that she could not do without
them.

The rehearsal dinner was the only thing that even
remotely identified Zan as Jessie's mom! It was held on the
beach beyond Incubation with a large bonfire lit just as the
sun went down. Bonfires had become more and more illegal
since Zan and I first arrived in Sarasota, but as long as it
was on private property, there was nothing illegal about it.
However, I chuckled to myself, Zan would probably have
had one even if it had been illegal!

Boy, was there food! Every kind of seafood imaginable.
Vanessa and Zan had eaten out a lot and knew every good
restaurant on the Island. Restaurant folks loved Vanessa and
anything to do with her, which included Zan and Jess. Our
favorite restaurant, the Sandbar, catered most of the rehearsal
dinner, but Anna Maria was full of personalized chefs as well,

a growing group of specialty people who cooked for the tourists pouring in. Tourists who didn't want to cook but didn't want to go out to eat either. All of those chefs wanted to be part of the celebration and vied with one another to provide the most exciting, the very best dish. One concession Jess allowed as different to the norm: she did not have a wedding cake; only Key lime pies. Lots of them, all made by bakers from the island. I have never eaten so much or so well in my life!

All the girls were beautiful! Jessie wore a traditional dress with a long veil, carrying orchids that were radiant in a wide variety of colors. The girls, Addie, Brooke, and Sera, wore various colors picked up from the orchids; not one wore the same color or style. To center everyone on Jess, the girls did not carry flowers but wore crowns of flowers in their hair. They were so radiant no one even noticed they didn't carry flowers. The music was live musicians, again from the island. Even the wedding march was nontraditional, as was Zan walking Jess down the aisle, her father not invited. The dance usually reserved for the bride and her dad was a poignant waltz between Zan and Jess; then Jeff's father cut in to dance with Jess while Jeff danced with his mom. Zan and I took several spins around the dance floor, gazing deeply into one another's eyes, sure of our friendship and the special love we shared.

One of the funniest parts of the reception was my girls dancing: Brooke, Addie, and Sera danced, spinning, laughing, gulping in almost hysteria. Then the music took an abrupt dive, the girls became serious, the lights dimmed. Sera stepped forward. She announced that part of her wedding gift to Jessie was a beautiful choreographed dance involving her, Brooke, and Addie. It was so powerful, the music so lilting, so bittersweet, I could not stop weeping. I looked over and noticed Jess and Zan crying too. I had known for years that Sera was a wonderful dancer but never before had seen her talent so artfully displayed, had never been shown what she herself choreographed.

Jess and Jeff left almost immediately for an Alaskan cruise; having lived most of their lives on one of the most beautiful beaches in Florida, a beach destination did not have any appeal for their honeymoon.

Even though Zan and I hardly did anything for the wedding, we were exhausted. I wanted to visit and show my family (and Reagan) around but could hardly get out of bed. That was not a problem for Sera—she was not tired and appointed herself tour guide, loving that she knew every nook and corner that was an interesting place to take them. Liam had his own personal agenda: he was going to college in a few weeks and had already been accepted to Ringling School of Art. Because of his interest, they all stayed on the whole next week; he had an appointment at Ringling on Monday.

Monday after the college tour, the whole family moved back to Incubation. Matt found me in my room and quietly closed the door. "Well, I learned two interesting things today that I'm sure you do not know about." His voice was grim enough that it scared me a little.

"What? What are you talking about?"

"You're not going to like either one, so, sit down." I did. "For starters, Reagan's moving here with Liam. They've been looking at apartments. Rented one today. The freedom Vanessa's money is giving Liam made him able to make such a decision without our approval."

"What do you mean? I thought that money was for college."

"It is, but he got a hefty scholarship to Ringling, and Vanessa left the money in his name. He and Reagan both signed the lease. He needed her signature since she's the older of the two." I groaned.

"How's he going to get around?"

"Reagan owns a car. They are going back to Atlanta to load it up and come down here right away. You know what a big bike rider he is—he loves the flat land around here and will probably bike everywhere. That's not the biggest problem..."

"What do you mean not the biggest problem? I think Reagan living with Liam his freshman year of college is a pretty big problem. What could be bigger than that?"

"Sera isn't planning to return to Atlanta either."

"What? What in the hell are you talking about?"

"She's going to Bradenton High School. She's already registered there. She showed me the school and asked if I wanted a tour. Did you know anything about that?"

"Not just no, hell no! I've never heard of that plan at all. Without us registering her, how on earth did her registration go through? If I'm not mistaken, a parent has to register a child."

"Zan and Jessie, Vanessa too, are so well-known around here, she registered telling the school she had moved into Incubation with her mother. They are expecting her to bring you in soon with her shot records, birth certificate, and stuff."

"Oh my god! What about Brooke?"

"Brooke knows she has to go home. She has parents who expect her—any day now, I might add. Grady High School starts in a week. Brooke told me she plans to be there."

"What do you mean Brooke has parents who expect her home? So does Sera!"

"I'm just telling you the type of independent children we have raised and their decisions."

"Sera's only fourteen—she can't make decisions like that!"

"On the other hand, we've always encouraged our children to express themselves. To live with their own opinions, their own choices. It's been such a big part of their life, how can we react negatively when they take the initiative and make their own decisions?"

"Are you saying you are okay with her staying here? I was coming home in two weeks and, in my ignorance, thought she was too."

"I know. However, I am trying to think like the unusual parent I think I am. What if it is okay for her to stay here?"

"What's the motive? Jessie and Jeff won't be here. He has a church in Daytona where he's been hired, so they aren't going to live here."

"This may thoroughly surprise you, but she wants to join the circus! She's been taking dance her whole life and has a fascination with circus life. She's been going to circus training all summer with Zan. She goes to watch twice a week, even tried out the trapeze."

"How old do you have to be to join the circus? Certainly not as young as fourteen, I should think!"

"Here's what I think," Matt said.

I bristled at his quiet, serious introspection then remembered he'd had at least four more hours of knowing about this transition, four more hours than I had as well as a lifetime of acceptance and patience I could only imagine. "Okay, Matt, tell me what you think."

"I think we should let her try it out. You stay down here...you're getting a lot of work done here anyway, and then you can keep an eye on Liam and Reagan without them knowing that's what you're doing."

"What about my studio? Losing me and Reagan at the same time? How is that going to work?"

"Keep your lease. Real estate in Atlanta is so exorbitant at the moment you can't afford to give it up. In any case, move your work here. I'll transfer your orders and your business to this address at least until you come home, and then it will be easier to adjust without Reagan. You can hire her. If you move your whole business down here for the fall, you might need her. You know she'll need the work."

Again, how did Matt do that? He always made the most sensible decisions, the most realistic responses to some of the most ridiculous experiences—and Reagan and Sera moving to Sarasota, that, in my mind, was ridiculous! However, once I thought about it and mulled it over, I realized that my staying was as good a solution as any, especially since Matt felt Sera should stay. I had not yet begun to reconcile myself to Addie—to her writing, to the fact that more than likely she was my child! It would give me time to come to grips with that.

So what did I do first? I talked to Zan, and she was eager for Sera and me to stay; she was going to miss Jess horribly and did not like the idea of being alone in the main house. In the end, it wasn't really very different from the Briarcliff House, especially in the beginning when I had my studio in our backyard. I did make the decision not to hire Reagan. I was confident I could keep up with the work without her, and I did not want to interfere with (or even be near) her and Liam setting up house. It wasn't long until Reagan got a job anyway (at Carla's Clay in Sarasota), and that kept those two mostly in Sarasota (again, they only had one car). I knew Matt wanted me to keep an eye on them, but if I was in Atlanta,

I wouldn't, so I wasn't going to do that here either. Next, I went to register Sera at Bradenton High School. I decided I was not going to make anything easy for her, so I made it clear she had to ride the school bus. If I was staying because of her, I wanted to start work whenever I was ready, not cart her around, cater to her. This was her decision, not mine. She had never ridden the bus in her life, but she wanted to be in Bradenton so badly she conceded. She had other restrictions: dance and gymnastics came before watching circus practice, and top-notch grades were even more important than that. She didn't seem to be worried—she had always been an A student in Atlanta even when she was involved in loads of dance activities, extracurricular and at school. She thrived on being busy. Wonder who she got that from?

Now, Addie. What about Addie? Was she my child? Did I even broach the subject knowing that if we were not related it might backfire and ruin our wonderful friendship? Would it affect her friendship with Sera? The first person I asked about all this was Zan (of course). I did not let her read Addie's story (that was given to me privately), but I did tell her that Addie had ended the piece with the possibility that she might never want to know the truth about her heritage.

"Then why the hell do you want to bring it up? You read her piece, you know what she wants!" Zan admonished me.

"I think she is my child, my own flesh and blood. If I traded places with her and I was adopted, I would want to know. At least know if it was a possibility, especially know why it happened the way it did."

"Do you think that should be your first step?"

"What do you mean?"

"Maybe you should talk to Jonathan first and tell him it's possible that he's Addie's uncle. Ask his opinion. He is very, very close to Addie."

"Oh god, the thought of that makes me sick! Jonathan? I could live the rest of my life without seeing him again."

"I think that's where you should start. Tell him what happened, get his opinion on how to face Addie, if you should face Addie."

"I'm not starting that monkey ride without talking to Matt first. He deserves to know."

"I agree. Talk to Matt."

Matt called a few nights later. "Matt, when you were here, I did not share what has been going on with Jessie's friend Addie. She lives at Incubation and is a writer. She and I have become very close, close enough she shared her writing with me. She looks Native American but was adopted by two very redheaded, fair-skinned people. I have a sneaking suspicion she's my child."

"That might be great, Katrina!" Matt, always positive, reacted with love and support.

"How do I open that door? What if I suggest that to her and she rejects the idea? What if it turns out to be untrue? Zan thinks I should talk to Jonathan first. He knows Addie well and might have a good read on what she'd want."

"Jonathan as in Jonathan whose brother slept with you when you were thinking it was him?"

"The very one."

"Why would you bring him into it?"

"Addie revealed in her writing that she is so close to him she feels as if he is a surrogate father. She fantasizes that since he is Native American, and she might be, he might be her dad. She has become so close to him that in her writing she says she may never want to know the real origin of her birth."

"Let's think on that for a while before you make any decisions." Again, Matt, ever the sane one, the logical scientist.

"I think you're right," I told him.

Sera adjusted to high school like a surfer to the next big wave. She made friends instantly, especially since she hailed from the big city of Atlanta, lived downtown there and knew that territory intricately. She also appealed because she lived at Incubation. No other teenagers lived at Incubation; most of them had parents who wouldn't even let them step foot inside the property. That didn't stop Sera; she immediately made the dance team, took two dance classes, a gymnastics class, and, when not otherwise engaged, went home with a multitude of friends. The same friends whose parents would not let them visit Incubation. I could tell from Sera's stories that even though they did not approve of where she lived, they loved her! Who wouldn't? These same parents were open and thrilled to meet me, as long as it was at dance practice, in the school parking lot, or at a coffeehouse. They just were not interested in discovering Incubation. Sera and I by implicit understanding never talked to them about it.

I did spend time wondering what assumptions they made about where we lived. Why did they forbid their children to come to our residence? This was just the beginning of communal living and was so new it was often highlighted on the news. Of course, given the way news is, communes were never highlighted in a positive way. I'm sure these parents (maybe even their children?) thought we all shared partners, lived not only together in the house but in one another's bedrooms. Maybe they thought we spent most of the time in the nude. I had to giggle at this image: I figured working in the pottery studio or standing at an easel would be highly uncomfortable without clothes on!

In an interesting turn of events, Addie solved the dilemma of approaching the topic of her birth. I was glad this was how it happened as this topic was frequently on my mind. She approached me one evening when Sera was out and we could visit alone.

"I know in my writing I wrote that I didn't want to find my birth parents," she started the conversation, "but with these new DNA kits, I thought I might try and find something out."

"What DNA kits?" I had never heard of this.

"You know what DNA is, right? Now you can have tests and find out your background, your ancestry. People like me who haven't a clue can find out anything we want to know."

I panicked a wee bit but tried not to show it. I had a strong sense that if she went this route and the tests were specific, she would find out that I was her mother. I figured it was time for me to have a meeting with Jonathan. I'd rather tell her myself than have her find out from some random mail-order kit.

To Addie, I said, "Humor me. Give me a week to do some research, and let's talk again before you take one of those tests. Okay?"

"Why?"

"I have some thoughts, some ideas on this, and want to check it out before you do something like that. Just trust me, okay?"

"Okay, I'll trust you." She crossed her arms, seeming to fold into herself. I hated to put her off. I noticed her frown and concentration, but I needed time to resolve this before she went ahead with this idea.

I went to see Jonathan. His mom's store was where it had always been, and he was there the morning I dropped in. You should have seen his face! His jaw dropped when I arrived. "What are you doing here? Did you forget this is the store I own?"

"I'm here to see you. Is there somewhere we can talk privately?"

"Sure, we can go sit on a bench looking out over the beach. Will that work?"

"Yes."

"Let me just call my assistant from the back and have him watch the store for me." I knew the minute I saw his assistant it must be Dibs because he did, indeed, look like Addie. Jonathan and I walked to the bench in silence.

"So, what's so important that you seek me out after all this time? If I remember correctly, you turned your back on me at Wally's funeral."

"Indeed, I did. What I have to talk to you about is why I ran from you. On that trip long ago to Oklahoma, I met your brother, Brett. Remember you and I had a falling-out almost as soon as we got there and I went home early? Before I left, I was hoping we'd say goodbye, and I thought we did, thought we were together my last night."

"What do you mean?"

"Brett came to the tent, courted me, and took me up on a hill, and we made love. Only I thought it was you I was making love to. A goodbye tryst. Right at the end, I saw a scar on Brett's back and realized it wasn't you. He said every year you both traded women and he got lucky."

"What are you talking about? What was Brett talking about? I never knew he did that. Oh my god!"

"That's what he said. An older woman, your grandmother, confirmed it. She took me to the bus station the next morning and said Brett made it routine."

"Brett was lying. I guess my grandmother knew he did that…I never did. She had a lot to do with raising him, they were really close. A lot closer than I was to either of them.

"I am so, so sorry, Katrina. God, if I'd known that happened, I'd have taken you to the bus station myself. Thrown myself down in front of you and begged for mercy. I had no idea any of that happened. Brett never said a word."

"You and Brett didn't compare conquests? I was sure that's what he said. He strutted around like I was a trophy or something. Told me he was going to tell you how good a fuck I was."

"I never thought what you and I did was fuck. I can tell you that much even though our time together was brief and ended badly. Where Brett is concerned, we didn't grow up together. Never spent more than a few summers in the same place, and since I was younger, I always got brutalized by him. His father brought him up, our mother, me. He was so jealous I was raised by our mother he would do anything to make my life miserable. Did my grandmother tell you about the time we were at her house and he held pillows over my face and tried to suffocate me? Actually, tried to suffocate me. She had to pull him off, and I always thought if she hadn't been there, he would have killed me. After that, I never spent much time with him—never spent the night in the same house where he was. He was messing with me by being with you. Oh god, I am so sorry."

"Jonathan, that's not all. I got pregnant. I was back at school just a few weeks when I realized that I was carrying his baby. I stayed in school until spring and then came to Sarasota, lived with Zan, and had the baby here."

"You had a baby? My brother's baby? How come I'm just now finding that out?"

"Because I never wanted to see you again. I knew I'd never see Brett again. I gave the baby up for adoption. Had the baby here and signed it away with adoption papers."

A strange look crossed Jonathan's face. "Was the baby a boy or a girl?"

"A girl."

"That's why we're having this conversation, isn't it? You think I may be Addie's uncle. You may be her mother." He stared at me, then up at the sky.

It took me a minute to speak. I was still processing that he had not been an active participant in his brother's deeds, in my being raped. After a long pause, I found my voice. "Yeah, that's right. You're right. She wants to do one of those DNA searches for her identity."

"Wally knew all about this, didn't he?"

"Yes. He wanted to marry me and keep the baby, but I felt that would rob him. I wanted him to have a life being married to someone who wasn't just his best friend. Later when he met Gia, and they had a wild, romantic marriage, I was glad I said no."

"That's what happened between me and Wally." Jonathan scrubbed his face with his hands, and next I heard deep, gulping sobs wrenching from him, his shoulders heaving, tears streaming down his face. He leaned down over his knees, as though to keep from fainting. "No one's fault but my own and Brett's. We did not have a good family dynamic, and you suffered from it. Boy, I have screwed up my life! Lost my own son for twenty-five years, and now I'm finding out I may have lost my niece for just as long! Why are you finally telling me?"

"I am going to tell Addie to go through with her search, but I am going to let her know what she might find once it's completed. I wanted to tell you first because if my name comes up, your family's will too. She thinks of you as a father. I wanted you to be prepared. I didn't know if we should get Brett involved."

"Brett can't be involved. He died shortly after you left. He got into it with another guy over some woman and was knifed to death. He lived a hard, rough life. You saw the scar, remember? That's how he lived. We all thought his days were numbered. I just never knew he left a daughter as a legacy, left me a legacy as valuable as that: a niece, my niece. I may be Addie's uncle."

"Do you think I should tell her in case it turns out I'm her mom?"

"Have you seen Dibs? Did you just see him in the store? He and Addie look so much alike I think you better tell her so she has an inkling of what might happen."

"I also want to tell her why I gave her up. She has been writing a very deep piece, and some of what she explores is trying to understand why she was given up for adoption."

"Yea, I think you should tell her. Do you think I should come with you?"

"I appreciate the offer, I really do. I think this is something I must do by myself."

"If she gets upset, tell her to call me. I can be there in a heartbeat."

"I will. Jonathan, I am so glad we talked so I could find out the situation was not as bad as I have always thought it was. I was so hurt, enraged. I thought you sent Brett to pick me up like used goods, thought you were in on it. That's what he said, and I never questioned it. Now, knowing the truth makes me feel better about what happened so many years ago."

"Maybe we can be friends after this? After all, you may find a daughter, me a niece."

I paused. "Let me think about it."

Next was Addie. How on earth was I going to tell her, talk to her about my suspicions? I did what I often did when I faced complexities in my life. I called Clayton and told him what was going on.

"Hey," he said, "Annabella and I need a vacation. Why don't we come to Incubation for a few weeks? I'd love to see you, of course, and it'd be fun to see Liam, Sera, and Zan. Besides, I have been interested in Incubation since you first wrote about it. If you need me to, we could do some type of ceremony whenever you wanted…before you talk to Addie, after you talk to Addie, when you talk to Addie, whatever. What do you think?"

"That would be great. Wow! That's not even why I was calling, but that is exactly what I need. Let me ask Zan about you coming down, then if she says yes, come soon. Addie's getting antsy about her DNA search."

Of course, when I asked Zan, she was thrilled! I called Clayton back, and he said he and Annabella would come that weekend.

Addie knocked on my door a few days later. "Okay, what's up? You asked me to give you a week, so I have."

"I am working my butt off on my research, and I'm almost ready. A dear friend of mine is coming down this weekend…you've never met him, but he and I studied together at Penland. I specifically want to meet with you and him at the same time, to share some things with you. I know you are very private, but for me to talk to you about what we need to talk about, I need his support."

"Things are getting curiouser and curiouser. What could you and a man I've never met have to do with my ancestry?"

"I know this all sounds odd."

"Hell, yes, it sounds odd! What do you know that you're not sharing? What is going on? Why are you keeping me in the dark? My mind is racing with possibilities, and I don't like what I'm thinking."

"My friend always keeps a situation calm, peaceful. I promise I will share with you as soon as he gets here. It is not all negative—at least I hope you won't think so. Clayton is coming this Friday, just two more days. We will meet with you Saturday. How about it?"

"Can you give me some idea of what's going on so I don't burn up inside?"

"Yes, Addie, I can. I know more about your birth origin than I have let on."

"What the hell?"

"Just bear with me. Give me two more days. I will tell you everything then, I promise."

As Addie walked away from my room, she shot me a look I could not read. It was full of suspicion, lack of trust, even grief. I hated to do this, but I needed Clayton to keep the situation calm, hopefully even loving.

That Saturday, we met at Island Coffee Haus. It was early enough that it was quiet and we could have privacy. I maneuvered it so Addie drove and met Clayton and me there. I thought it important that if she needed to escape, to run, she wasn't trapped because of riding with me. Jonathan had a cell phone by then (a relatively new invention) and had both me and Addie on speed dial so he could be reached instantly. I introduced her to Clayton, who came with me to the coffeehouse.

"Okay, what's the secrecy? What's up?" We sat together at a table; I was beside Addie, Clayton sat across from her. She was tightly wound—arms crossed, leaning back in her chair, her body language closed off from us.

Clayton started by taking Addie's hand, but she abruptly pulled away from him. "Addie, I don't know if I'm sorry or pleased to tell you that Katrina thinks she may be your mother."

Addie leapt up and ran out of the coffeehouse, spilling her hot coffee everywhere. Clayton sat at the table as I ran after her; I am sure he felt Addie and I needed this time to ourselves. Addie fell down on a bench. I eased down slowly beside her, close enough to hug her but far enough for her to stay distant if she wanted. Her dark skin paled, her eyes flitted from me then away quickly.

"So, you might be my mom—and, is that man my dad?"

"Well, that's complicated."

"Complicated? Katrina, how can that be complicated? That's a yes-or-no question."

"If I'm your mom, Jonathan's brother is your father, not Clayton."

Addie fainted, dropped off the bench and straight onto the sidewalk. Clayton ran outside, looked at me, and said, "You'd better call Jonathan. I think he might help." I had Jonathan on speed dial (I had a cell phone too), and he answered immediately. "Get over here, quick."

"What happened?"

"She's fainted." Just then she roused.

"Who are you talking to?"

"Jonathan. I thought you might want him here."

"Hell, yes, I want him here. Tell him you two have some explaining to do."

Jonathan must have been hanging close to Island Coffee Haus because he arrived in less than five minutes. "How can I help?"

"Hug me first, Uncle." Despite her obvious chaos, Addie was funny and in high spirits; she even managed a light giggle.

He looked at me. "Lord, you told her? What did you tell her?"

"Not much," Addie responded. "I still don't know what he's doing here…" She pointed at Clayton, who was gracious enough to blush as much as a black man can.

"In my defense, Addie," Clayton said, "I met your mom shortly after she had given you up for adoption. We spent a lot of time talking specifically about you and about her making such a life-changing decision. How about we go back into the coffee shop and talk together? We haven't paid yet, so I'm sure they haven't given up our table, and it will be more private in there." We walked back in, Jonathan supporting Addie and helping her sit down in the chair she had recently vacated. He sat on the other side of her, and Clayton was again across from her.

"Tell me everything! Oh my god—everything! Does this mean Sera and Liam are my siblings? My brother and sister? Dibs, my cousin?"

Lord, I hadn't even thought of that—now I had to tell them too.

Jonathan picked up the story. "Katrina and I dated one summer, a mad, loving relationship that died as soon as we travelled to Oklahoma together. I got caught up with other Indian women I had known all my life and left Katrina in the dust." At this Jonathan squirmed, but I had to credit him, he was telling the truth. "My brother had a one-night stand with Katrina, but to complicate things, Katrina didn't know it was my brother. We looked just alike. Until the very end, Katrina thought she was with me. Then she noticed a scar on my brother's back. She knew I didn't have one. My brother did all this intentionally—was with Katrina on purpose, but until a week ago, I never knew this happened. My brother and I never got along. He was very jealous of me. He did all this to hurt me. He didn't expect Katrina to call him out."

I picked up the story from there. "I came back to Georgia to go back to college and soon found out I was pregnant. By a man I didn't even know. I didn't have any way to reach Jonathan—he had dropped me cold in Oklahoma. I wasn't going to contact his brother—he meant nothing to me. Remember too this was twenty-five years ago, so no cell phones. We had never even thought about them."

"Trust me," Jonathan continued, "my brother never shared any of this with me. He died only weeks after Katrina returned to Georgia. If it's true and if you are my niece, I have to tell you, Addie, it's one of the greatest things to happen in my life. It's as great as discovering Dibs."

I continued, "To have you, I moved in with Zan in Sarasota, in the spring of 1972. I gave birth to a baby girl on April 22. I had such mixed emotions, but it was 1972. The only unwed mothers I knew were those who got pregnant in high school and were forced to marry their high school sweethearts. You live in such a different age you have no idea how things were in the early 1970s. I didn't have anyone… no high school sweetheart, no real father for my child, my parents never even knew I was pregnant. Zan and I decided adoption was the only route for me."

"What day did you say you gave birth?"

"What?"

"What was your baby's birthday?"

"April 22."

"That *is* my birthday! So, you think I'm your child? I was born the day you gave birth, here in Sarasota. I have even thought that Jonathan might be my father."

"What do we do next?"

"Well, my mom and dad have my real birth certificate. Did you fill one out?"

"Yea, I did. I am listed as mother. Father is listed as unknown."

"They have never given me a chance to look at it, but they have promised I could whenever I was ready, whenever I asked. I figured I might take a glance at it after I took the DNA test. Or, maybe before and save all that money taking a DNA test."

Clayton burst out laughing. "You know, Addie, I like you! You have brought humor to this whole scene. All day. You are just as quirky as...as..."

"As my mom? As Katrina?"

"Yea, as your possible mom, Katrina."

"So, what do we do?"

"How about you meet with your parents and take a look at that birth certificate? If it says what I think it will, then we can go to dinner with Sera and Liam."

"One reason I'm here is because I do ceremonies," Clayton told Addie and Jonathan. "Ceremonies for celebrations, grief—anything. If you want to celebrate discovering your mom and uncle, if indeed that is what you find out, I'm your man. I can plan anything you want."

"So, that's why you're here." Addie chuckled to herself.

"I do like you, Addie. You are unbelievable! Another really strong woman."

*****

Addie didn't waste any time meeting with her parents, sharing with them that she might have met her mother, someone they had met too. They did not hesitate to show her the birth certificate. There it was in black and white:

Mother: Katrina Wheeler;
Father: Unknown

Addie was so excited she almost crowed. She called me: "I want to have a simple ceremony—no big bonfire, no fireworks, even though I feel like I have fireworks going off inside of me! Dinner at Incubation: you, Jonathan, Sera, Liam, Dibs, Randi, and Zan. Have your interesting friend Clayton plan it. He can come too—even bring his wife. But that's it. No one else. I am not even inviting my parents. This is a celebration but a quiet one, an intimate sharing of something extremely important to me and I hope to you too."

Important to me? Something I'd spent the last twenty-five years yearning for, reaching for, anguishing over. My daughter, my Addie, my firstborn!

The celebration was just as Addie wanted with one slight variation—with Addie's permission, Matt flew down and joined us, wanting Addie to know he'd be a father to her too. Liam and Sera took it like champs—Sera already loved Addie, and Liam looked forward to getting to know her. What an extended family! I looked forward to sharing the rest of my life with these people—even Jonathan. We could be friends, just as he asked. Especially now that I knew he and Brett did not swap women.

Addie, Jonathan, and I had a commitment ceremony, one that was twenty-five years in the making. It was not closure, more an opening, flavored with love, joy, and yes, I must admit, fulfillment—finally. Jonathan wore a tuxedo, I wore a simple flowing (yes, hippie) dress, and Addie dressed all in white. Clayton's family joined us too, and we had the ceremony on the beach right in front of the property Matt and I owned. The finale was a dance Sera put together with friends from her high school. She had invited her friends and their parents, and since we stayed at the house next door to Incubation, the house on our own property (a single-family dwelling), they came after dinner to perform the dance. Again, as at Jessie's wedding, the dance was powerful. After her friends danced to a frenzy, at the end when all the other dancers dropped to their haunches, Sera drew Addie, Jonathan, Matt, Liam, and finally me in, circling in simple dance steps we could follow. A cheer erupted on the beach, and Matt left our circle to light fireworks that lit the sky for several minutes. Addie opened her arms to Mr. and Mrs. Woodbridge, who had come for the dance; I reached for Zan; Jessie and Jeff came for the dance too; then finally everyone on the beach was encircled in a spirally dance that ended with Addie at the center, crying, laughing, even gulping in her joy.

EPILOGUE

*T*here you have it—my life with a wide smattering of other characters beginning when I was just twenty years old. I think a lot of people feel they would like to relive their experiences when they were teenagers as the adults they become, but I know I would never want to relive the Sarasota summer even with the knowledge I have today. What happened then impacts me now, but it is what was, what was meant to be, what makes me the person I am.

Liam went to the Ringling School of Art, graduating from there and staying in Sarasota. He and Reagan still live together (it's now been seven years)—both artists and only now considering the possibility of blessing me with grandchildren though they have never mentioned marriage. Theirs is one of the few youthful romances I trust to survive. Two years ago, Reagan told me, "You know, of course, why I love Liam so much, don't you? He's your son. I love you, so it was only natural…"

My heart flipped, and some of what I sought from Reagan was realized. She did love me, just not the way I fantasized when we first met. Now, I have three daughters, my own son, and sons-in-law.

Sera? Never went to college; she did join the circus as a trapeze artist the day after she graduated from high school. She married the master of ceremonies, and they are expecting their first child. Of all of the children, she travels the most, seeing the world and never staying in the Sarasota area long. She is on the road, lives on the road, and thrives!

Addie became a cub reporter at the *Sarasota Daily News* after I mentioned to Zan that her writing was succinct, clear, desirable for the field of journalism. Zan made one well-placed phone call that led to an interview. Addie is invaluable there. She's thrived in the newspaper setting particularly as a political reporter. She now has her own column three times a week, which has been picked up throughout Florida and is being looked at by national syndication.

She never lost her idealism and love for the Native American culture, but she married Clayton's son after he visited Sarasota and fell in love with both Sarasota and Addie. Jay is the straitlaced, tie-wearing child I always knew one of us would have (but thank God he's not Republican). He's a banker (funny how this all started with my job at a bank). His security gives Addie what she wants: the ability to write and live primarily as a mother, having three dark-haired children already (she's thirty-two) with one more due in April. She and Jay have applied to adopt two siblings who have been tied up in the foster care system most of their lives. These children have never lived together, and Addie wants to give them that chance. You guessed it—they are Native American, one of the few Floridian children left whose parents are both Natives. She qualifies because she is 50 percent Native American (of course, not my side)! Once we proved that Brett and I were her parents, Jonathan and Addie got all the proper paperwork for her to claim her Native American heritage.

Yes, I know that makes six children, but Addie is excited and dedicated. Her interest in having so many children is a direct result of the loneliness she felt as an only child. Once she discovered Incubation, Sera, Brooke, Jessie, Liam and Reagan, Dibs (the list goes on and on), Addie wanted her own huge family in a big, sprawling house with lots of room and lots of kids. Jay is happy if Addie is happy.

She has six people who her children call grandparents, so she has lots of babysitters! Me, Matt, Jonathan and Randi, and yes, Mr. and Mrs. Woodbridge. Only we are now dear friends and call them by their first names: Madeline and Thomas. They have dinner at Incubation at least once a week, and I value and love them for taking care of Addie when I could not. As I mentioned earlier, Jonathan and I are friends. Not bosom buddies, but we spend time together with the grandchildren, and we have quiet walks on the beach sometimes, each in our own world, daydreaming, loving our lives.

Suffice it to say, given my history, my children are complex, challenging, realistic, self-assured: they are firecrackers that sparkle with life.

Matt and I moved to Bradenton shortly after Sera started high school there. I rapidly realized with Addie, Liam, Reagan, and Sera all there, I just couldn't go back to Atlanta. Initially Matt moved into Incubation with me; we redesigned the house on our own beach property and eventually moved in there. We sold our share of the Briarcliff House to Joy and Ed. We do have a room there, so we always visit when we need their socialization or business calls.

Business calling? That's another story. In moving to Florida, Matt took a teaching job at New College, and he and Zan started a skin-care line (her herbal knowledge, his undergraduate chemistry degree) that has taken off by storm. Everyone wants it—who wouldn't when it is a natural, age-defying line of products that help keep the wrinkles away and gives everyone a chance to have a bit of Zan's lively sass? That's what it's called: Sass! All anyone has to do is take a look at Sass's senior model (Zan) and want what she has! I have always felt that way from the first time I met her.

Joy and Ed still live at the Briarcliff House with their adult children in and out, but they never replaced us for more communal living. After all these years, now it's just the two of them. Of course, just the two of them is rare as they have company all the time. Joy does a great job of filling the house with artists, actors, actresses, other people's children who need a place to crash. So life is different every day—never boring—ever changing. Has it ever been different for any of us? Not really.

Joy's business continues to thrive and she found herself owning a store in the midst of some of the hottest real estate in Atlanta—only able to afford the location because she bought her storefront years and years ago. Joy, ever creative and giving, embarked on a project for each of our children when they graduated from high school (it took her their whole senior year to complete each one). She gathered twelve-by-twelve-inch muslin squares from all their friends—their peers, boys and girls, their friends from childhood, adults and children, with instructions and return postage to Briarcliff House and deadlines so she had time to sew it together piece by piece. She made each child an artistic quilt (too pretty, too sentimental to ever sleep under), which we hang in the Briarcliff House foyer and at Incubation until the children marry and move away. Then they find a wall or space in their own homes to display their quilt. Except Sera, of course. Hers is and probably always will be at Incubation. Liam's was first—such a complete surprise, he wept over its beauty. Since all the other children were part of Liam's, they knew theirs was coming, but it did not matter: the impact of such a display of love from most everyone they know never failed to touch them deeply. The chosen one would take in a deep breath, and then would let out a deep sob from within a place deep and private. It was the perfect expression for a rite of passage. As a wedding gift, we made one for Addie and Jay, who display it prominently in their home on Siesta Key.

Gia has grown old in Columbus, Georgia, never remarrying but earning a strong following as an artist. She has been at the forefront of developing and preserving Pasaquan and Eddie Martin's artistic estate. She works tirelessly with all the arts organizations in Columbus, but Pasaquan has remained her passion. She credits Eddie with the later developments in her own work, moving from small pottery people to much larger installations. She spent time with Bread and Puppet Theatre in Vermont learning about puppetry art, so she and her daughter, Katie, often work together producing breathtaking puppet shows, combining Katie's theatrical bent and Gia's artwork.

Katie is one who has stayed at the Briarcliff House on numerous occasions until finally she moved in to one of the spare bedrooms. Joy missed her own children so much she loves having a young adult living under her roof. Plus, it means Gia visits, often. Katie, with Joy's help and contacts in the theatrical world, launched her own career as an actress and storyteller, finally appearing at the International Storytelling Festival in Jonesborough, Tennessee. She was included in our quilt-making, a project Gia embraced and added her three-dimensional touch to—oh, is it a work of art!

Clayton is still in Charleston but travels most of the time with a tremendous amount of recognition for his artwork. He is one of those artists who can acknowledge that he has "made it" before he dies. I am fortunate to know him; he enhances my artistic endeavors, throws contacts my way as often as he can, and enriches my life with his friendship and support. Since his son married my daughter (Jay and Addie), he visits Sarasota often.

As Matt and I grow old, we grow more in love, not less, much to the disgust of some who keep thinking we'll tire of one another. We're too different and, at the same time, too comfortable to grow apart. Fortunately, we don't declare war—silent/steaming or hostile screaming as many couples do who have been married as long as we have. Instead we embrace one another—our lives, our differences, our similarities (we do have a few) and love one another with all our hearts. I have come to realize that that's a special gift God bequeathed us, a rarity, and now what I value most in my life. Other than my children (including Addie), my grandchildren, and of course, those grandchildren yet to come.

Menopause is finally a thing of the past, though Matt and I both feel it should be called women-a-pause. I look forward to growing old with the right—the honor—of saying what I think, no holds barred. Walking along and farting, giggling at my indiscretions, but—God forbid!—never apologizing.

I am Katrina as Zan is Zan. Thankfully our daughters are strong in their individualism too—women living, crying, agonizing, laughing, sharing. Women. Friends. No more Bread Legs, we embrace all that we are and forever will be!

ABOUT THE AUTHOR

K. L. Watkins is a professional storyteller who has told stories throughout the country. She travelled to Russia with a storytelling delegation through People to People Ambassadors. She has published numerous articles and short stories in professional journals. She retired as a cultural arts director for Parks and Recreation, Gwinnett County, Georgia, where programs included all the arts with a strong writers' group established in 1989. You can learn more about K.L. Watkins on her website: Watkinswrites.com.

Author photo by Madison-Rhea Koehler.